RUN POSY RUN

CATE C. WELLS

This book is a work of fiction. Names, characters, places, and incidents are the product of the author's imagination or are used fictitiously. Any resemblance to actual events, locales, or persons, living or dead, is coincidental.

Copyright © 2021 by Cate C. Wells. All rights reserved.

Cover art and design by Clarise Tan of CT Cover Creations.
Photograph by Golden Czermak.
Edited by Nevada Martinez.
Proofread by Kayla Davenport.
Special thanks to Katee, Sara, Nina, Kara, Erin, An, Layne, and Elisabeth.

The uploading, scanning, and distribution of this book in any form or by any means—including but not limited to electronic, mechanical, photocopying, recording, or otherwise—without the permission of the copyright holder is illegal and punishable by law. Please purchase only authorized editions of this work, and do not participate in or encourage electronic piracy of copyrighted materials. Your support of authors' rights is appreciated.

❦ Created with Vellum

1

POSY

Today is a great day. It's finally stopped raining, the daffodils are blooming, and the town car is in the drive. Butterflies swoop to life in my belly.

I guess Dario's meeting didn't last as long as he thought it would. I'm gonna make him steaks for dinner. I'll light a few candles. Wear the red dress with the slit up the side. Maybe he'll take out the pale blue box I found in his sock drawer when I was rummaging for a pair of wool socks to thaw my frozen feet.

Is he going to get down on one knee? I can't imagine Dario Volpe ever doing that, even to propose. He probably won't ask at all. He'll drawl "marry me" while compelling me with his dark, hooded eyes.

Tingles skate over my skin. Dario's a throwback, but damn, he does it for me.

I can't wipe away my cheesy grin. Lord knows I've kissed a lot of frogs. I'm due a prince.

I skip up the polished marble stairs, swinging my shopping bags, and magically, exactly when I reach the top, Ray opens the front door.

"Perfect timing," I sing, sailing past him.

I want to get a shower before I find my man and ask him about the steaks. My hair's in a messy bun, and I'm not wearing my face. Dario's second generation, but he thinks like my grandparents—you don't leave the house looking less than your best. He's a bespoke suit, not a tracksuit kind of guy.

I'm a few steps in when Ray wraps his hand around my upper arm in a punishing grip, jerking me to a halt. I raise my eyebrows at my boyfriend's driver. That's Ray's official job. He drives like an old lady, though, and he spends most of his time skulking around the house. I don't question it. I was born and raised in a connected family. My lack of curiosity is genetic.

"He wants you in his office," Ray says, his craggy face blank and his voice gruff. Ray's never friendly, but this is different. Not good.

My stomach plummets.

"What's wrong? Is Dario okay?"

Has he been hurt? It's always a possibility. Dario's a money man, but even money men can catch lead.

"He's fine. Come on." Ray's already propelling me through the cavernous front hall with the crystal chandelier and the marble floors that shine like glass.

"Are you sure?" He's scaring me. His grip is too tight—as if he thinks I might bolt.

"Don't worry about Dario." Ray won't look at me, and the way he says it implies that I *should* be worried. Maybe for myself. I didn't do anything, though.

I am not the kind of Catholic with the guilt. My dad's side of the family tried their best to teach me shame and how to be a "good Italian woman," but Mom hated being nothing but a wife and mother. She never had the balls to help herself, but she did her best to break the cycle. She snuck me a copy of *Our Bodies, Ourselves* when I was thirteen, and when we were supposed to be going to confession, she'd take me to the park so I could play chess.

My heart twinges. I miss my mom every day. Dad, not so much. Life got easier once he was gone.

But these are bleak thoughts. I try to shake them off as we get to the imposing oak door to Dario's office. He mostly works from home, so he spends a lot of time in this room. It's more like a library. Tons of bookshelves and a workstation for his assistant, Miles, as well as Dario's own gargantuan desk.

Dario's bent me over it on several occasions. It's a little too high for comfort.

I have the sense I'm not being called to the office for a quickie. Ray's face is way too disapproving.

I draw in a calming breath. This is Dario. I didn't do anything wrong. He loves me. I don't need to worry. Whatever has happened, I can handle it.

Coming from a mob family and having been with my share of made men, I know that's not entirely true, but the mantra soothes me enough that I'm able to smile brightly when Ray hustles me in and deposits me in front of Dario's desk. Ray shuffles off, and I hear the soft snick of a door shutting. My nerves jangle.

Dario doesn't look right. He's rumpled. His jet-black hair is always neatly combed back, but it's tousled, as if he's been running his fingers through it. His tie is loose, and two buttons on his white collared shirt are undone, one more than usual. My wariness surges.

"Is everything okay?" I blurt.

He stares at me, his brown eyes a dark pool. Dario is always inscrutable. He's not an easygoing guy. That's what I bring to the relationship—fun and relaxation. He's always serious, but this glare is different than his usual baseline intensity. It's smoldering. Angry.

Fear trickles down my spine. My palms grow damp.

He doesn't answer me right away. I squirm in my flip-flops. I wish I'd been able to change before he saw me. He hates me in T-shirts and yoga pants. Whenever he catches me wearing them, he asks if I need him to increase my allowance.

I hate that he calls it my allowance. I do plenty around this house, and I'd still be working if he let me. But he's right—he's too important in the organization for me to be in public without protection.

After what feels like an eternity, he exhales and cracks his angular jaw.

"Come. Sit." He pats his lap. The gesture's affectionate, but it doesn't match his eyes or the tension radiating from his body.

My mouth goes dry. Something's very wrong. He never wants to snuggle. Not even after sex. Something inside me says I should stay where I am.

But this is Dario. He's a dangerous man, but not to me. I've dated bad men before. Too many. Dario isn't like that. He's hard—and insensitive in a manly-man kind of way—but he's never intentionally cruel. He's never raised a hand to me, and while I annoy him all the time, he doesn't yell.

I ease around the desk and hesitantly perch on his knees. He drags me back until I'm plastered to his chest, his arm curled around my waist. I inhale the spice of his aftershave and his natural musk, and some of the worry seeps from me. This is my man. I'm where I belong. I relax against him, letting my legs dangle and rest against his.

"You love me, don't you, Posy?" he murmurs, his breath hot on my ear.

"Yes, baby. Of course I do."

"And you'd never betray me." His voice lowers, and his hold tightens, pressing uncomfortably on my lowest ribs. I shift, try to give myself some breathing room. It doesn't hurt —quite. But it's not pleasant either.

"Never."

He grips my chin in two fingers and turns my head so he can reach my lips, pressing a soft kiss to my lips. He closes his eyes, something awful contorting his features. The expression is there for only the briefest second then gone.

"What's going—"

He shushes me. "I want you to watch something with me."

His laptop is in front of us. He taps the mouse, the screen comes to life, and as soon as I see the split screen, my heart drops, the air whooshing from my lungs.

There's no way. It can't be. I blink, but the image is still there, grainy and poorly focused but unmistakable. That's me looking into the camera, clumpy black mascara starting to run, trying so hard to look sexy and failing so badly.

I buck to get free of his arms, but he wraps a second arm across my chest, pinning me flush to his chest. His rapid heartbeat thumps against my back.

"That's you, isn't it?" he says.

My face burns and tears fill my eyes. "Turn it off."

"No. I like it. You look pretty with brown hair. Is it a wig?" His voice is ice cold, preternaturally calm.

On the screen, a woman moans. It's me. *I'm* moaning. In pain.

Blood rushes to my head, and my stomach heaves. "Stop it, Dario," I whimper.

"No. Watch it with me." His voice is mocking. Mean. "I only got it a few minutes ago. Frankie 'accidentally' airdropped it to everyone in the organization. I imagine everyone's watching it right now. Forwarding it to friends. You're gonna go viral."

Oh, Jesus. This isn't happening. Hot tears streak down my cheeks, and I can't wipe them away because Dario has me pinned. I'm trapped, watching a younger, dumber version of myself trying so damn hard to not look like she's suffering.

Acid scores my throat. I can't puke. I have to breathe through this until it's over.

How is it even possible? Giorgio swore he deleted the video when I got hinky about it. I watched him delete it off his phone. And I believed him, didn't I?

And how did Frankie Bianco get the video? Are all my exes sharing revenge porn? This video has been around for years. Has everyone seen it already, and it's just new to Dario and me?

Fucking Giorgio Fusco. Except for his dick, you can't even see him. He could be anyone. But that's *my* face. Clear as day.

"Can you make them delete it?" I whimper. It's too late, but how can I live with this picture in everyone's head? In Dario's head?

I can't tear my gaze away, horror and shame slamming into me in waves as my brain leaps from one nightmarish thought to the next.

Even with the split screen, it's clearly an amateur video. On the right, I'm grimacing in pain, teeth clenched to stifle my screams, tears in my eyes. Giorgio has my ponytail wrapped around his hand, and he's yanking my head back to make sure I'm looking straight into the camera.

On the left, Giorgio's struggling to wedge his cock in my ass.

There's a muffled rumbling, Giorgio's voice, though you can't make out his exact words.

"Yes," eighteen-year-old me lies. "I love it."

Another mumbling.

"Your cock in my ass. I love your cock in my ass."

In the here and now, I rock my full weight against Dario's unrelenting grasp. "Let me go. I can't watch this."

"Oh, no. There's two minutes and thirty-six more seconds. I watched the whole thing. You can watch it with me."

"Why are you doing this?" I sob, straining to see his face. He's a possessive guy, but he's not unreasonable. He's the least emotional Sicilian I've ever met.

"Everyone's doing it, Posy. Everyone is watching you beg for a cock in your ass."

"He said he deleted it," I blubber.

"So you knew about it?" he asks, his voice acidic with disgust.

Of course, I did. I'm looking into the camera, just like Giorgio coached me. He said he wanted to save the memory of when I gave myself to him fully in all ways. I was so young. I thought I was in love. I knew he'd never, ever betray me.

Loyalty is big in my world because no one has much.

On screen, a fat tear drips down my cheek and leaves a streak of mascara. My chest heaves with the effort of holding in silent sobs. I was such a dumb, trusting kid. I wish I could go back and rescue her. Tell her she deserved better.

I can't watch anymore. I force my gaze to the carpeted floor. "Please turn it off. Why are you doing this?"

"Why did *you* do it?" He bites back at me.

"What do you mean?"

I was stupid, and I believed a man I trusted.

I don't understand why Dario's being like this. He knows I had a lot of boyfriends before him. We met officially when I was dating Frankie Bianco. This isn't the fifties. He's never complained that I know what I'm doing in bed.

Dario tightens his grip, shaking me a little. On purpose. I freeze. This is new. He's never been rough with me before. Not in anger.

"I mean, did you wait for me to get on the plane to take this guy's cock in your ass, or was it in there as soon as I was out the door?"

Hold on. What?

I crane my neck until it hurts, but with the way he's holding me now, I can't meet his eyes. I can only see his profile, sharp angles tense with barely suppressed rage.

"December thirteenth," he says. "I flew to New York that day. Bought you a fucking ring."

My jaw drops, my brain scrambling to catch up. December thirteenth? I look back at the video, squinting, trying desperately to ignore the sight of Giorgio's fingers digging into my ass, leaving red marks on my pale skin. In the lower right-hand corner. There's a time stamp.

It says December thirteenth. Of *this* year.

I shake my head. "No. Dario, this video is five years old. That's why my hair's brown. I used to dye it in high school."

"Don't lie to me." He tightens his arms again, truly constricting my breath. For the first time, panic rises. I'm in trouble.

"I'm not lying," I gasp. "That's my high school boyfriend. Giorgio Fusco. I told you about him. The two timer."

Dario shakes me so hard my teeth chatter. "Stop lying, Posy."

I tense, instinctively trying to curl up and protect myself, but I can't. He's got me immobilized, facing the laptop, and all I can hear is the soundtrack of my pathetic whimpers as I beg Giorgio to hurry up and cum. That, and Dario's furious, jagged breath in my ear.

My stomach lurches again. I'm definitely gonna puke. I'm going to have to swallow it. If I don't, it's going all over myself.

"I swear to you," I pant. "I've never cheated on you. That date is wrong."

"I gave you everything, Posy. I brought you into my home. Treated you like a queen. And this is what I get?" He shakes me again. My head bounces, smacking against his bearded jaw, but he doesn't seem to notice. "This is what I get for laying down with a Santoro dog."

I wince. He's never brought my father's family up before. And since we've been together, no one else has either.

"Dario," I plead. I'm not sure for what. Trust. Mercy. Release.

He flings me off his lap, and I land on the floor with a jarring thud, arms and legs akimbo, my wrist bending back the wrong way. A sharp shooting pain radiates up my arm.

He rises to his feet, six-feet and two-hundred pounds of lean muscle and cold rage. I scramble up, dashing to put the desk between us, cradling my wrist.

I've never seen him like this—on the verge of violence. He's motionless, except for the twitch of his fingers as if he wants to reach for his gun.

Panic screams in my head. Run, run. My stupid heart

reaches for him, though. This isn't the man I know. Where is my Dario? Where is the man who plays games with me for hours and delights when I beat him, who comes looking for me at random times during the day to make love?

"Dario, please, just look at it again. It's an old video. I don't look anything like that now."

"You want me to watch that filth again? Watch you beg for cock in your ass?" His voice rises. "This is what I get for bringing a slut into my house. I should have expected this. You can't help being what you are—a dirty, lying whore."

He's bites out the words, lips peeled back in disgust, refusing to even look at me. My heart cracks.

This is the man who bought me a diamond and gold watch for our third date because I had a habit of being late. When he was trying to convince me to move in, he had the gardener replace all the flower beds with nothing but posies. He plays canasta with me for hours even though he hates canasta, and when I ask him, he reads novels aloud in Italian to help me fall asleep at night.

This is *Dario*. He should believe me. I've never lied to him. Not once.

"You have nothing to say for yourself?" he spits.

"Dario—" My voice cracks. "You *know* me."

He sneers. "I know you. I should have expected this from Frankie Bianco's sloppy seconds. Honestly, the last name Santoro should have tipped me off."

Each word is a blow to my soft belly. My shoulders curve, and I hug my aching wrist to my middle. My legs want to run, but fear has me frozen to the spot.

I don't know this man at all.

All the blood that normally flows through my veins has sunk to my feet. I'm sweating, and I don't know if it's from fear or shame or the sickening sensation of the other shoe dropping.

How deluded have I been?

This is why everyone tiptoes around the house. Why dangerous men square their shoulders and speak with respect, hats in hand, when they come for meetings in this office. Why the other waitresses at L'Alba cast worried glances my way when I started talking to Dario Volpe but would never say a word against him.

He's none of the things I tell myself he is—a gentleman, a shy genius who needs a girl like me to bring him out of his shell. A little old-fashioned in his views, but decent and generous. He's an *asshole*.

He's a *dangerous* asshole.

And he's seething, but he hasn't lost an ounce of control. He threw me on the floor on purpose; it was a move calculated to demonstrate his contempt. He's not falling into a rage. If anything, he's more self-contained now, as still as a cobra waiting to strike, deep brown eyes narrowed and glinting, devoid of any trace of fondness, let alone love.

He might actually kill me.

My gaze darts around the office. Files. Books. Overstuffed leather chairs and a low table. Nothing I could use to protect myself. Nowhere to hide.

I know he's carrying. A revolver holstered in the small of his back and a semi-automatic in an ankle holster.

We're in the suburbs of Pyle, but the house is big, the grounds expansive. There's nothing to stop him from squeezing off a single shot. No neighbors close enough to hear and call the cops. Lord knows Ray and Ivano wouldn't stop him. They'd bury the body, my body, for him.

My heart slams against my rib cage, deep grief welling up on the heels of terror. Where did my Dario go? Did he ever exist? If he loved me, could he be this cold and cruel? Could he believe I betrayed him so easily? Wouldn't he *want* to hear my side of the story?

But he's cut me out like the gristle from his steak.

I sashayed into this office thinking he loved me, and a quarter hour later, I am staring at a man who seems to be weighing whether or not I'm worth the effort of scrubbing blood stains out of the carpet.

I swallow against a wretched cry. No time for that now.

And besides—I cannot be this shocked. This is how life goes. Delusion and then disappointment and despair. I want to sink to the floor. Surrender. Beg for a mercy that I don't need and should never have to ask for.

I want to go back in time. Unbreak this thing between us. But I don't have the power.

He has it all.

I force myself to drag down a deep breath. I am not going out like this. I might have been named after a flower, but I don't wilt like one. I'm walking out of this room.

"Dario—" I start, pausing to lick my dry lips. I don't know what I'm going to say.

He holds up a hand. "I don't want to hear another word from your whore mouth. I'm going to tell you what's going to happen." His tone doesn't match his words. There's no scorn, only bloodless determination. "You're going to turn around. Walk out the door. Ray is going to drive you and your shit into the city. You're going to get out, and I'm never going to have to look at your lying face again."

He waits patiently. For me to answer or for me to leave?

I'm not an idiot. I'll take an out when I'm offered one. I nod and ease back toward the door on legs like jelly. I almost make it. My hand is on the knob when he says, "Wait."

For a second, my silly heart leaps, warmth hitting my chest like the heat from a shot of tequila.

The soft part of my brain I've never been able to fix spins off into a fantasy. He can't do it—he can't let me walk away. It's only been eight months, but what we have is real. I've never felt this way before, as if I'm punch drunk twenty-four-seven, walking on clouds. He's angry now, but deep down, he *knows* me. He'll take a breath. Think it through. He'll realize it's all a mistake. He's the smartest man I've ever known. He won't let a misunderstanding tear us apart.

I turn back to him.

"Come here." He beckons me over.

I approach slowly, equal parts dread and mad hope. His face is a cold mask.

I stop a foot away. He's on his side of the desk; I'm on the other. He skewers me with a vicious glare that triggers every instinct for self-preservation that I have, his lips curling in a contorted smile, dashing the hope. This isn't second thoughts. This is something else.

He taps the desk with one long finger. "The watch."

It takes a moment to sink in. He wants the Rolex back. It's on my wrist. I never take it off, except to sleep and shower.

My lungs seize as if it will hurt too much to take another breath. I don't know what's stronger—the humiliation or the death of the dream. He was the one, wasn't he? The jewelry, the flowers, the late nights, the box in the drawer. I've been hurt so many times, but it was worth it because it led me to him.

As my fingers fumble with the clasp, reality rearranges the pieces in my head. I wasn't living a fairy tale. I was high on a delusion that *this man* loved me.

The watch hits the wood with a soft thud.

"Earrings, too."

I touch my lobes. I'm wearing the studs he gave me for Christmas.

I can't take them out quickly enough. No matter what he thinks now, I'm not a gold digger. I've never asked him for anything. He made me quit my job. He insisted on the "allowance."

I hate this feeling. I fight it, force my hands steady as I pair the posts with the backs, already stepping away.

Dario's hand darts out, his rough fingers wrapping around my forearm, squeezing hard enough to bruise.

"People don't make a fool of me and walk away, Posy *Santoro*." He says my last name like a curse. "If I see you again, you're not *walking* away. Capisce?"

I jerk a nod. He drops my arm as if it burns him, and jerks his chin toward the door.

"Get out," he says, his attention already on his phone. "And shut the door behind you."

∽

RAY IS WAITING for me in the hall, his weathered face blank. For a second, the relief of escaping the lion's den rocks me on my heels, but it ebbs quickly, leaving a tangled mess of shame and loss and shock. My lip trembles, and a fresh wave of tears threatens to spill down my face.

For a brief second, I want to dash up the stairs, throw myself on the bed, and sob into the comforter like I did when I was in junior high and kids were mean to me at school. I want to let myself dissolve in pain until I'm too worn out to hurt so bad.

But I can't do that. I can't crumble.

I fight the panic back one breath at a time.

I'm not a child anymore. There's no mama in the kitchen to make me hot cocoa. I have to get myself out of here. I don't have the luxury of self-pity. I need to get angry. Quick.

I square my shoulders. Done giving me a moment to collect myself, Ray gestures for me to follow him back the way I just came.

Did he see the video?

My cheeks burn. Ray's old enough to be my father. Oh god. How many people have seen it? I bet Ivano couldn't get enough. He's always brushing by me too close. Watching my tits when I come down the stairs.

It went to everyone, Dario said. All the men who used to drink with my dad before our family's fall from grace. All the honorary uncles and cousins have seen me take it in the ass. My stomach gurgles ominously even though I didn't stop for lunch. I was rushing back to make myself up before Dario got home.

I trail in Ray's wake, numb, brain spinning. This is better than the vortex of feelings. I can handle this.

What am I going to do?

How could Giorgio do this to me? I haven't seen him in years. And how could Dario have believed it?

I'm not a liar. He knows that. Dario's a genius. He's a quiet man who keeps his own counsel but somehow knows everything. He spends his days playing the markets, master of a system none of us understand. I'm simple in comparison. What you see is what you get. How does he not know me by now?

I'm only half aware of leaving the house, stumbling down the stairs, and waiting beside the town car for Ray to unlock the door. He's taking a suitcase and a duffle bag from Ivano and stowing them in the trunk. It's the luggage I came with. Dario's bought me a huge wardrobe since I moved in, way more than two bags worth. Guess I'm leaving with what I came with.

My mouth is bone dry, my limbs still weak from the aftermath of the adrenaline rush. I need to sit. As soon as Ray clicks the key fob, I open my own door and collapse in the back seat.

Where is he taking me?

I look out the car window to the front of the house, the tiniest bud of hope poking up in my chest, as if I can't help but torment myself. Maybe the door will burst open and Dario will run out, shouting, "Stop!"

He'll drag me from the car, clutch me to his hard chest, gentle and careful this time, begging me to forgive him. He got carried away in a jealous rage, but he knows I love him. I might have gotten around, but I'd never cheat. He knows that because what we have is real. The connection is *real*.

He's not going to just let me go.

It's a hope that pricks like sorrow.

The door doesn't open. Ray pulls out, and I keep it in view until we turn onto the street, but there's no sudden flurry of activity.

Of course.

I've been here before.

I've been ghosted, slow faded, two-timed, dumped, and kicked to the curb enough times to know the drill.

This relationship was no different than every other disaster I've thrown myself into. Dario and I aren't a love story. It's the other kind. Girl meets mysterious, brooding mafioso. Convinces herself they're in love. Lets him take over her life.

And in the end, mysterious is criminal. Brooding is cruel. And the mafioso is a monster.

This is definitely not the first time I've tripped my happy ass down this crooked path.

Giorgio Fusco, the one who took all my virginities, swore he loved me. He'd take care of me. While he was swearing his undying devotion, he was doing the same with Angie Serra and Teresa Fiore. Danny Ricci loved me until his friends called him "pussy-whipped" and ragged on him for dating a Santoro. Hunter Vanzetti loved me until I showed him up a few too many times, won a few too many poker games.

I hopped from guy to guy—lapping up the love until the tap ran dry—until Frankie Bianco. He was a man, not a boy. A made man. A big deal. Possessive and intense. Pushed all my daddy issue buttons.

He backhanded me when I questioned what he was doing all night at the strip club. He punched me in the stomach when I was out with the girls and my phone ran out of charge so I didn't respond to his texts right away.

I told him I had to visit my sick aunt. I actually went to the Jersey shore for two weeks. I figured he had a short attention span, and I was right. He dumped me for his ex Jen Amato before I came back. Jen pranced around L'Alba like the cat who got the canary, talking shit behind my back. She still does.

Back then, I thought I dodged a bullet. I guess I didn't learn to not jump in front of them—I hooked up with Dario not much later.

Up front in the car, Ray fiddles with the radio and gets onto the highway.

By some miracle, I'm calming down.

I rest my aching wrist on my lap. The throb is fading. It's definitely not broken, and it probably isn't even strained.

This is a bad situation, and when I have time, I'll cry a

river, but I'm not destroyed. I've picked myself up from every relationship disaster so far, and I can do it again.

I have my phone. There's almost two hundred dollars cash in the case. I assume Dario will cancel my credit card. When I get where I'm going, I'll try to take out a cash advance. Maybe I'll get lucky and he won't have thought to cancel it yet. Hah. He'll have thought of it. He thinks of everything. Except why I'd wear a wig to cheat on him—and videotape it. That doesn't make any damn sense at all.

I have no guilt about taking his money. I'd still have my waitressing job if I hadn't let him talk me into making myself dependent.

The first flicker of genuine anger flashes to life in my chest. I'm not sure if it's toward him or myself, but it's energy, and I am bone weary, so I cling to it. Nurture it like a spark in tinder.

I will pick myself up. Find a place to stay. A job. A car. I've gotten them all before.

Car.

"Guess I don't get to keep the Beamer?"

Ray startles, his gray eyes glaring at me in the rearview. His thick eyebrows knit together like I'm talking crazy.

"Guess not," I sigh. I let them trade in my Honda when Dario bought me the convertible.

Ray's lips thin in disapproval. I know I sound like a gold digger. If he saw the video, I don't see how his opinion of me is getting lower, though.

Still, my gaze drops to my lap.

I miss my mom.

If she were still here, I'd be heading to our old apartment that smelled like cooking spices and incense. She'd make me a cup of tea and give me a biscotti from the tin hidden on top of the china cabinet. She'd let me cry my eyes out, and then she'd tell me the same thing she always did.

You're a smart girl, Posy Santoro. You've got a good heart and you're not afraid of hard work. Keep your head up. You'll be fine.

My mother loved the hell out of me. My father thought I was nothing but a pretty face, worthless like all women. The kids at school hated me for being a Santoro. When my uncle stole from Dominic Renelli, he cast shame on the whole family, even the kids. My cousin Andres had it worse, but I had it bad enough.

I've been alone before. I've been called names. I've been cast off.

But I *am* smart. I *will be* fine.

I'll break down later once I have a bed for the night.

I'm so lost in thought that I startle when the silence is broken by the rip of the emergency brake. Ray's pulled into a parking space along River Street, the congested boulevard that runs along the waterfront. This is the center of the city. Tall buildings line the north side, a promenade on the other. The Luckahannock glints silver in the late afternoon sun. It's wide and deep here, and on the far bank, mansions sit high on a bluff.

That's where the capo of the Renelli organization lives. Frankie's family, too. I never understood why Dario chose a place on the outskirts of the city so far from Saint Celestine's. He doesn't like people. That could be it.

It doesn't matter. Not my concern anymore.

Ray pops the trunk. I check for oncoming traffic and get out.

I feel like a zombie. My body's moving, but my brain's unattached, wandering off in all directions. My stomach's starting to really ache with hunger pangs.

Did I have breakfast? Or was I too excited to go shopping? The game store had called to tell me that the bespoke backgammon set I ordered for Dario had arrived. He was going to be so stoked. He'd give me one of his tight smiles, the slightest curve of his firm lips, but I'd know he was pleased.

There's a sharp stab to my heart. I breathe through it.

That should have been my first red flag. What kind of man never shows his teeth when he smiles?

I walk around to meet Ray behind the car. He sets my rolling suitcase on the sidewalk and props the duffle bag on top. His hand rests on the extended handle.

He stares at me, brow furrowed, looking every inch a grizzled detective from a 70s TV show.

Ray and I aren't friends by any means, but we've developed a rapport over the past few months. I'm cheerful. He feigns annoyance. I refill his coffee the way he likes it with sugar and cream. When I forget to return an umbrella to the stand or hang my keys from the labeled hook, he helps me out, keeping the peace. Dario likes things in their proper place.

Guess I don't have to give a crap about that anymore.

I reach for my suitcase, and Ray reluctantly releases the handle, his troubled gaze still resting on my face. He seems to be struggling with himself.

"Well, bye, Ray. Catch you on the flip side." I lift my hand.

He clears his throat, and his eyes dart around as if he's checking to make sure we're alone. There's plenty of tourists and business people on the sidewalks, some rushing, some strolling. No one familiar.

"Listen," he says, ducking his head down, leaning closer and lowering his voice. "You need to leave town."

My eyes widen. "Why?"

"Dominic Renelli. He doesn't like loose ends. You're not with Dario anymore. You're a loose end."

Icy fingers stroke down my spine.

Dominic Renelli had my Uncle Marco killed. Everyone knows it. He beat my father within an inch of his life before he let himself be convinced that Dad had nothing to do with the scam. Renelli let Dad live, but Dad was out. When Dad passed, he was working for peanuts at one of the laundromats the Renelli's run as fronts. There was no cash in an envelope for his widow. The cancer took Mom because we couldn't afford the treatments.

Dominic Renelli ruins lives without a second thought. The guilty and the innocent.

All of a sudden, the fear from Dario's office comes rushing back.

"Renelli will not let you walk away. Not when you've had a front row seat to his business and your last name is Santoro."

I sway on my feet, barely holding myself up with the handle of my suitcase.

Ray nods. "I see you grasp the severity of the situation," he says.

"I understand," I manage.

A shadow passes over his face. He opens his mouth to say something else, but he must think better of it. He returns to the car without a backwards glance. Instead of pulling away, though, he sits in the driver's seat and scrolls on his phone. I guess he has orders to wait until I walk away.

I drag down a steadying breath. There's a nip in the air as the sun lowers. I loved the feel of sunshine on my bare feet earlier, but now my toes are frozen. God, I hope whoever packed my bags didn't forget shoes. I'm not getting far in flip-flops.

Or with two hundred bucks.

I am well and truly fucked.

I had half an idea to get a hotel room for the night, but if Dominic Renelli is after me? Every second counts. I don't have time to waste. I need to move.

I shake myself and take note of where I am. Ray has dropped me in front of La Armada, the fanciest hotel in the city. Dario and I stayed here after he took me to the opera a few months ago. The singing I could take or leave, but the hotel was my jam. Heated jacuzzi tub. Soft mattresses. A spa, a chocolatier, and a jeweler on site. If that wasn't enough, there's a pedestrian walkway connecting the place to the glitzy shopping mall next door.

And under the hotel—a subway station.

Bingo.

I head for the rotating doors, head high as I pass the valets. In a T-shirt and yoga pants, I don't look like I belong. Not with my discount store luggage. But I keep it moving and act like I know where I'm going.

I remember the layout of the place well enough. There's a hallway past the bar that leads to the elevator. There's a bathroom and an ATM. I head that way, praying. It hasn't been that long. Is Dario really going to get on the phone with the credit card company to cancel my access right after he throws me out of his house?

I pull the black credit card from my cell phone case, sliding it into the machine with trembling fingers. Come on. Big money.

Declined.

Dario is fast. And a vengeful prick. I drop the card in the trash.

I need to get out of here.

What else?

Come on, Posy. Use that brain.

I need money. I need to figure out where to go and how to survive when I get there. I need to cover my tracks.

I duck into the ladies room. It's empty, thank goodness. I lock myself in a stall and sit to think. My mind isn't working right. I can't focus.

Dominic Renelli cut off Freddy Izzo's hand for brushing it against his wife's ass by accident. At least that's the story. And when I was with Frankie, Joe Palumbo disappeared, and Frankie and his friends joked for months about how fat the fishes in the Luckhannock were getting.

Freddy Izzo and Joe Palumbo were made men. I'm a woman. A Santoro. I'm not gonna make it into the river. They'll throw my body in a dumpster like trash.

Finally, it all hits me in a wave, my stomach revolts, and I whirl, hunching, barely making it in time before my guts seize, and I puke acid and coffee into the toilet. It burns my throats. My eyes water.

I'm not crying, though. I suck down breaths between violent heaves, and when there's nothing left in my stomach, I spit a few times. I grab blindly behind me for a wad of toilet paper, wipe my mouth, and flush.

Then I press my clammy forehead against the cool metal partition and force my brain to work.

I need help.

I can buy a bus ticket. Maybe get a few states away, but after that, I'll be broke and screwed. I'll need a way to make money, and if I have to stay off the grid, my options are tricks or panhandling. Maybe eventually I'll be able to find work under the table, but I need ID to get a real job.

I can't use my own. I can't leave any breadcrumbs for Renelli.

Who can help me?

My immediate family is gone. My mom's side cut us off when Dad's brother ran afoul of Renelli. They'd turn me over to him in a heartbeat. Dad's side is down to a great uncle in a nursing home.

I've got friends, girls who deign to overlook my last name since I've been with Dario. We go clubbing, get manicures. They're not the type you can go to in an emergency.

Except. Maybe. Nevaeh?

Nevaeh and I used to work together at L'Alba. She's with Carlo, the Renelli's accountant. We get thrown together a lot at dinner parties where we're the only women our age. She's nuts. I used to think she did a lot of cocaine, but it's just her personality.

She might help me for shits and giggles. She's the kind of reckless that doesn't gauge risk well, a kindred spirit.

I've been by her place. It's in a rough neighborhood. Carlo hasn't moved her in with him yet. I kind of get it. She's a lot to take.

It's worth a shot, though. Even if she turns me away, it's a place to go right now where Renelli won't think to look.

I steel myself, leave the stall, and rinse my mouth out with lukewarm water. I don't look good. I'm pale, and my eyes are huge. I look strung out. My messy bun is half undone and listing to the side. I take a second and tug it back into a tight ponytail, debating whether I should root through my suitcase for a hoodie.

I've wasted enough time here, though. I need to move. I can dig through my stuff on the subway.

I head out toward the elevator, hustling as fast as I can without drawing notice to myself. I take a second and surreptitiously drop my phone in the trashcan next to the ATM, wincing.

I've never *not* had a phone, but there's a Find My Phone

app, and Dario's never hesitated to use it when he's too lazy to go looking for me in the house.

I'm not going to make this easy on them.

I'm not taking a bullet to the back of the head today.

Not for Dario Volpe.

I'm not doing a damn thing for Dario Volpe ever again.

2

DARIO

I stand behind my desk, staring at the shattered laptop and the crack in the drywall, fists clenched so tight my knuckles ache, the cords in my neck straining.

There's a dull roar in my brain, as irritating as a vacuum in the middle of a meeting or a lawn mower outside an open window.

I miscalculated.

I never miscalculate.

Posy Santoro was always a risk, but that's what I do. I manage risk. I excel at it. Low risk equals low reward. I make big bets. If Dominic Renelli knew how much of his money I lose in a given day, he'd shit himself. But I make him twice as much by the time the market closes, so everyone's happy.

If this was Wall Street, I'd be king, but this is the Renelli organization. I'm the wizard behind the curtain.

I don't mind. I don't like people. My work suits me.

I should have fucked Posy Santoro a few times to get her out of my system and then dropped her. That was my intent. It would have made sense. Everyone knows she's loose. Her family name is garbage, and it's not like she's a mafia princess. No one would bat an eye if I had hit it and quit it.

She was good at chess, though. Very good at Stratego and Risk. She can master the rules of new games in one session of play, and her winning percentages range from about thirty percent for Scrabble to almost fifty percent for Risk.

And she's a great lay.

It was inconvenient to invest hours in wining and dining her so that we could get to the games, so I moved her in. She doesn't bother me when I'm working, and she's hot. Better looking than any of my associates' wives or girlfriends. Their horny side-glances amuse me.

It comes rushing back. The video. My chest tightens. The urge to beat and destroy flails inside me, fighting for release, dark and loud and mindless. I didn't get enough.

I want her back. I want to break her again and watch her cry. Hear her beg for mercy.

I want her terrified and cowering, covered in snot and her own piss.

She wasn't sorry at all. She feigned innocence and played the victim. So predictable. You'd think someone as skilled at strategy would be a better liar.

Everyone has seen her take a cock in her ass now. Frankie airdropped the video to the whole organization. Everyone has seen another man taking what's mine.

It's good I sent her away. If she were here, I'd kill her. After him. Frankie's already fucking dead; he's breathing on borrowed time.

I need to go downstairs to the gym. Expel this rage on a punching bag before I do something stupid. Like call Ray to bring her back.

She had the nerve to narrow her eyes at me when I

asked for the watch. As if she was disappointed in me. White hot fury races through my veins. I let her get too comfortable. Kept my mask too firmly in place. She doesn't like to play when she's cranky or hormonal, so I bail when she irritates me. I should have let her taste the back of my hand once or twice. Fear is a much better motivator than loyalty.

If I'd treated her like everyone else, she'd know to be afraid. Then I wouldn't be here with this goddamn deafening roar in my brain.

I don't have time for this. They haven't rung the bell in New York yet, and I'm expecting a rally of the stock I've been shorting. I grit my teeth until my gums ache.

I should call Ray and have him drag her back. I let her off too easy. She needs to pay for messing up my equilibrium. It was satisfying to break her heart—torch those dreams she's been spinning in her head—but it wasn't nearly enough.

She'll just fall in love with the next man who pays her any attention. As easy as transferring funds. Like she did when she went from Frankie Bianco to me. I knew I had her when she mooned at me the exact same way she'd mooned at him, big blue eyes drugged with her favorite delusion.

With a sigh, I squat and collect my broken laptop, plucking each shard from the carpet. Hurling it at the wall was foolish. I lose millions a day, and I don't break a sweat. With risk, loss is inevitable. Posy was a bad bet. That's all. I don't dwell on bad bets.

I did like this laptop, though.

As I drop the last of it into the trash, there are three loud knocks at the door. Ivano. He bangs like the cops.

"Enter."

Chapter 2

I don't have time for this—whatever this is. Posy stole hours of my day, and my time has a steep price tag.

The door opens and a half dozen guys shuffle into my office, stinking it up like cigarettes and old man's cologne. I don't need this right now.

"I don't have you on my schedule."

There are a few chuckles and they part, allowing Dominic Renelli to make his way through. His veined hand shakes where it grips his ivory cane. I force myself to straighten and clasp mine in front of me in a show of respect. It's expected. Habits ingrained from youth are hard to break.

Renelli never makes the trek out to my domain. I meet him in the city. He leaves me to my own devices, and I make him a god among men. It's a convenient arrangement.

"Dario. My boy." He grabs my shoulders in a surprisingly firm grip and kisses my cheek. He smells sour. "Let's sit."

His shuffling steps are careful, and he eases himself down, sighing as he sinks into the cushion. He's getting old. Tony Graziano, his balding consigliere, takes a seat beside him. They're remnants of another age. Cufflinks, suspenders, and pocket handkerchiefs.

The others spread out, making themselves comfortable. Lucca Corso takes the armchair across from me. His second, Tomas Sacco, looms behind him. A memory from school flashes in my head. Lucca tearing down the soccer field, breaking for the goal, Tomas driving his shoulder into the torso of a guy coming in for a side tackle. Inseparable then as they are now.

Frankie Bianco props his ass on my desk. The brass balls that motherfucker has, showing his face here. I'll deal with him in good time. A sickly sense of satisfaction fills me at the prospect. I'm gonna cut his dick off and shove it in his ass. I'll take a picture and be sure to send it to the group chat. I flash him a smile so he knows I'm thinking about him.

Vittorio Amato rounds out the number. He stands by the door with Ivano, surveying the scene and straightening his cuffs. In his day, Amato was the man. Now he's short-tempered and reeks of booze. And he's been making mistakes.

I'm the money man. I don't concern myself too much with operations, but I hear things. Amato's not as razor sharp as he was when we were coming up.

Renelli eases back and rests an arm along the back of the sofa, exhaling noisily and sweeping his bland gaze around the room.

"Two generations, eh?" he says. "The older and the younger. The circle of life."

Renelli's not a big talker. I appreciate that about him. When he does speak, though, he sounds like a philosopher. Like some don from the movies. I've never heard the man talk about pussy or the ponies. It's all loyalty and honor and other meaningless shit.

He seems to be waiting, so I incline my head. Lucca, Frankie, Tomas, and I came up together. Lucca broke my first bone. I torched his first car. We're not friends, but we have history. There are secrets and debts between us.

"We're brothers, eh?" he goes on. "If not by the blood in our veins, then by the blood we spill. True?"

Everyone mumbles affirmation like we're at mass. What the fuck is this?

"I understand there's a video," he goes on. "I've not seen it myself. I leave the internet and the email to Tony, yeah?"

Tony nods, his shark eyes gleaming. He's seen the video.

Chapter 2

My muscles bunch, and acid rises in my throat. I swallow it down. Incline my head in acknowledgement.

"Tony tells me about this video, and I think to myself—these modern times are crazy. We didn't use to tape the evidence." He barks a laugh, and Tony joins him with a braying guffaw. Renelli bobs his gray head. "So different from when I was young. But some things never change. We don't let whores come between brothers, eh?"

He waits, piercing me with his rheumy, hooded eyes. He wants an answer. So that's what this is. He's forbidding retaliation.

My skin heats. Fuck that. Frankie Bianco disrespected me. I don't let that shit pass.

Renelli raises a gnarled finger, pointing it at me. "I see what you're thinking. I was a young man once myself. You can't let a thing like this go. I understand. It's a matter of pride. But with the wisdom of age, you'll see. This thing of ours comes before these petty considerations. This idiot nephew of mine has done you a favor. Saved you from marrying a whore."

"Bullshit. He didn't come to me like a man. He clicked a button like a bitch." I smirk at Frankie while I say it. He rises to his full height and squares his shoulders. He's got forty pounds on me easy from hanging at the gym for hours. I'd still take him out in thirty seconds. He's slow, complacent, and overconfident.

I bare my teeth and wink at him. I'm gonna take a video of him bleeding out with his castrated cock in his ass and put a soundtrack on it. Some special effects. Like those dance videos.

There's a nudge at my calf, and I startle. Renelli is tapping me with his cane. "Be that as it may, it's a squabble between brothers. Go to the gym. Kick his ass in the ring.

Get it out of your systems and leave it behind." His last three words are an unmistakable order.

Frankie snorts at the idea of us in the ring. No one else does.

It's been a long time since Saint Celestine's when I was the kid with his nose in a book and Frankie Bianco was getting sucked off behind the bleachers. Frankie's still the man in his head, but the rest of us have moved on.

The other men in this room know what I am. They understand what I'm capable of. Frankie does too, but he's too stupid to have developed a sense of self-preservation.

"Are we clear, son?" Renelli presses.

I nod. It's clear. I'm not going to drop it, but I have no problem waiting for revenge. I'm a big fan of antipasti. I like all kinds of things cold.

It's almost better when an enemy's been lulled into a false sense of security. The surprise in his eyes when he feels the blade slip between his ribs. It gets me hard every time.

"Good." Renelli reaches over and pats my leg. "Forget the whore. You won't see her again." He deftly changes the subject as my blood runs cold. "Now, how's my money?"

"Good, good." That nagging buzz in my brain that never quite subsided roars to life. *You won't see her again*. It was an assurance. He's sent men after her.

My gaze flickers around the room as I sprint through the calculations. Our best men are here. Renelli sent soldiers. Ivano I've never been a hundred percent sure of, but Ray's mine, and no one but Ray knows where I told him to dump her off. If Renelli made the call when he saw the video, he could have had eyes on her for hours. She might have a bullet in her brain now.

My pulse pounds in my ears. I'm chatting with Renelli,

rattling through my recent trades on autopilot, and if not for those years in my father's house, I wouldn't be able to hide the rage that's broken loose in my chest.

He dares go after what's mine?

An image flashes in my mind. Posy on the ground, a hole in her head, blood in her blonde hair, her blue eyes sightless.

The buzz in my head becomes a wild roar.

No. I'm not done playing yet.

Is she dead already?

If she's dead, so are they. Every motherfucker lounging in this room as if they're bad, wearing suits and gold watches and diamond rings paid for by the money I make. Any goon can collect a debt. I've built these apes a financial empire.

I decide when the game's over. If they take Posy from me, I'll burn it all down and throw their limp corpses on the fire for fuel.

Renelli's staring at me askance. I realize I've stopped talking. His brow furrows, and then he offers me a wry smile.

"Of course, my money's always good in your hands. I don't understand a fuckin' word you say half the time, but I understand zeroes enough. Keep 'em growing, my boy." He nods to Tony and struggles to his feet, joints cracking. "We'll leave you to it."

I stand. The men fall in behind Renelli, careful to avoid my gaze. Except for Frankie. He smirks and licks his lips.

I'm going to bury him out back under the hostas so I can take a piss on him while standing on the edge of the deck.

The men shuffle out the door, and I go to crack the window. I can't think with this reek in the air. I need to call Ray. I need to know she's alive.

The footsteps grow softer as I reach for my phone. As soon as Ivano sees them out, I need to know. My nerves stretch with the seconds, my chest tightening.

I almost don't notice Lucca Corso hanging back, Tomas lingering behind him.

He's in the doorway, hand resting on the frame, casual, as if he's had an afterthought.

I tense. Lucca's not as stupid as the rest of them.

He quirks his lips, flashing his bright white teeth. It's his way to flirt with everyone—man, woman, and child. It's how he convinces people to underestimate him.

"What?" I snap. "I have work."

He smiles wider. "All work and no play makes Johnny a dull boy."

"Get the fuck outta here, Lucca."

A trace of real amusement sparks in his dead eyes. "You do better work when you get to play your games."

What is he talking about?

He takes a half-step forward. "Yield on the growth funds has increased at least twenty percent over market average for the past two quarters."

It's true. But what's his point? I raise my eyebrows.

"You said it yourself just now," he says by way of explanation. "But I read the prospectuses. I've noticed." He rubs an invisible speck from the doorframe and then slips his hand in his pocket. "Some men value loyalty above all. Honor. Brotherhood."

He expels a cynical sigh. "But we're not brothers, are we, Volpe?"

His words conjure the ancient past, fetid and foul. Bitterness floods my mouth. "No. We're not."

His mother was married to my father, but no—we were never brothers.

"We see things the same, you and I."

He's speaking in riddles, and I don't have time for it. Is that his game? He wastes my time while Renelli's men narrow in on Posy?

The roar in my brain becomes a howl. I force my hands to relax, slow my breathing, give nothing away.

When I don't respond, he clicks his cheek. "It would be a shame if our bull market came to an end." He shrugs. "But I suppose no good thing can last, eh?"

He blinks as if rousing himself from a daydream. "I'll leave you to it," he says and heads off down the hall, Tomas falling in to walk by his side. The movie star and the street fighter. Odd fuckin' couple.

My phone's immediately in my hand, and I'm dialing. Ray picks up after one ring.

"Do you have her?" I growl.

He only misses a half beat. "I dropped her at La Armada."

"When?"

"I don't know...Twenty minutes ago?"

"Where did she go?"

"Into the hotel."

Why would she do that? She has no more than two hundred dollars cash. Maybe she doesn't realize I cancelled her credit card.

"Was anyone following her? When you dropped her off?"

"No, boss."

"Go back. Get her. Bring her back here."

"All right."

"How long before you get there?"

"I'm still parked out front."

"I told you to dump her and leave."

"I was reading the paper," he grumbles. "Don't bust my chops."

"Go now." I hang up.

Twenty minutes. If she tried to book a room, her credit card would have been declined. She'd head somewhere else. It's busy downtown this time of day. Ray might luck into her, but she could be blocks away by now.

I click the app to track her phone. I should've done this first. My brain is slow. Thick.

By some miracle, she's still at La Armada. I text the coordinates to Ray, and I pace, the cacophony in my brain ebbing and surging with the erratic beating in my chest.

He'll bring her back to me. Within the hour, she'll be here.

No one takes what's mine without my permission.

I decide when I'm done with that bitch.

And by the time I am, she's going to be very, very sorry for all the trouble she's caused.

3

POSY

Nevaeh Ellis lives in a dump. I thought I was roughing it before Dario moved me in, but this is a shithole. Elevator's out of service. Narrow hallways with stained ceilings and warped tiles. I made the same salary she did at L'Alba. What does she do with her money?

I haul my suitcase up the last set of stairs and head for her apartment. As soon as I got off the subway, my panic ebbed. I'm hella more likely to be mugged in this part of town, but I'm a hundred times safer. The Renellis don't bother with this neighborhood. There's no vig on zero.

Still, I keep looking behind me. I'm not gonna stop until I'm far, far away.

I knock, sending up a short prayer. This is a hail Mary. Nevaeh instantly replied with her address when I texted her for it earlier, but I didn't tell her what was going on. Once she hears, she very well might send me packing.

If she told Carlo that I'm visiting, and he knows what's going on, I might be delivering myself to Renelli on a silver platter. I didn't dare ask her *not* to tell Carlo, though. That would definitely make her leery. She's not stupid, just flighty.

At first, there's no sound, but then there's a thump and a scramble and the door flies open.

"Posy Santoro!"

A small woman with big, bouncy black hair yanks me inside. She's grinning, and her breath reeks of weed. She's wearing joggers, a hot pink crop top, and socks with red pom poms on the heels.

"Oh, crap," she says, stretching the vowel, her eyes rounding. "You're in trouble."

She peers into the hall and then slams the door shut.

"What did you hear?" I ask.

"Nothing, but I know that look."

"What look?"

"Like *shit* hit the *fan*!" She drags me over to her futon, toeing aside dirty clothes and random debris strewn across the floor, and tugs me down beside her. Nevaeh's not big on personal space. Or moderating her volume.

Dario is very insistent on both of those things, so naturally, he loathes her. Makes me like her even more now.

"What happened? Tell me everything. Did you and Dario break up? Did he cheat?" Nevaeh's nose wrinkles. "Did you find the bodies? That dude must have one hell of a count." She shudders. "No offense."

My brain struggles to catch up. Nevaeh's mouth operates on high speed. You have to listen quickly. "None taken."

"I guess you need money."

I flush, but she's right. "He kicked me out."

"What did you do?"

"Nothing." I crane my neck and stare blindly above me

for a second. What did I do? I trusted the wrong man. Again. "He thinks I cheated."

Nevaeh snorts. "You don't have a death wish." There's no doubt in her voice.

Hurt bubbles up through the fear and anger. Nevaeh doesn't even know me that well, and she can see I'd never do something like that. I'm crazy for Dario—

Correction. I *was* crazy for Dario.

But even if I wasn't—even if it was a casual thing with him—I don't mess around. And I'm definitely not risking a relationship that's going somewhere for sex. I mean, sex is okay. Better with Dario than most of the other guys I've been with, but I'm not gonna piss off a mobster for some strange.

"There's a video," I confess, screwing my eyes shut.

"Show me."

I groan. "I don't have it. Ask Carlo. Frankie Bianco airdropped it to everyone."

"Revenge porn?"

"I guess." This would be so embarrassing if it wasn't Nevaeh. She's a walking, talking no-judgment zone. "It's me doing anal for the first time with my high school boyfriend."

"Hot." She thinks a second. "No, hold up. Not hot. Gross. Were you a minor?"

"I was eighteen. And I was in love." I draw out the word, a bitter smile twisting my lips.

"Love makes you do stupid shit," she sighs.

All I can do is nod in agreement.

"I mean, I've never shacked up with a psychopathic serial killer, but this one guy convinced me to join a spin class where they all talked like motivational posters and banged each other afterwards."

"I—"

What?

"Dario's not a serial killer."

Well, not in the "bodies in a freezer" sense. He's a bad man, but he—

No. Nope. Nuh-uh.

There's no "but." I'm not making one more excuse for that man. Eight months of telling people they're wrong about him, he's great once you get to know him, he's introverted, that's all—and he proves everyone right in five minutes.

He's a heartless bastard. A cold, unfeeling jerk.

My eyes prickle.

"Oh, honey." Nevaeh squeezes my hand. Her palm is sticky like from candy. That is so weird. "Did you take the jewelry?"

I shake my head as hot tears dribble down my cheeks. "He made me give him my watch and earrings back."

"Oh, that's brutal. I'm so sorry. Carolyn has such excellent taste."

My brow wrinkles. "What do you mean, Carolyn?"

"Carolyn buys jewelry for all the guys. Even Renelli himself. She does everything. Remembers special occasions, books the trips, makes the dinner reservations." Nevaeh blinks. "I thought everyone knew that."

"Carolyn from L'Alba?" She's a matronly woman who does payroll and the books. She fills in as hostess in a pinch. She's on the phone *a lot*.

"Yeah. She got me a really nice tennis bracelet when Carlo fucked up and called me Angie in bed."

A piece of the puzzle plinks into place.

Dario's always seemed like Dr. Jekyll and Mr. Hyde to me. There was the mad genius who only wants to fuck dirty and play board games, who never talks about his feelings or *really* laughs. And then there's the sweet guy who sends me a bouquet of posies and seasonal flowers on the sixth of every month, the anniversary of our first date. The man who always makes sure my favorite snacks are stocked in the kitchen. Who leaves the new releases from my favorite authors on my nightstand for me to find as a surprise.

Oh, Carolyn is *good*.

I should have seen it.

I know for a fact Dario doesn't know my sign. What are the odds he knows my birthday? He pours me red wine all the time even though I tell him every time it gives me migraines. And yet the posies in the flower beds are my favorite pink and purple? The jewelry? The shoes in my size and the clothes that fit as if they were tailored for my body?

A dozen casual conversations with Carolyn float through my mind.

That bastard has been Cyrano de Bergerac-ing me.

I swivel and collapse on the futon. "Holy shit."

It's like I pressed the lever at the end of Connect Four. Everything clatters out the bottom. I wasn't in a relationship. I was in that movie where the guy finds out his life is a reality TV show.

Nevaeh winces. "Sorry if I ruined the romance."

"Oh, no. Getting thrown out on my ass and having my life threatened did that."

"Oh, man." Nevaeh's eyes pop, and she finally starts looking uneasy. "But Dario kicked you out. Don't take this the wrong way, but if he was gonna kill you, you probably wouldn't be here right now."

"I'm not worried about Dario." Much. I help her put the pieces together. "Dominic Renelli doesn't like loose ends."

Nevaeh's gaze flies to her phone. It's peeking out of a

stack of magazines on a coffee table covered in rings. "Are they looking for you?"

"Probably."

"You have to get out of here." There's an edge of panic in her voice. She gets it now.

"Yeah." I wrestle my exhausted body upright. She bounds to her feet and roots in her purse. "I have thirty... seven bucks." She shoves a wad in my hand.

"I'll pay you back."

"Just—you gotta go. This town is not that big. Posy, you in danger, girl." She checks her phone. "Shit. There's a text from Carlo."

"What does it say?" I lean over to peer at the glowing screen. "What is that?"

"Eggplant emoji." She huffs and rolls her eyes. "He thinks he's cute. It means he wants to bone."

"No mention of me?"

"Just dick veg."

We exhale in unison.

"Nevaeh, I would never ask you this, but—"

"What do you need?" she interrupts. She's right in my face, earnestly making eye contact, so close I can see every freckle on her nose. She's such good people. I wish we'd had a chance to hang out more.

"I need your driver's license. And you can't ever tell anyone that you gave it to me. Say you lost it."

"I've totally done that before." She grins, and my lips curve in response.

"Here." She hands me her card. "We look nothing alike."

"I'll dye my hair when I get where I'm going." She's older than me by seven years, shorter by three inches, and then there's the mass of kinky curls.

"Maybe get a perm, too." She fluffs my lank ponytail.

Chapter 3

"I'll only need this to rent a place. And maybe so I can get a job until I can find something under the table."

"If I catch shit for it, I'll claim you stole it." She squeezes my shoulder.

I gnaw my lower lip, staring down at the little piece of plastic. "Are you sure?" I meet her eyes, hold her gaze.

A current of understanding passes between us. We both know the Renelli organization doesn't play. And we've both been surfing a dangerous wave in a crazy world, just trying to steal a little joy before we get dashed on the rocks again.

Well-adjusted women with happy childhoods don't fuck mobsters.

She knows the risk. She folds my fingers around the card. "Now can you get the hell out of my place before you bring the organization down on me, please?"

"I won't forget this," I swear.

"If Renelli ever catches you, please do."

I laugh, 'cause that's all you can do, and I smack a kiss on her cheek as I head out the door.

Next stop—somewhere far, far away where they've never heard of Dominic Renelli, and I can pretend the bastard I fell in love with doesn't even exist.

I'm starting to understand that maybe he never actually did.

∽

I TAKE the subway to the bus terminal downtown. It's bustling even though it's almost eight at night. I adjust my hoodie, making sure my hair is tucked away. I'm not kidding myself. This disguise won't hold up to any kind of scrutiny. I served Renelli's men for years at L'Alba besides dating my way through a decent portion of the crew. They know me well.

I have to leave now, and two hundred thirty bucks isn't going to get me far. The last discount bus has left for the day, so I've got to ride in style on Greyhound. A one-way ticket to New York City is ninety bucks. Chicago is ninety-five.

I've never been outside of Pyle. All my family is—*was*—here. I didn't go to college. That was never on my radar.

I imagine a city would be a great place to hide, but wouldn't that be what Renelli expects? Everyone runs off to the Big Apple. And the more people around, the more folks who could rat me out.

You know what no one ever does?

Run off to the country. Except for that movie where they send a woman in witness protection to an Amish farm. Or something like that.

I'd stick out like a sore thumb on a farm, obviously, but what about a small town out in the middle of nowhere? I'd need a good story. Something simple. Why do strangers end up in bumfuck? Maybe I'm heading for California or Florida, and I ran out of cash. I'm only in town until I can save enough to move on.

This is good. I wander over to the map hanging beside the vending machines. There are too many possibilities. I check the list of rates. It's thirty-seven bucks one way to Stonecut County. The last bus of the day leaves in fifteen minutes. Kismet.

I hustle over to the ticket counter, hand over Nevaeh's crumpled cash, and jog to the terminal. The bus is not even half full. I get a row to myself in the back, and although the cloying sweet smell of air freshener wafts from the toilet, the heat's blasting, warming my chilled fingers and nose, and the upholstery is clean.

Chapter 3

I hunch down in the seat and stare out the window. The sun is going down, and the sky is a deep blue-black. In the high rises around the terminal, lights blaze in offices being cleaned. I love this city at night. Ever since I was a little girl, if I happened to be driving through after dark, excitement would swirl in my belly.

It was so mysterious. Buildings busy during the day were abandoned, and sidewalks empty during daylight teemed with laughing men and women at night, chatting and smoking in sparkly dresses and sharp suits.

Growing up a Santoro, I didn't make it to adulthood with many dreams intact, but one persisted well past the time I should have known better.

I'd meet a mysterious man, and he'd ask me out. He'd pick me up in a shiny black limousine and show me the town. We'd dance in the clubs, surrounded by laughing people under glittering chandeliers, and he'd tuck my hand in the crook of his arm and walk me down the darkened streets, the stars smattered above the tall buildings, and he'd kiss me, enchanted, swept away by the special thing inside me that only he can see.

As the bus pulls away from the curb, I squeeze my eyes to hold back the tears.

Damned if I didn't try to shove Dario Volpe into that mystery man's shoes. I can't be too hard on myself. Dario had the car. He took me dancing when I asked enough times. He never went so far as to shake me off when I held his elbow as we walked. He'd only pick up his pace so I'd have no choice but to drop his arm.

And he was very comfortable in the dark.

I think he likes being in the shadows. He likes watching people without them noticing. Gauging, measuring. Like a venomous snake considering a strike. Not invested. Just doing calculations in his cold, serpentine brain.

I saw. I *knew* this. But I was different. Special. He moved *me* into his house. He treated *me* like a princess.

Until he decided to strike.

Dirty, lying whore.

I don't want to hear another word from your whore mouth.

If I see you again, you're not walking away. Capisce?

Shame floods my body, and suddenly it's too hot on the bus, the smell from the toilets too floral. I break into a sweat.

I have no reason to be ashamed. It was stupid to let myself be videotaped, yes, and humiliating. But if I hadn't been knocked so off-kilter by Dad's passing followed so suddenly by Mom's, I wouldn't have ever been suckered by a sweet-talking piece of shit like Giorgio Fusco.

The series of guys after? Honest mistakes. Long shots that didn't pan out. Good times gone bad.

And then there was Frankie Bianco. He was handsome, charming, on his way up. All the girls at L'Alba were hot for him. I knew what he was, but I was twenty-one, working at the hottest club in Pyle, living the dream. I took the good with the bad until he did me a favor and cut me loose. I cried, doused my sorrows in ice cream, and fell in love with the next pretty face to notice me.

Dario Volpe.

What's my excuse for him?

A rebound? Youth? I can't claim inexperience.

I *knew* better. A face like a dark angel, and none of the girls crushed on him. That first night at Il Destino when he asked me to dance for him, and I did while he assessed me with that icy stare, his bodyguards impassive at his sides, gazes averted.

I thought it was hot.

Chapter 3

He was auditioning me, testing whether I valued myself cheaply enough to go along with whatever he wanted.

And I did. With a smile.

That's why the shame is eating me up.

All of this did not come out of left field. He's a bad man. It was only a matter of time before he did something bad to me.

The further we get from the lights of the city, the sharper the image becomes in my mind, the clear line from getting on my hands and knees in Giorgio's dank basement bedroom to caking on the makeup after Frankie made a point with the back of his hand.

It leads straight to the back of this Greyhound bus.

If my father were here, he wouldn't be surprised in the least. Wherever she is, though, I know I'm breaking my mom's heart. She never did better for herself, but she wanted so much more for me. Nothing material. Only love. Happiness. Kindness. Peace. She had no idea how to get it for herself, and I have to face facts—neither do I.

I slump against the highbacked seat, drained. Despite the lingering adrenaline, the whooshing of the wheels on the asphalt is lulling me to sleep. I'm hurting, but there's a part of me that's springing to life, a tendril of strength, buffeted and trampled but alive.

Maybe Dario did me a favor, ripping the veil from my eyes now.

I would have quite happily tripped down the aisle to him. Carried his babies. Settled into life as Mrs. Volpe, blessing my good fortune every day.

Sleeping blithely next to a bastard, growing more dependent year after year until a single blow would break me.

Despite all her prayers, all her whispered affirmations, I

was on my way to becoming my mother, stuck forever with a man who—deep down—thinks she's garbage.

Fuck that.

I'm going to Stonecut County. I'm starting over, and I'm never going to ache like this again.

Never.

4

DARIO

"She's gone, boss."

I hurry down the stairs to meet Ray in the foyer. It's almost four in the morning. Ivano and a dozen men are still scouring the city. Posy has vanished without a trace.

I stride over to Ray. He has her cell and credit card in his hand.

"They were in a trash can?" He told me on the phone, but I ask anyway. I'm trying to figure out this problem with the facts available even though it's impossible—like putting together a puzzle with only three pieces from a box of a thousand.

"Next to the ATM in the hotel," Ray confirms again.

"No blood? No signs of a struggle?"

"Renelli's men wouldn't leave any." We both know that, but I had to ask. I'm—unsettled.

Ray sniffs and shrugs off his trench coat. He's rumpled. Exhausted.

"Coffee!" I bark at one of the staff, and there's a scurrying.

I need Ray alert. He's my best man. He knows Posy.

"Where would she go?" he asks me.

How the fuck would I know? I pace to the front window. Her car is still in the drive. I forbid her to park it in the garage herself. She's scraped the side panel twice.

"Does she have a best friend?" Ray probes, sinking onto a bench with a muffled groan.

"She has friends."

He takes out a little pad of paper and a golf pencil. He looks like Columbo. "I need names."

Jesus. I don't know their names. "There's the one with the hair. And there's one with big tits. Ask Carolyn."

Ray tucks the pad back into his pocket, rolls his shoulders, and stretches his legs. "Maybe you want to let this go, boss."

I glare at him. He straightens up.

He pauses a long moment and then sighs. "I'm just sayin'—if she's dead, do you want to know? And if she's gone, do you want her back?"

Yes. No. It doesn't matter right now. She's mine. I decide if she lives or dies.

"Do we have a man at the airport?"

"Yes. And the bus terminal. We got guys paying visits to the car rental places. Hotels. It's a needle in a haystack, though. I say we hang back and wait for her to tickle the system. Miles is on it. As soon as she buys a ticket or rents a room, we got her."

"If she's alive."

Ray gives a short nod. "If she's alive," he repeats.

Posy's smart. She'll figure out the risk, and she'll leave town.

But where would she go?

I don't know how she spent her days. Shopping, I guess.

As long as she was home when the markets closed, I didn't care.

Does she like the beach?

She used the pool every day before the weather turned. I'd catch a glimpse of her from my office window, and I'd come out, bend her over the back of a chaise lounge, hook her wet bikini to the side, and sink into her tight pussy. She'd be so hot wrapped around my cock, her thighs and back cold to the touch as the late summer air dried her skin.

I adjust myself and pace back to Ray. "Where does she like to go?"

His thick brows knit together, and he shrugs a shoulder. "The mall. The Promenade. Stansbury Park."

"Stansbury Park?" A memory sparks and my lip curls.

"Yeah. She plays chess with the old guys."

"She wins?"

"Usually."

My grandfather took me to Stansbury Pavilion to play chess. I learned Fool's Mate and the Sicilian Defense there, stuffing myself with hot roasted peanuts Nonno bought for a quarter a bag. It feels like a hundred years ago, not twenty. I imagine Posy cross legged, playing with the old guys as the pigeons peck the ground.

An unfamiliar tightness grips my chest.

"You had someone comb the park?" I ask.

"She's not there." Ray shifts uncomfortably in his seat. "She's a clever kid. She probably left town as soon as I dropped her off."

"But you didn't see her leave the hotel?"

"I wasn't watching. And there's the subway station underneath."

Of course that's where she went. The subway. The simplest solution. That's how her mind works, why she's such a formidable opponent. Most people can be distracted with gambits. You can switch strategy midstream and seize the advantage during the lag as they adapt. Not Posy. She operates independently of her adversary, always pursuing the straight forward, elegant win. She's an instinctual player. It's an extraordinary thing to watch.

Again, there is a discomfort in my chest. An after effect of the rage, I'm sure. I didn't expect it. I haven't lost myself to it since I was a junior at St. Celestine's, dousing Lucca Corso's Ferrari in gasoline. It was stupid beef, a throwaway insult to his mother that became a beatdown and ended in arson. Sister Mary Francis made Lucca and I clean the chapel for the rest of the year, and our fathers paid for a new floor and bleachers in the gym.

Lucca and I sparred in the narthex when we got bored with polishing pews, and I discovered a way to channel the rage. It was a relief. The blankness left behind was vastly preferable to the mindless fury that arose unbidden and drove me to behave—without due consideration.

As I did when I sent Posy away.

I call up the image of her face in the video. Her hairline. That wasn't a wig. Her hair was brown. She was wearing a lot of makeup, but she did not quite look like she does now. It could be the—duress—for lack of a better word, but she seemed young.

And—the realization crashes on me.

I made a mistake.

She was clearly in pain, and it was clearly a challenge for the man I had assumed was Frankie Bianco to get his cock inside her. Posy doesn't love anal, but she's not unaccustomed to it. I take her ass when the mood strikes me, and she asks for lots of lube, but she doesn't act like she's getting reamed.

Chapter 4

That video wasn't from December.

She was telling the truth.

The time stamp is a fake. Frankie's fucking with me. Now why would he do that?

I picture my visitors from earlier. Renelli and Graziano next to me on the sofa. Lucca and Tomas across from us on a chair. And all the way across the room, leaning on my desk, Frankie Bianco, contender for the crown.

I'm a piece in play. And they dare to use Posy to get to me.

I need her back now.

"Get the CCTV tape from the station for the half hour after you dropped her off," I order Ray. "Bribe whoever you have to. Money's no object. Find out where she went. Do it yourself. Call everyone else in."

"You're sure, boss?" Ray's already dragging himself to his feet. He knows me. I'm always sure. Asking is just his way of complaining.

"Sleep when you're dead." I say over my shoulder as I head toward my office. The European markets are about to open, and I need to focus myself so I can figure out this mess.

I will find Posy soon. We're on her trail. It's only a matter of running her to ground.

She's not dead. Renelli's soldiers move slowly. They think that if they drag their feet enough, he'll keel over before they have to do any real work. It's been this way for awhile now. Since Amato lost his edge.

Still, it makes my skin crawl that she's out there because of my misjudgment. All my efforts for the past eight months blown in minutes. She saw only what she wanted to see, and I had exactly what I wanted. I knocked over my own tower of blocks.

How hard will it be to lull her back into her happy fantasy?

Not hard. Posy's a good tactician, but she's also soft. Emotional. Weak. She cries easily. A splinter in her palm. A commercial with a kitten.

Frankie and the others said she was easy. Daddy issues. The kind that'll suck your dick for a kind word.

It's true as far as it goes. They think that makes her worth less, but then again, they don't use their own brains, so what use would they have for a woman's? Posy is the only person who's ever been able to beat me at cribbage. And she's one of the few who even knows how to play.

I want her back now.

I scroll idly through my portfolios. The letters and numbers blur.

I push up from my desk. This is pointless. I can't focus. Posy is not where she's supposed to be. She's always asleep upstairs when the London Stock Exchange opens. Always.

Fuck.

I only know one way to excoriate this feeling. I slip on my jacket and grab the keys to the Bugatti from the peg in the kitchen. I'm dialing as I head to the garage.

"Miles? I need an address for Giorgio Fusco."

I'm going to have a little chat with the director of Posy's movie, and then I'm going to stab him in the throat so he sprays blood like a hose as he dies.

On the drive back, I'll call Carolyn. She'll need to make Posy fall back in love with me.

It shouldn't be hard.

She falls in love at the drop of a hat.

5

POSY

I rue the day I ever met Dario Volpe, but not nearly as much as the day I decided to come to Stonecut County. I lay on the lumpy mattress of the foldout sofa in my pay-by-the-week efficiency, breathing through my mouth so I don't inhale the room's mystery scent of stale piss and black mold.

On the bright side, my plan was sound. No one is going to come looking for me here.

No one who has a choice is coming here *ever*.

Stonecut's county seat is cute enough. It's a sleepy bed and breakfast kind of a town with a picturesque river and a fancy restaurant in an old mill. The bus dropped me off in the town square next to a white wooden bandstand with stars-and-stripes bunting.

It would've been stupid to stay at the end of the line, so I hitched a ride in the back of a redneck's truck. He said he was going "up the mountain." That's where I ended up—in a one-stoplight town called Anvil at the base of Stonecut Mountain.

Apparently, there's a big deal motorcycle rally here each

fall, so it's like a beach town, half-abandoned in the off season. Most of the storefronts on Main Street are shuttered. My boss, Randy, at the gas station says they open as bars and souvenir shops during the weeks bookending the rally.

As far as I can tell, moonshine is the other major industry in town. There's a flea market in an abandoned discount store parking lot on Saturdays, and every vendor has a crate of mason jars underneath their folding table.

I've gone to the flea market every weekend since I arrived six long weeks ago. The lady in the big straw hat has the best hooch. It's caramel apple flavor. She sells it for a reasonable price, but she gouges you on the Mary Kay. Makes you pay for samples.

I feel like I know everyone, not by name, but by sight. I'm scared enough of Renelli to keep my head down, but in a town this small, there's no real anonymity. I'm sure I'm the new chick at the gas station, just like my neighbor is the drunk Libertarian and the clerk at the grocery store is the woman with the Playboy bunny tattoo.

I really am doing okay, considering. I'm renting this efficiency on top of the one of the vacant stores, and I'm averaging thirty hours a week at the Gas-and-Go. My basic needs are met. And I don't have a choice.

I don't want to die, and life in Anvil has really proven how much. I end every day doing what I'm doing right now —staring at the bulging ceiling tiles, tossing and turning, unable to pass the time even by falling asleep.

I miss my life.

I miss seeing people and going places and doing things. I miss having *stuff*. I had the idea that I'd hunker down for a bit, save my money, let the Renelli business die down, and then head for Vegas or Cali. I didn't realize I'd be living hand to mouth. I'm going to have to become a cam girl or something, or I'm never leaving Anvil alive, so to speak.

The absolute worst is that I miss Dario.

Not the flowers and gestures that all turned out to be bull crap. Or the sex or the awkward silences whenever we were alone with nothing to do—like at dinner or during long car rides. But I do miss the games, the hours of just the two of us, his brown eyes glinting, dark eyebrow quirked, lips turned up, almost smiling. He loved winning. He loved it even more when I beat him.

No one ever paid more attention to me than Dario Volpe when we were in the middle of a game. I was the center of the universe, and this exquisitely beautiful, powerful man was desperate to know what I was thinking.

I hate him.

I hate him more than all my exes combined.

I was his toy.

He didn't love me. He doesn't even know me. How could he? We never talked about anything that mattered.

He sure figured I was bought and paid for, though. When he thought someone had touched his plaything, he didn't want it anymore. I was the new sneakers that never came out of the closet again after another kid at school showed up in them.

It's so messed up that a man can be so interested in what's going on in your head but he doesn't give two shits about how you feel. After a hard-fought game, he'd spend a full thirty minutes grilling me about my strategy, but he didn't have even thirty seconds to listen about that video. He just banged the gavel and threw me away.

And he gets away with it.

My life is over, and he gets to continue on, king of all he

surveys, everyone pussyfooting around him because he's the moneymaker.

I should have screamed at him.

I should have taken his precious laptop and thrown it against the wall. No, at his head. At his cold, unfeeling face.

I was so accommodating, so quick to hand over my watch, my earrings. I was scared. And that was definitely the right reaction.

Still. I wish I could go back. But with a gun. I'd tell Dario Volpe exactly what I think of him, and I'd take *his* watch *and* his damn phone. He was on it all the time, too busy to bother with his toy if we weren't playing a game.

Oh god, how am I going to stay here until I get enough money to leave? I'm going to go crazy, staring at the ceiling, railing at Dario Volpe in my head, getting myself all worked up, and there's nowhere to go and no way to get even—not even a little bit.

I need money. There are no second jobs in Anvil though. There are only side hustles. I've got nothing to sell at the flea market. I can't even sink to stripping; there's no place to do it in this town.

Maybe the cam girl idea isn't the worst I've ever had.

Hold up.

I click on the lamp on the floor next to my makeshift bed, reaching for my cell. It is an idea. I'm hot enough. It's not bragging. I check the boxes—blonde, big tits, tight waist.

It's something my girlfriends and I have always joked about when money's tight at the end of the month. *Well, that's it. I'm gonna have go put an application in at La Dolce Vita. I need to get a TopFollower.*

The waitresses at L'Alba were always talking about starting a TopFollower. I think Teresa went ahead and did it. It must've been a bust since we never heard much about it.

Chapter 5

She wasn't desperate, though. She wasn't cleaning the hotdog grill at the Anvil Gas-and-Go for minimum wage.

I'm motivated. And seeing that video broke the last part of something inside me that's been holding on by a thread for a while. What does it matter what anyone sees anymore? It's just flesh. Meat and bones. My body's not *me*.

My fingers fly on the keyboard. I set up a throwaway email account and then get started.

Username?

PosyVolpe.

I grin and sit cross-legged in my shadowy apartment, blocking out the scuttling in the walls. For the first time in weeks, I'm fully awake, and it's past midnight.

Bio? Hmm. *Twenty-something trophy girlfriend/slut interested in anal and revenge.*

I take a selfie flashing my middle finger, and I upload it as the profile pic.

Then I have to set a subscription rate. One thousand dollars a month. Nope. There I go undervaluing myself again. *Five* thousand dollars a month.

It's so easy. I have the link in no time. I send it to Dario's work address. On paper, he's employed by a company called Ridgemont Limited. Ridgemont is the name of his neighborhood.

I settle in and create content. Who knows? Maybe there's a bored billionaire somewhere who'd really like to see my cute, pink painted toes. Why didn't I think of this before?

The clock on the microwave above the stove blinks, and the drunk Libertarian stumbles down the hall, bellowing about those cocksuckers in Washington, D.C. He might be wasted, but he's not wrong.

I peel off my T-shirt and try to get a good shot of my cleavage. The lighting in here sucks.

I'm aware that I'm punch drunk, bordering on manic, but I can't seem to calm myself down. These past few weeks, I feel more and more like an astronaut and the cord connecting me to the spaceship has been cut. I'm drifting, and there's nothing stopping me from floating on forever. No one will miss me. No one will even wonder where I went.

I'm a loose end.

And then my phone pings. I have a new follower. Holy crap.

Another ping. He wants a face-to-face. You can set a different rate for live video. Whoa. This is really happening. I smooth my hair and tuck it behind my ear. I'm still topless. I grab for my shirt, but then I stop.

What do I charge for live video?

Whoever it is just paid five thousand bucks to see my coral toenails and a practice shot of my kitchenette. I'll flash them a little black lace bra. It has a lining. They won't see much.

Is it Dario?

It has to be, right? But there's no way he'd just click a link. For one, he hates me. For another, he'd think it was a scam. He always suspects a trap. That's why I can beat him sometimes even though he's so much smarter than me. He can't stop himself from defending against sneak attacks, wasting his time while I go straight for the kill.

Ping. Okay, okay. I type in five thousand bucks again.

Instantly, his face appears on screen. Black eyes. Perfectly trimmed beard. Not a hair on his head out of place. I gasp and drop the phone.

"Posy." It's an order. His voice drips with menace.

I didn't really think he would—I press my hand to my chest, try to contain my galloping heart.

What have I done?

Chapter 5

No, no. I'm okay. He can't trace me. I bought this phone at the flea market, and I'm paying for minutes. I can hang up anytime and never speak to him again.

"Posy," he repeats, insistent. Louder. I toss a pillow to the foot of the bed and prop the phone on it. Then I prop my back against the couch part, drawing my knees to my chest. I'm not so brave now, and there's an ache in my chest, a stupid wave of hurt feelings.

He's at his desk. There's the painting of the schooner behind him. He's wearing a white shirt with the collar unbuttoned. No tie. It's so late, but he doesn't look the least bit rumpled. He looks angry. Even on the small phone screen, I can tell his eyes are flashing. A cord in his neck throbs.

My heart stings. He's still the most beautiful man I've ever seen in my life. Aquiline nose, chiseled jaw, high cheekbones. An angular face with no softness. No give.

"Posy, where are you?"

A hysterical sound flies from my mouth, half snort, half chortle. "I'm not telling you that."

"Let me come and get you. Renelli's men are hunting you down." He says it so evenly. As if he's updating me on the weather.

My stomach knots. I knew Renelli was after me, but it's a whole other thing hearing it from Dario's mouth.

"Call them off." My voice quivers. I don't want to sound weak, but I can't seem to act brave. I'm alone. It's late and dark and I don't know what's going to happen to me, and I'm scared. And maybe I don't know who Dario really is, but I know his face like the back of my hand. "Tell Renelli to leave me alone."

"I can't. But he won't touch you if you're with me. Text

me the address. I'll pick you up." His tone is so even and reasonable. It pricks my temper.

"You kicked me out. I cheated on you, remember?"

His jaw tics. "Don't be dramatic."

My eyebrows fly up. "You said you wouldn't let me walk away again."

"Posy." He stretches his jaw and then levels his gaze, radiating menace. "Be smart. It's only a matter of time before he finds you."

"So I should serve myself up on a silver platter?"

"I can keep you safe."

I'm surprised at how hard the words hit. That's what I want more than anything—what I've *always* wanted. And it's such an obvious lie. I blink furiously and force a smile. "I don't believe you."

He sighs in frustration. "I spoke to Giorgio Fusco. I know it was a fake date stamp on the video."

"Good for you." I wait for a sense of vindication, but it never comes. Only uneasiness. A twitch under my skin. I stretch my legs. I don't need to huddle like I've been beat. Dario can't touch me anymore. Not in any way.

"Frankie Bianco bought the video off him and shared it to—" He searches for words. "To sow discord."

I swallow. My throat is tight. I told Frankie about the video, early in our relationship when I thought spilling all your secrets was how you got close to a man.

"Don't worry." Dario flashes his white teeth, baring his sharp incisors. "I'll kill him."

"Don't do it on my account. He did me a favor."

Dario's eyes narrow. "What do you mean?"

"If he hadn't shared the video, I wouldn't know what you are."

"And what's that?"

I shrug. "I don't know. What do you call a person who can't feel? Who fakes it? A psychopath?"

He blinks, his expression unchanged. Ice shoots down my veins.

I stumbled on it, but I think I'm right. I've had a lot of time to think. When you take away all the things Carolyn did, all the pretty stories I told myself, what's left? A man who used me and put me away when he was done, neatly, like any of his games. A man with no close relationships, no friends, no interactions except for business.

He's defective. Missing a piece. How did I not see it? I was raised with petty criminals and mobsters. I was always easy to take advantage of, but never naïve. I know what men can be; I just can't resist hoping for better.

I'm my mother's daughter.

My shoulders slump.

"What are you thinking?" he asks.

"I should hang up."

He taps his keyboard. My phone pings, a notification flashing that I've been tipped five hundred dollars.

"What are you thinking?" he asks again.

"I'm not going to tell you."

His jaw tightens. "What do you want? To make you come back?"

"What do I want? Like an apology?"

He can't really think this thing between us is repairable. It has to be a ploy. Does he think if he offers me enough money, I'll trot my happy ass straight back into the lion's den? Is he on Renelli's bad side because he lost track of me?

"If you want an apology, I can do that." He drums his fingers on his desk. "Give me your address. Every minute, Renelli's men get closer. Do you know what they'll do when they find you?"

My heartrate kicks up a notch. It's a good threat as far as psychological warfare goes. But it's not logical. Renelli's men are only getting closer if they're heading in the right direction. If they're not, they're getting farther away. Statistically, the latter is much more likely.

I ignore the attempt to rattle me. "Yes. I would like an apology."

"I'm sorry."

"For what?"

He glances to the side of the screen. Is there someone else there?

"I was wrong to accuse you of cheating."

I huff a laugh. It's the most unsatisfying apology I've ever heard. It's a statement of fact. There's no regret, not even any awkwardness in his tone. He's not capable of remorse, is he?

I didn't know him at all.

"Now tell me where you are," he demands.

"No."

His gaze darts to his left again.

"Who's there? Ray? That creep Ivano?"

"No one."

"Yeah?" Bullshit. Who's standing there, coaching him on what to say? How to approximate a human with real feelings? I bet it's Ray.

Thinking back, the only truly genuine emotion I think I've seen him express was that day in his office, watching the video. He was seething with rage. Not because he thought he'd lost my affection, but because I was a *whore*. I'd given away what belonged to him. And everyone could see.

He hated that.

I have an idea.

I press my lips so he can't see my smirk, and I switch to my knees, bending over to readjust the camera so it tilts up.

"What are you doing?" he asks.

"Earning my tip." I slide my legs apart and slither my fingers up my hips and side. Goosebumps break out across my bare stomach. It's freezing in here.

Dario's face is stone.

I cock my head and reach behind my back, undoing my bra clasp, waiting for his eyes to dart to the side.

"Tell Ray—if that's him—that I expect a tip from him, too."

I curve my shoulders and let my bra fall to the mattress. The air hits my breasts and my nipples pucker. I'm full and achy. I'm due for my period soon, and I'm tender. Light blue veins are visible through my pale skin. Can Dario see?

I cup my breasts, let my thumbs brush my nipples. My belly quivers. I'm not turned on exactly. It takes a lot to get me going. But the sensation is interesting. Better than the dull misery that's settled in my soul since he kicked me out.

His gaze is locked on my hands, tracking as I massage my breasts. I don't really know what to do so I do what feels good. His face is as hard as ever, but his eyes gleam.

"Does Ray like this? Does he want more?"

"Posy—" he breathes, his voice tight.

"What?" I ask when he doesn't go on.

"Show me your pussy."

Heat floods between my legs. "No."

"Then touch it."

"I don't want to. This feels good."

He swallows. I see his Adam's apple bob. He might not have any feelings, but he's into this. Me.

"Tell me where you are." His voice is lower now.

"No." I like this, his eyes burning and intent on every move I make, my hands stroking soft, goose-bumped skin, my pussy swollen and aching. I like making myself feel good while I tell him no.

"It was a mistake. I'll make it right."

My breath is coming faster. I haven't been this turned on in a long time. When Dario and I first got together, he made me hot just by looking at me. Then I learned he was a taker in bed—like most men—and the novelty wore off.

Is it knowing that there's someone else in the room watching? Is that what's got me going?

Or is it the expression on Dario's face? Not cold and collected for once but raw. I can see the banked rage. The frustrated desire.

He flashes another glance to the side.

Who's there? He clearly doesn't care if they see my tits. I guess I'm not worth getting possessive over since everyone in the organization has seen me take it in the ass.

Suddenly, the room is too cold. This isn't exciting. It's sad, and I'm pathetic.

I snatch my T-shirt and drag it over my head.

"Posy—" he says and reaches for the screen.

"Show's over," I say, tugging my hair loose from the collar.

My phone pings. Another tip. This time a thousand dollars.

I don't like this game anymore. I reach forward, tap a button, and Dario's face disappears.

The memory of his dark, burning eyes haunt me until I finally fall asleep huddled under a scratchy comforter, listening to the mice in the walls.

6

DARIO

"You can turn around. She's gone."

Ray's been facing the wall since Posy went to her knees. I didn't have to tell him. He figured out before I did what she was about to do.

I don't understand her. She doesn't particularly like sex. She's always willing, but she only comes once in a while, and she has to play with her clit for ages. She's not horny wherever she's hiding out; she's not trying to make me miss what I can't have. She sees now what I am. She's figured out that I don't love her. I don't have those kinds of feelings.

No, she's playing a game.

My lips twitch.

I love to play games with Posy Santoro.

She thought someone else was watching her. She was right. She flashed her tits to flush them out. It was a decent maneuver, but built on faulty assumptions. Ray's seen her tits before, and I don't care. I've fucked her pretty pink pussy in every room in this house. Most everyone in the house has gotten an eyeful at some point. I guess she never noticed, face down with her ass in the air.

I drum my fingers on the desk. This has gone on too long. I want her back. I can't focus on work. I'm taking ill-advised risks. For the first time in years, I'm getting trounced by the Dow.

She's going to pay in flesh when I get her back. Every lost minute, every bad trade, she's going to work out on her back.

I don't want to wait anymore. I shouldn't have to. I'm throwing hundreds of thousands at the problem, and the best investigative minds in the country are acting like she's the Jackal. I shouldn't be so critical. She is brilliant. They underestimated her at first. It's a common mistake.

"Where are we?" I ask. I know, but I like to hear we're getting close. It keeps my cock hard.

Ray sniffs and strokes his stubbled chin. "If I had to guess, within a ten-mile radius."

"And where are Renelli's men?"

Ray scoffs. "Exploring a hot lead down on the Gold Coast. They seem to think she's in a strip club in Miami. They're making sure to check them all."

I shake my head. Renelli's not going to stay on top much longer, not if his men have the audacity to waste his money with such impunity. He needs to replace Tony with Lucca now before Lucca decides the time is ripe to give himself a promotion.

It's not my problem, though. As long as I'm left to my own devices, I don't really care who wears the ring. I have my own concerns.

"How much longer?" I press.

Ray shrugs. "There's an element of luck involved. Could be weeks. Could be tomorrow."

"We should send more men."

"You could spook her."

"Then put more eyes on the tapes."

Posy was clever, running to the middle of nowhere. In this modern world, no one disappears, though. There are cameras everywhere.

We found her on the subway CCTV, but we lost her on the platform when the recording glitched. We found her again at the bus terminal. Tracked her to a rural county a few hours away. She hadn't even left the state. It should have been easy to find her once we were at the end of the line, but Stonecut is a small, sleepy town. We've had to be discreet. We don't want to tip her off.

Renelli's men have been bungling their way down the eastern seaboard so I've been content to move cautiously. I'm not so patient now.

I click the "request private meeting" button again on this TopFollower app. I'm taking the two thousand five hundred dollars out of her ass, too.

No response.

I recline in my chair and exhale. I haven't been sleeping. I'm too wired. I should call La Dolce Vita and have them send some women over like I used to do before Posy. Work out my energy. I'd spar with Ivano, but it's late, and he's probably asleep. And my cock is hard with no sign of subsiding. It'd be weird.

The European markets open soon, though. And I hate strangers in my house.

"She looks the same," I observe.

Ray's eased himself into the armchair across from me, waiting for instructions. He grunts.

"She should have cut her hair. Dyed it, at least." I stare at her ridiculous profile pic.

Her hair is still long with soft, golden blonde waves.

She's lucky she didn't change it. If she did, I'd punish her for that, too.

"She's lost some weight." I scroll through the photos she's uploaded.

Posy has a perfect hourglass shape, generous breasts, hips like the curve of a cello, a waist that nips in neat and tight. A woman can't have tits and an ass like hers if her body doesn't carry a few extra pounds. There's always a gentle swell to her belly, a slight jiggle in her thighs. I could count her ribs, though, when she arched her back to show me her hard nipples.

"That apartment looked like a shithole." Ray grunts again in agreement. You couldn't see much, but there was a crack in the wall behind her, and her bed was a sofa.

"She's not in love with me anymore."

Ray shifts in his seat and coughs into his fist. He's been with me since I became a made man, but he doesn't understand what I am. He treads lightly, careful of my feelings. He hasn't accepted that I don't have any.

"I'm sure you'll win her back, boss."

I laugh. "I'm going to break her."

Ray bends, bracing his elbows on his knees. He's exhausted. He's been keeping my hours, but he's not a young man anymore.

"Not if you're careful," he says.

Is he deliberately misunderstanding me?

I shrug it off. It hardly matters. Soon enough, Posy Santoro will be under my roof again. Mine to do with as I please.

I held back before.

I don't have any reason to now.

My mouth waters. I can hardly wait.

Chapter 6

It's been a week, and the investigators I employ are no closer to finding her. She won't accept my requests to chat live, but she's playing with me. I check my phone. No new pic. She usually posts late at night. She can't sleep either.

I straighten my tie and slip on my jacket. Renelli has requested my presence at a dinner in town. We're entertaining a new cartel who's looking to do some business. I never understood why I'm needed at these things. My equivalent in their organization has access to our numbers. They know what we can do for them.

"I'm driving," I say to Ray, holding out my hand. He tosses me the keys.

"Any word?" I ask.

"None."

I knew that, but I need him to feel the urgency. No one rests until Posy is back where she belongs.

I shift into gear and peel off, enjoying the squeal of rubber and the dismay on Ray's grizzled face.

"You got a complaint, old man?"

He's clutching the grab handle. He shakes his head. "It's your car, boss. You strip the tires, it's your business."

I glance over. "That's right. It's mine. I do with it what I please."

Ray is soft when it comes to Posy. I've noticed him cover for her. Kick shoes she carelessly left in the foyer under a bench so I don't see. She's going to be home soon. He needs to understand how it'll be.

"If I want to handle my ride a little roughly, it's my prerogative."

"Yes, boss."

I flash him a tight smile. He almost conceals his discomfort.

I enjoy Ray. He's an oddity in our world, a man motivated by loyalty and honor. The mafia code that exists only in his mind and in the movies. It makes him predictable. Reliable. Comfortable like a broken-in pair of boots.

When we arrive at Il Destino, I don't hassle him about insisting he park the car. He doesn't trust valets. He thinks they'll burn the clutch.

I make my way to a private room on the second floor. It's a Wednesday evening so the club is low key. The happy hour crowd. This is where I had decided I wanted Posy, but it was packed that night. Past midnight in the middle of a heat wave.

She was out with the girls, barely decent in a short white dress, side slits cut up to her hip, the neckline draping almost to her belly button. The thinnest spaghetti straps. It must've been held onto her tits with tape. She had looked like a porn star in a Greek goddess costume.

I'd been watching her for a few months. I knew I wanted to fuck her, but she'd been with Frankie Bianco. And she's a Santoro. There were good reasons not to scratch the itch.

She noticed my eyes on her. She wandered closer and closer. She'd smiled at me, drunk and giddy. I told her to dance for me, and she did.

I drove her home, fucked her face, then took her pussy. She made these fake little moans. She was tight, and it was good, but not earth shattering.

Her place was cramped and disorganized. It made my skin crawl. I didn't even take my pants off. I was buckled and set to bail when I saw the chess set on her coffee table. A cheap plastic and cardboard number.

Chapter 6

We played. She beat me. Twice in a row. I won the third time because she started drifting off to sleep.

It was like finding a twenty lying in the gutter. A diamond in the rough. I moved her in with me as soon as I could, and I started polishing.

I grind my teeth so hard pain shoots through my jaw. It was a fool's errand. She's messy like her apartment. The kind of woman who lets her boyfriend tape her taking it up the ass. Who lets a mook like Frankie Bianco smack her around. And I was going to marry her?

I was out of my mind.

When I get her back, things are going to be different. She's going to know her place. She's not going to dare to pull a stunt like this ever again.

I check my phone one last time before I join the party. No new posts. My left eye twitches.

"Here he is now!" Renelli greets me, his cheeks flushed from wine. Antipasti has been served. I'm not late enough. I like to arrive when the entrees are served.

"Gentlemen." I incline my head and take my seat.

My role here is easy. I stay sober. I nod. I accept the plaudits for my financial acumen. They ask me jokingly for a hot tip. I give them a stock, and then I buy heavy and run it up the next day to reassure them that I am a genius.

The room is packed tonight. Tony, Vittorio, Lucca, Tomas, Frankie and at least six guys from the cartel plus wives and dates. They've even invited Carlo, the smarmy accountant, and his cokehead girlfriend with the crazy hair.

If Carlo's not skimming already, he will be soon. He's a college boy playing mobster. He doesn't have the healthy fear of the men at this table born from experience. The money will be too much of a temptation.

I'm seated in between his girlfriend and Perla Amato.

Perla glances at me uneasily and tries to surreptitiously inch her chair closer to her husband. Idiot woman. I have no interest in her.

As a waiter fills my wine glass, I check my phone. Nothing.

"Got somewhere else you want to be?" Carlo's girlfriend nudges me with her elbow. She's tipsy. Maybe drunk. She's flushed, and her eyes are shining. I glance over at Carlo. He's absorbed in conversation with Lucca. Kissing ass.

I'm about to ignore her when a memory tickles the back of my mind. She works at L'Alba. She must know Posy. Now that I'm thinking about it, she's one of the giggling, shrieking women that Posy invited to the pool in the summer.

I force my lips to curve. "Don't we all?"

She snorts indelicately and leans in as if we're instant confidantes. "I know you," she stage-whispers.

"You do?"

She pokes me in the chest. "You were mean to Posy."

My pulse kicks up, and under the table, my hands curl into fists. I'm careful to keep my face neutral. "Why do you say that?"

"You made her cry."

I want to drag this woman outside and shake her until she tells me what she knows. Instead, I offer my best approximation of a rueful smile.

"Never intentionally."

"Yes, intentionally." She rolls her eyes. "You said she cheated on you. Posy's not like that."

Adrenaline surges through my veins. Did the key to finding Posy just drop itself into my lap?

"I know. I made a terrible mistake." I furrow my brow

and look down, hoping it's close enough to an expression of regret.

"You did. She'll never forgive you."

I nod in somber agreement. "Still, I'd like to apologize, but I don't know how to get a hold of her. Do you…?"

"Nevaeh," she supplies. "Nevaeh Ellis." She gauges me with bleary eyes, her thoughts flickering across her open face like tickertape. Sympathy. Consideration. Mistrust. I hold my breath. Finally, she sighs. "No. Sorry. I don't know where she went."

She's lying. She knows something. I tuck her name away for later. I'm not going to wring her scrawny neck here in the middle of dinner. I can wait an hour. Maybe two.

I shrug and refocus on my meal. Veal cacciatore. Too much garlic. Not enough rosemary. A little underdone.

My phone's silent in my pocket. No vibration indicating a notification. Around the table, everyone is absorbed in animated conversation. Occasionally, a sly look is cast my way. The video must still be news. I note who smirks. I file those names away, too. I will take great pleasure in wiping the smiles away. All in good time.

I let my fork clatter to my plate. I'm full, no one's asking for stock tips, and it's too loud. Too stuffy.

I push my chair back. Tony casts me a look and slides his gaze meaningfully towards the gentlemen from Sinaloa. I raise an eyebrow. He lifts his eyes to the ceiling. He understands how it is. I don't answer to him.

There's a hierarchy in the organization. Every man has his place. Well, every man except the capo and me. I answer to the market. If the numbers are good—and even now, they're good—no one tells me what I can and can't do.

I stroll off toward the hall to the john. Next to a vintage cigarette machine, they've kept the original wood and glass telephone booths with the folding doors. Framed ads hang where the phones used to be. I slip into one, slide out my phone, and squat on a red velvet stool.

No new posts. I click "request private meeting." I don't expect a response. Posy's gone radio silent. Maybe she wised up.

I almost startle when her face appears on the screen. She's flushed, and her hair is pulled back in a tight ponytail. She's breathing heavily.

"Are you fucking someone?" I demand. An asshole skulking in the hall, holding his woman's purse, smirks in my direction. I shove the door shut with my shoe.

"Yup," she pants. "Just hopped off a dick. What are you doing?"

"You're not funny."

"I'm hilarious. You have no sense of humor."

The screen shakes and then she's lying flat on her back, her chest rising and falling, tits flattened by a black sports bra. She's wearing low cut yoga pants. Her stomach curves in, her hipbones visible through her pale skin. I was right. She's lost weight.

"You're working out." I relax against the wall of the booth.

"Ding, ding. Gotta keep it tight for the fans." She blows me a kiss and winks.

My gut sours. I knew the veal was undercooked.

"Where are you? The bad guys are closing in. You don't have time to play around." I inject my voice with urgency.

"I'm in your brain, stalker." She grins. "I'm all up in your gray matter. I bet you can taste me."

She's baiting me. Why? Hell, I don't really understand why she's reaching out to me at all. A smart woman would cut all ties. A truly smart woman would never have gotten involved with me in the first place. Good for me Posy is a smart woman with one hell of an Achilles heel.

"Hey, you sent me the link," I say.

She scrunches her nose. "You clicked it."

"You showed me your tits."

"You've sent me one hundred nineteen private meeting requests in the past six days."

"They're very nice tits."

She struggles against a smile and loses. A strange feeling sloshes in my stomach.

"Tell me where you are, Posy. Let me come get you." I lower my voice. "You like it here with me. You like the pool. And the kitchen."

I'm not sure about the kitchen, but she's always in there, rooting around in the fridge. She knew what she was doing, grazing all day, keeping those curves round like I like. She's clearly on a tight budget now, and she's lost weight. Too much.

"When's my birthday?" she asks.

"Why are you changing the subject?"

"When is our first date anniversary?"

"If I guess the right answer to the third question, do I get to cross a bridge?" This is typical female bullshit. I don't know when her birthday is. Does she know what credit card gets charged when she orders delivery?

"What's my middle name?" she throws down. It's an accusation.

I glare at her face on the screen, fight to keep my grip on the phone steady. It's infuriating—flinging barbs at each other over a video chat. She's growing quite a false sense of security. When I catch her, I'm going to shove my cock down her throat until she remembers how to talk to me.

"How much are the property taxes?" I snipe back

because that's all I can do in this fucking booth. "How about the utility bill? What's the name of the company insuring your car?"

Her eyes darken. "I didn't want to quit my job."

"I didn't make you." I did convince her it'd be a security risk—that someone could use her to get to me—and she's softhearted. It didn't take more than one conversation for her to give notice.

"You're a manipulative asshole."

"Why did it take you so long to figure that out?" I'm genuinely curious. She's a brilliant strategist, but with people, she sees what she wants to see.

She sighs and rolls on her side, propping the phone and folding her hands under her cheek. Her eyes are huge on the screen, blue and sad.

"I don't know. Wishful thinking."

"I would think that with your experiences, you'd have learned to be wary by now."

She tenses. I probably shouldn't have said that.

"What do you mean?"

"How your father treated your mother. The boyfriend in the video. Frankie. All the failed relationships."

I might not know her birthday, but I listen. When we first got together, she went through a confessional phase. Told me her life story. She cried, but I think she felt better afterwards. She didn't bring it up again.

On the screen, her eyes shine and her chin wobbles.

"I'm sure you were warned off," I point out. The women in our circle are terrified of me. They think I'm a monster. "But you fell in love with me so easily."

"I don't love you anymore." Her voice is small.

I grit my teeth. That may be so, but it's incidental. It'd be easier to go back to normal if she was still nursing a flame, but it's not a requirement. Fear works as well as love as a motivator.

"Good. Then maybe you can think rationally. You're in danger. Come back. I can protect you."

"Why would you? You hate me."

"I don't." It's the truth, as far as it goes.

"You know what I think?" She sniffles, but the tears never fall. They gather until her eyes are blue pools like rounded glass. "I think you can't stand that I flipped the script. You threw me away, and then you changed your mind, but I was gone. You're butt hurt that the trash took itself out."

"What are you talking about?"

The phone's moving. She's maneuvering herself upright up on the bed.

"You don't care what happens to me. I doubt you care what happens to anyone. But you need to call the shots, don't you? You can't *stand* that the girl who let everyone walk all over her won't lay down for you."

"Posy—" She's spouting nonsense. I need her to focus. "Can you stop with the woe is me for a minute? You're in real trouble."

"I'm not feeling sorry for myself," she denies, indignant, even though she knows it's a lie. She can't help herself. The denial is a kneejerk reaction.

She has this front, and it's paper thin. Everyone can see through it. That's why men take advantage of her. She's defenseless, and it's obvious, but it's a matter of pride for her to take whatever she's dealt and shrug it off.

Someone taught her a long time ago that she'd better not let on when it hurts, but she never got any good at hiding the pain. She's made herself a convenient victim.

I'd undo the damage if I knew how. I don't need her to

pretend. I like her raw feelings—all of them. They turn me on. That's what makes her different from every other person in the world.

Besides, I don't need her pretending she's a tough cookie when she clearly isn't. She doesn't need to be strong. I *am* strong. I can destroy anything that threatens her—if she just fucking tells me where to come get her.

I inhale and slowly exhale. My left eye's twitching. How much longer does this part of the game last?

When I don't reply, she feels compelled to argue the point. "It's only the truth. If you don't like it, that's on you."

"Okay. If you say so."

"I'm not feeling bad because we broke up, if that's what you think. I'm pissed because you can't tell when something is obviously photoshopped, and now my life has to be over."

"Fine. Where are you? I'll bring you home. Smooth things over. I'll set you up in your own place, and you can take your car."

I'm lying through my teeth, and she's not even listening. She's stuck on our relationship. It's like when I need the numbers from Miles, and he wants to talk about his draft picks.

"I know that Carolyn bought me all the stuff. You don't know me at all, do you, Dario?"

I know her perfectly. Better than she knows herself. She's a tangled ball of self-doubt, foolish pride, dumb hope, brilliance, masochism, and blind affection. And I'm obsessed.

I need her back.

I drop my voice, lace it with menace. "I know what's going to happen if you don't come home. You'll be found. There will be no conversation. You won't even feel the bullet in your brain. You'll be dead before the synapse can fire, and your life will, in fact, be over."

"Don't threaten me." Her voice rises. I knock my forehead on the glass door of the booth. There's no reasoning with her.

I change tack. "Do you need me to apologize again?"

"Don't bother. It didn't make me feel any better."

"I do regret the mistake." My rush to judgement has grossly inconvenienced me, and it's put a piece in jeopardy that I did not intend to permanently lose.

"Your apologies are completely unsatisfying."

"I don't know how to do it any better."

"I believe that." She looks bitter. And tired. There are light bruises under her eyes. Is she not sleeping either?

My fingers twitch. I want her closer. If she were in my arms, I wouldn't feel this—empty-handedness.

"Are you even capable of actually feeling sorry for hurting someone?" She cocks her head, as if considering a new idea. I can see her doing the math, searching for a memory to prove herself wrong and coming up short.

She's getting it now.

"No." A thrill skates down my spine. It feels good to admit it.

She blinks at me, finally, really understanding.

"But you can feel angry?"

"Yes."

"You were angry because you thought I let someone touch what belongs to you."

"Yes." It's almost sensual, the way the naked truth feels on my lips. Like skinny dipping in broad daylight, the way the sun feels on your bare skin.

"Not because you loved me."

"I don't love anyone." I never have. I understand the

concept and I can recognize the emotion in others, but I just don't have the capability. I imagine it's like colorblindness. You eventually learn what green is, but you never actually see it yourself. And it has no real impact on your life.

"But you can hate," she asks.

I shake my head. I enjoy revenge and aggression, but more as sport than as emotion.

"So all I've got to work with is rage?"

Her soft lips quirk up in a sad smile, but there's a twinkle of mischief in her eyes. It goes straight to my dick.

"What makes you mad, Dario? Does it make you mad when I don't accept your private meeting requests?"

I don't dignify that with a response, but no, it doesn't. Toying with me is how she's playing this game. Her tactics interest me; they don't anger me.

"Does it piss you off that I can make you go away by pushing one tiny button? I bet you just can't stand it that this *slut*, this *whore,* can turn you off with one little tap on the screen." Her hurt mingles with her delight in what she's about to do.

"Posy—" I warn as if I can stop her.

She wiggles her fingers. "Bye, Dario."

The screen goes dark. She's gone.

I hit refresh. Nothing.

She's gone again. And I still don't know where she is.

Again, without warning, a storm crashes through my chest, a vision of my phone flying from my hands through the glass door erupting in my mind.

My grip tightens until my knuckles blanch. I don't lose control. I don't lose, period.

Except to Posy. And it's good when she wins. It makes her want to play with me more.

Chapter 6

The red tinting my vision slowly seeps away, and my lungs loosen enough so I can draw in a deep breath.

This isn't a bad development.

After all, Posy loves winning. I never let her, so when she does, it's real, and she knows it. She crows about it. Losses roll off her shoulders, but when she beats me, she gleefully rubs it in.

Is that what she's doing now? Strutting around that shitty apartment, giddy that she's bested me?

A smile plays at my lips.

I bet she is. I bet she's skipping around, glowing with the satisfaction. My cock presses hard against my zipper.

She can enjoy her win for the moment.

Ray says it's only a matter of time. It's going to be so sweet, collecting my prize.

She better enjoy this small victory. It'll be her last for a long, long time.

7

POSY

I think I did manage to piss Dario off. He hasn't requested a private meeting in a week. Part of me is still riding high, but the other part is sinking back into the despondency that seems to blanket this whole town.

I can't stay here, and I can't afford to leave. I'm beginning to realize that almost everyone in Anvil is in the exact same situation. It's Hotel California with unreliable internet and no liquor sales on Sunday.

TopFollower pays on a ninety day lag. By mid-summer, I'll be able to move on, but for now, I have to pray that Nevaeh Ellis keeps her mouth shut and my hours don't get cut at the Gas-and-Go.

I'm working late tonight, but at least it's something to do. My boss Randy called out drunk. He told me to lock up at midnight and take the key home with me. He'll come by for it tomorrow.

Even though it's a Saturday night, the town is dead. The only customers tonight have been two guys my age looking to buy energy drinks and the cheap single cigars they buy to roll blunts. It's good they were high as kites and incapable of doing much more than ogling my tits and snickering. I'm alone, and the Vape Emporium next door closed at nine.

I only have a half hour until close. I pass the time taking pictures and posting them on TopFollower. A crumpled bag of chips. A dead cockroach smeared on a baseboard. I try to make it artsy.

I need a plan, but my brain refuses to cooperate. I'm stuck on that last conversation with Dario.

The asshole had a point. I should have known better than to get involved with him, and I sure as hell shouldn't have fallen for him based on flowers, fancy dinners, and expensive gifts. Am I that shallow? I never thought I was, but what else can you call it?

If I had put the trappings aside for a minute, it would have been glaringly obvious. Dario never spoke about his past. His family. His feelings. He has no friends. No dog or cat. He works, he plays games, and he fucks me. Sometimes he reads. Nonfiction exclusively.

To a degree, I felt sorry for him. I assumed he must be lonely. I was bringing fun and laughter to his empty life. I completely ignored the fact that he is one hundred percent content with everything exactly as it is.

How did I not see? Because he treated me like a princess?

Or wasn't it more like an exotic pet?

When he was done working, he took me out and played with me. And I lapped up the attention, didn't I? And never once demanded anything like intimacy. I was so grateful for the crumbs he fed me from his table.

I set myself up. The red flags were flapping in the wind, and I ignored them. Again.

It's a depressing thought, but I guess it doesn't matter

now. That chapter of my life is over. I've got other worries now.

I begin closing up a few minutes early, helping myself to a chocolate bar. I've been living on microwave noodles and snacks from work. By some miracle, I've managed to lose weight. Probably because I spend so much time walking around town. I can't bear being in my apartment, especially when it rains. The damp smell is oppressive.

It doesn't take long to cash out the register and sweep. I flick the lights. I don't want to go home now, either. I could go to the bar, get a beer with the locals. I've considered it when the boredom gets really bad, but I can't help but think I'd be inviting trouble.

All in all, Anvil is a sleepy town. The people are the same as anywhere, a mixed bag. Randy warned me to watch myself at night, but besides some half-hearted catcalls from passing cars, no one's bothered me.

I'm not worried walking home alone in the dark. It's only three blocks, and it's the main drag. There are streetlights. I hoist my purse on my shoulder and head out.

It's a beautiful night. It's clear and cold, and the stars are out, a bright smattering bedazzling the dark outline of the mountain. I breathe in crisp air and expel the stale nastiness of the store.

I slow my steps. There's nowhere I want to rush. In the distance, a screen door slams. A car shushes past, and then it's quiet again.

And then a whistle cuts the silence. A shiver shoots down my spine.

It's not a catcall. Not a warning. It's a tune.

And then Dario's voice echoes against the darkened buildings. My heart leaps into my throat. Driven by instinct, I bolt, rubber soles slapping the pavement.

Chapter 7

He's humming now, and then he sings. Soft and deep as his heavy steps pound behind me. *Run, run, run—you'd better run.*

I already am. I'm sprinting as fast as I can towards home, hair whipping my face, the night air burning my lungs.

A laugh rings out in the empty street. He's close. How did he get so close?

I part my lips to scream, but then an arm snakes around my waist and a rough palm covers my mouth.

"Got you," he says, breath hot on my ear, and for just a second, my traitor body melts into his hard chest, my fear catching fire and flaring into something else, an unbearable anticipation that crystalizes into horror as he drawls, "Now what am I going to do with you?"

I flail, kicking, bucking. I'm not a tiny woman. I throw my weight, but he's stronger. Taller. And he's not afraid of hurting me. He squeezes my middle until the pressure is unbearable. He's going to crack a rib. He's going to do worse.

I fight harder, jerking my head, trying to dislodge his hand so I can scream, so maybe someone will hear me.

And then there's the press of cold metal against my back.

"Stop struggling." He sounds so matter of fact. Ice cold. "If I shoot you from this angle, I'll shatter your spine. Is that how you want to go? Bleeding out on a dirty sidewalk, your legs useless?"

He'd do it. In that moment, there's not a doubt in my mind. I can almost hear it in his voice, the curious musing, as if he's picturing exactly what that would look like. He's a monster, and I should have never baited him. I should have never let him lull me into believing that this thing between us was a game.

I'm dead. Maybe not in the next minute, but soon. Did I think this was chess? Winning isn't putting me in check. It's putting me in the ground. I go perfectly still. Raise my hands the little I can with his arm pinning them to my sides.

His grip loosens slightly, allowing me to finally expand my lungs and take a shallow breath.

"Why are you walking home alone?"

What?

The muzzle of a gun is digging into the soft flesh above my hip, and he wants to know why I'm walking home alone?

"I—I closed tonight," I stammer.

"It's dangerous."

A hysterical giggle flies from my lips. Dario makes an irritated sound and nudges me forward with the gun. "Walk. At the end of the block, turn left."

What's left? Nothing. An empty lot. The vacant discount store. He's going to shoot me. Leave my body in a field strewn with cigarette butts and beer bottles.

My knees go weak. I can't propel myself forward. My legs won't do it. I won't walk calmly to my death.

"What's wrong with you?" Dario tries to urge me forward with a hand on my back.

"I d-don't want to die." I wish I could be brave in the face of this, but my voice is broken. Desperate. The sound of it stokes my panic, makes it all too real.

Dario reaches for my arm and pulls me up short, spinning me to face him. We're under a streetlight, and it casts every hard, unforgiving line of his perfect face into sharp relief. He's beautiful, and he has no feeling. None at all.

He cocks his head. "I'm not going to kill you," he says and smiles, revealing even, white teeth. "Where would be the fun in that?"

Then he shoves me forward, and when I stumble, he drags me back to my feet, prodding me forward, around the corner into the dark.

Chapter 7

He propels me down the sidewalk cracked by weeds, and I struggle to stay on my feet. I know if I fall, he won't ease his grip. He'll hold on while I rip my shoulder from the socket.

He's parked behind a vacant fast-food restaurant. The block is silent, not a car on the road. The nearest vehicle is in front of the house at the corner. There's a light on upstairs. It's unlikely they'd hear a scream. I'll have to run. Dario will have to drop my arm sometime. That's the instant I need to make my move.

He pops the trunk of the sedan. I prime myself to bolt.

I don't have a chance. He slams his palm into my back and sweeps my legs so I upend into the car. The carpet burns my cheek. I kick, but he's wedged himself between my legs, and I can't get the angle right. My heels glance off him as he works.

I'm screaming now, but he has the back of my head, and he's shoving my face down, flattening my nose, muffling my voice. He's panting. Muttering curses. I'm not making it easy for him.

There's a rip, and his hand moves. I arch my back, desperately filling my lungs, but he's using his whole upper body now to pin me down as he snatches my wrists and forces them together. He binds them behind me. Something sticky and tight. Duct tape.

He slaps a strip over my mouth and then he relaxes, his chest crushing my back, the edge of the trunk digging into my lower belly. I can feel him between my legs through my pants. He's hard. He's getting off on this. His breath is heavy in my ear, and not just from the struggle.

He grinds his cock against the juncture of my khakis. I hold myself rigid.

He won't do this here. It's too exposed.

But what do I know? He's got me in a trunk. He's lost all his sense, all his caution.

I don't want this. I don't want him to hurt me. I shake and tears spring to my eyes.

He leans closer and smooths the hair from my face.

"You're scared," he murmurs. "That's understandable."

I can't help but moan.

"You didn't have a chance," he says, his voice jarringly detached. "You're weaker."

Then he backs off, forces my legs together, winds more tape around my ankles, and rolls me into the trunk, slamming it shut.

Claustrophobia hits me in a wave. I squirm, straining against the tape. There's no room. I'm up against a canvas bag. His golf clubs. I jackknife my body, and I knock my head against the side panel and taste copper.

How much air is there in here? It's hot, and it smells like fumes. Where is he taking me?

And where's Ray? Dario never goes anywhere without a bodyguard. I was under the impression Renelli decreed it so. Whatever Dario does for the organization, he's irreplaceable.

But Dario also does what he wants. And for some reason, he doesn't want a witness to whatever he's going to do to me.

My heart slams against my chest. The trunk is pitch black, and the longer we drive, the stiffer I become. I try to twist my wrists, but all I do is warp the tape so it digs into my flesh. I can't move my ankles enough to struggle.

Everyone's heard that if you're in a trunk, try to kick out the lights, but with the golf bag crowding me, there's not enough space to draw back. I try, but there's no force behind it. I wriggle to my back. There has to be an emergency release. A latch or something.

There it is, a neon green tab with a helpful picture of a stick figure jumping out of a trunk and running away. There's no way I can reach it. Dario taped my wrists and elbows. I can't even try to get it with my teeth.

I can't breathe; blood pounds in my ears. I'm going to suffocate. I'm going to slowly lose consciousness to a muffled bass beat coming from the front of the car, and then I'm going to die. He'll probably shove my body in the golf bag.

The trunk vibrates from the music. He's blaring the radio, and we're going fast. He's *enjoying* himself.

There's something about the idea that calms me down, lets me think.

I have enough air right now. I'm uncomfortable, but I'm okay for the moment. I can plan.

Odds are he's going to take me back to his place. Dario's a loner, and his home is his castle. He's angry. He wants to play with me. He'll want to be on his own territory.

That's good. I know every inch of that house. I never wasted the rare opportunity when Dario went to a meeting downtown with his men. I've explored every nook and cranny. I wanted to know everything about the man I loved. Discover his secrets. I was searching for a yearbook or a photo album. I never found anything.

I snort, and it's loud in the trunk despite the music, the purr of the engine, and the shush of the road under the wheels.

I'd actually felt sad for Dario. Poor lonely child with no living family, no mementos to remember them by, no evidence that he'd ever been cared for. I knew his father had passed, and his mother left when he was very young.

I only have a few boxes of my mother's things and some keepsakes from my grandparents. Nothing's worth much, but it means the world to me. My heart broke to think he didn't even have that.

I was so wrong.

He doesn't have keepsakes because he's a man-shaped shell.

He was telling the truth about anger, though. He was furious when he saw the video. It must have been injured pride. He'd lost face. It must suck to feel no love, but to be perfectly capable of feeling like a bitch.

I don't think he's even mad anymore. He's having a grand old time. This is another game to him. Tag. He won. A fresh wave of nerves unsettle my guts.

He gets bored when he wins.

Panic threatens to take over my mind again, but I beat it back. He's not done with me yet. He said so. If I'm alive, I have the chance to escape, and I will. I'm not going out like this.

~

At some point, I fall asleep. I'm jerked awake by the trunk opening and a rush of cold air. The sky is lightening to an ash gray. It must be near dawn. My eyes are dry and bleary. I groggily make to rub them, and the tape digs into my raw wrists.

Dario leans over and pats my stinging cheek. "Rise and shine."

He lifts me like a bride and sets me on my feet. I shriek to warn him, but my mouth is taped shut, and I'm not even fully awake. I list for a breathtaking moment, and then I crash to the ground. My legs won't hold weight. They're numb. My head cracks against the driveway and a blinding pain shoots through my skull. I tuck and curl like a shrimp as a wave of nausea rolls over me.

Behind us, a door opens.

"Boss?" It's Ray.

He'll help me. I call out on instinct, but I'm muted.

Dario crouches over me. "What's wrong with you?"

He nudges my leg with the toe of a polished shoe. "Did your leg fall asleep?"

He squats lower, fingers searching through my hair. "There's a lump. You banged it hard."

He narrows his cold eyes, and then his hands are everywhere, the cut on my forehead, the rash on my cheek. There's a snick. I peek through cracked lids. He has a knife. Oh shit. My stomach lurches.

I can't puke. I'll choke.

He considers me, head tilted, and I whimper, flopping on asphalt, trying to scuttle back. He stops me easily by rolling me to my stomach and pinning my butt between his knees.

"It won't hurt long," he says. "I'll be quick."

I freeze. Is this it? Does he gut me in the driveway?

My panties grow warm and damp. Did I pee myself? I moan.

There's a press of cold metal at my wrists, and then a burn as he rips away the tape, taking fine hairs and a layer of skin with it.

It does hurt, but the burn is nothing compared to the flood of relief.

"If you hit me, I'll hit you back," he warns, matter-of-fact. I have no doubt. I stay still as he removes the tape at my elbows and ankles. Finally, he flips me onto my back.

Pins and needles begin to prickle at the tips of my toes

and fingers. I couldn't fight if I wanted to. I might be able to move my arms and legs, but it'd be like swinging a slab of meat.

I hate this. I'm helpless, and he's on top of me, his hard dick digging into me again. Ray must be watching from the porch. If there weren't a high privacy fence, anyone driving past could see. We're in the middle of the driveway.

He can do what he wants. Hopelessness floods my chest, and all of a sudden, I'm cold to the bone, shaking so hard my teeth rattle.

Dario's eyes narrow. He tears the tape from my lips, leaving a strip of fire in its wake. My nose tingles. I'm not going to cry. Not in front of him.

He brushes a strand of hair from my face. "What's wrong with you?" he asks.

I sputter a laugh. "So much." I rotate my wrists, trying to get the feeling back. "But not nearly as much as what's wrong with you."

I brace myself, but he doesn't react. His expression remains inquisitive. His brown eyes are still dark, inscrutable pools, and his body's alert, but not tense.

"Do you have a headache?"

"Yes." It's more of a dull throbbing now, but it's awful. There has to be a goose egg on my head. I'm so thirsty my lips stick together which is not helping.

"Nausea?"

"Yes."

Is he checking to see if I have a concussion?

"Blurry vision?"

He is.

"No. I need water. And I need to sit up." I don't know why he cares. He's got me back. That's all that matters, right?

He rises easily to his feet and grabs me under my

armpits, hoisting me until he can scoop me into his arms. I'm not a small woman. His brute strength always surprises me. He spends hours a day at his computer or on the phone, but he balances it with time in the basement gym. He doesn't have machines. He flips tractor tires and swings ropes. That kind of thing.

I used to love his body. I was obsessed. I loved the ridges and lines other men don't have and how his boring suits hid such sculpted power.

I was sucked in so easily. A pretty face, a hot body, money, brains. I was a goner.

Well, maybe anyone would fall.

But all the women I know steer clear of him. They know something I don't. If he was just a dark horse, they'd be all over him. Frankie Bianco smacks women around, and everyone knows it, and the ladies still fight over him.

Until the video, Dario never laid a hand on me. He never even raised his voice. What did he do that is so bad that none of the shameless gold diggers in our circle tried their luck with him? Or am I so blind when it comes to men that I can't see what's obvious to everyone else?

Clearly, he's not right in the head.

Each step Dario takes jars my brain, increasing the throb in my brain. He carries me all the way upstairs while Ray follows in his wake. I need an aspirin. I need to sleep. I can't fight in this condition.

Dario brings me to our room and heads straight to the en suite. He sets me on the edge of the jacuzzi tub.

"You smell like gasoline and hot dogs. Take a bath." He fingers my split ends, his mouth screwed up in distaste. "And wash your hair. It's filthy."

"I'm too tired." I don't know what possesses me to say it. It's the truth, but I should use the time to search the bathroom. There might be cleaner I could throw in his eyes. Scissors. A razor.

I'm about to take it back when he grabs the hem of my collared work shirt.

"Arms over your head," he orders. I'm so woozy, I obey. He doesn't undo the top button, so when he pulls, the collar gets stuck around my head.

"Stop it," he barks, yanking harder.

"I'm not doing anything." I can't suck in my face.

Finally, he wrangles it loose, and I register the chilly air on my bare belly. Goosebumps pucker my arms.

All the tugging triggers a sharp pain in my temples. I wince, squeezing my eyes shut. It's blessedly quiet for a moment, and then there's a rummaging in the medicine cabinet.

"Here." He takes my hand and presses pills into my palm.

"I can't swallow them dry." I'm still so thirsty.

I hear the sink run.

"Open your eyes," he demands. He's holding out a glass of water. I grab it, draining it in three gulps. I don't even think to save a sip to take the painkillers.

He refills the glass. I drink more slowly this time. The water sloshes in my belly, and my guts cramp. I'm dizzy. I guess I did whack my head pretty good on the driveway.

That must be why I'm going along with this, sitting here complacently while Dario tries to care for me like a toddler with her first doll.

How did I never notice how awkward he is?

I guess our time together was always structured. Dinner. Games. Clear rules and etiquette. He pulled out my chair. Poured my wine. Even sex was somewhat scripted. He put me in position, and I took him. I came if I could get myself off. If I couldn't get to my clit, I didn't. He'd kiss me when he was done, and then he'd take a shower.

And I was okay with it. More than okay. I was in love.

Why?

Why is *this* all I wanted for myself?

I can tell myself I didn't know there was something wrong with him, but I wasn't asking any questions, was I?

"What are you thinking about?" Dario's leaning against the sink, arms folded, watching me drink.

"You." I don't have the mental bandwidth to lie.

"Are you thinking about how I won?"

"I'm wondering what made you the way you are."

His smile fades. "I don't see why it matters."

I shrug. "I guess it doesn't."

He stalks toward me, and I tense, but he leans past me to turn on the spigot. Water gushes into the tub, steam filling the air.

"Are you going to burn the rest of my skin off in the jacuzzi?"

He frowns at me.

"You turned the handle all the way to hot." I point out.

He sticks his fingers in the stream and sucks in a breath, snatching them back. "That's scalding."

"Yeah."

"The hot water heater needs to be turned down."

"Probably."

"Why didn't you tell me?"

I lift a shoulder. Truth be told, it never occurred to me. This isn't my home. I was a guest. I wasn't going to complain about the accommodations.

"Why haven't you ever noticed?" I throw back.

"I take cold showers."

Of course, he does.

He's adjusting the temperature, brow furrowing. At least the water isn't steaming anymore. He seems frustrated.

I'm not used to seeing him this rumpled. His shirt sleeves are rolled up, and his second button is undone, revealing the thin gold chain he always wears with a crucifix and Miraculous Medal. He's not religious. I asked him once why he wore the necklace, and he said habit.

"Give me your hand," he huffs, grabbing it before I can respond and thrusting it into the water. "Is it too hot?"

"It's fine."

Can he not tell?

"Strip. Get in," he orders, backing away. He's irritated.

I keep an eye on him while I peel off my khaki work pants and white cotton panties. Feeling has returned to my extremities, but I'm sore. I'm bruised all over. At least half of the marks I gave myself in that trunk. I scan my body quickly as I step into the tub and sink into the warm water, wrapping my arms around my knees.

Dario sits on the closed toilet, staring at me.

I don't want to be naked in front of him, but I'm not embarrassed. I'm on overload. Survival mode. The pounding in my head has mostly subsided, but there's still a dull ache. The lump where my skull hit the asphalt is still tender and hot to the touch. My wrists burn.

The water soothes some of the lesser aches, but I still feel like I've been through a war.

And Dario's looking at me like a science experiment.

"Wash," he says, impatiently. "Don't just sit there."

"If you're getting bored, you can leave," I mutter, but I reach for the body wash.

"You never bore me."

I blink and focus on his face. It's bland. Hard. Same as always.

Chapter 7

He's not sweet-talking me. Dario's sweet talk is cliché and repetitive. He trotted out the same phrases every time we had sex when we first got together. *You're so beautiful. I love being with you. You're perfect.* He stopped when I moved in. I figured it was a natural evolution of the relationship. Like peeing with the door open.

Looking at this cold man with his hands braced on his thighs, glaring at me, wound tighter than a drum, it's impossible to believe the words ever came from his mouth, but I remember vividly. We were skinny dipping in the pool when he said I love you for the first time.

No. He said, "I love being with you."

And we were about to have sex.

"What are you thinking?" he demands again.

I waste time by squeezing lavender-scented body wash on a loofah and kneading it in my hands.

"You never used to wonder."

"Because I knew." He says it with absolute confidence.

"You knew what I was thinking? All the time?" I run the sponge as lightly as I can over my shoulders. It's rough, and I'm sore.

He nods. "You loved me. You were anxious about other women. You wanted me to propose. You worried about whether I thought you were getting fat. Whether I was getting bored."

My face flushes. He's one hundred percent correct, and it's pathetic. I was dancing around, high as a cloud, happier than I'd ever been in my life, and that's the garbage that was on a loop in my head.

"I never got bored," he says, offhandedly.

"Why not?" It's out of my mouth before I can remind myself that I don't care.

"I don't know." He stretches his spine and rises to his feet. "You're going to take forever going that slow."

He stalks over, and I shrink to the corner. "Hand me that."

He grabs the sponge from my hand and begins scrubbing my arm. Hard.

"Stop," I cry, jerking away, curving forward to protect my breasts and belly, steeling myself for more rough handling.

He does. I gape. His shirt is wet, clinging to the ridges of his abs. He looms at the side of the tub, sponge dripping suds down his veined forearm.

"It hurts?"

"When you rub my skin off? *Yes.*"

He glares at the loofah. "Then why are you using this?"

I stare around the immaculate white tub. I don't know. It's what was here. I got nothing.

He sighs and perches on the edge, grabbing the bottle of body wash. He squints at the label, grunts, and squeezes some in his hand.

"Come closer."

My pulse kicks up a notch. I'd rather not. I don't understand what's happening here, and I'm naked. Vulnerable. Hurt and tired.

I stay plastered to the far side.

He makes an odd sound in the back of his throat, almost a growl. I tremble. The air is warm and steamy, but my insides are cold.

He sighs in exasperation, toes off his shoes, and peels off his socks.

"What are you doing?"

He splashes into the tub, pants and shirt still on.

"Whatever I want."

I scramble away, and somehow, he hooks me around the

waist as he lowers himself into the water, dragging me between his legs, trapping me.

"Stay still, or I'll hurt you." His voice is calm and even. I'm panting, chest heaving, and he works his hands together to lather them up again. Then he runs them from my shoulders, down my arms. Gently.

He stops just before he gets to the abrasions on my wrists, his fingertips almost touching the raw, red skin.

I shiver against his hard chest. Some primal instinct has me frozen in place, afraid to breathe too deep.

He rests his chin in the crook of my neck and then rests my hands on his knees, stroking back up the sensitive inside of my arms.

He emits a low hum and skims the bruises. He's *admiring* the marks he made.

"You like seeing how you hurt me?"

I tense. I shouldn't have said it. I have to get out of this alive; I can't let words fly out of my mouth.

"I like marking you." He says it as if he's discovering it himself, in this moment. "It might leave a scar. These tape burns on your wrists." He sounds pleased.

He sniffs and straightens, reaching for the body wash.

"You shouldn't have run," he says as if that answers for everything.

"Ray told me to."

Ray watched Dario maul me in the driveway, and ultimately, he backed away. He's not my friend. I don't owe him shit.

Dario chuckles. "Did he tell you where to go?"

"No."

Dario pours more soap into his palm, bemused. "He would have given you bad advice. You're much more clever than Ray."

"Thanks." It's a smart remark, but Dario either doesn't notice or doesn't mind. He rubs his hands and then strokes them over my breasts.

I suck in a breath.

Dario's hard cock presses into my back. It has been this whole time, but I've been ignoring it. Dario's different from the other men I've been with. He's not led by his dick. We were in the middle of sex once when the market in Japan opened, and he pulled out without coming because he was obsessed with some tech stock.

I try to ignore the feeling of his rough palms soaping my heavy breasts, too, but I can't. He cups me, lifting and molding, and then he smooths over my belly and glides down my thighs. He leans us both forward so he can reach my calves and feet, and then he straightens back up and returns to my boobs.

It's jarring. It's not affection. It sure as hell isn't love. His touch is almost clinical as he weighs me and plucks at my nipples until they're stiff and aching. I press my legs together. My pussy's throbbing, but that's biology.

He can touch me however he wants. He's stronger, and I'm beaten down. It doesn't mean anything, though. It doesn't mean I love him anymore. I hike my chin and stare at the stone tiles.

"Does this feel good?" he asks.

"Why do you care?"

"I don't know."

With no warning, he pries my knees apart, wedging a leg between mine to hold me open. I buck, but he wraps one arm around my chest, pinning my elbows to my side. He slips his free hand between my legs, thrusting two fingers inside me without warning.

I gasp.

Chapter 7

"You're wet," he murmurs in my ear.

"So?" It's a short syllable, but it shakes. I swallow. "I don't want to do this." I know it doesn't matter to him, but maybe it matters to me. That I at least say it.

"You fucked me all the time before when you weren't in the mood."

My stomach turns. It's the truth. "We were together then. Couples do that."

"I never fucked you if I didn't want to."

My body is so tense. His fingers are still inside me, probing. His thumb's seeking out my clit. I clench my thighs, but I can't dislodge him.

"Dario," I say softly, knowing it won't make a difference. "Please stop."

And it's a miracle. Like I've said the magic words. He immediately slips his fingers from me, ghosting the tips gently over my plumped pussy lips and then resting his palm right above my wet curls. He moves his legs so I'm cradled between them again.

"I'm going to put a baby here." He tickles the swell below my belly button.

My brain can't keep up. "No." Even though I'm utterly drained, alarm skitters my nerves. "That's a terrible idea."

He hums, unmoved. "Our children will be smart. And attractive."

"And humble." He's never talked about kids before. Despite the box in his sock drawer, we never talked about marriage either. And now—he's insane. We're not bringing a child into this disaster.

He laughs. "You can teach them how to be like you. They might be born like me, though, and then you'll just have to deal with it."

"Born how?"

"You know. Without—" He seems to struggle for words. "A conscience?"

"No one's born with a conscience. You develop one. It's learned."

"Well, then. Our future children will be fine. You'll teach them right from wrong, and I'll teach them all the important things."

The conversation is surreal. The water's cooling, and except where his hot skin touches mine, I'm shivering. Dario seems impervious. It's silent in the house, as always, and the sun is bright, streaming through the frosted glass panes above the alcove with the tub.

My brain is slow from sleep deprivation and the aftereffects of adrenaline. I should be fighting. At the very least, I should be on guard, but I'm limp in his arms.

"I thought you were going to make me suffer." My voice is thick.

"I was." He cups a palm and scoops cool water over my breasts, rinsing the suds away. I shudder. "I changed my mind."

"Why?"

"I'm not angry anymore."

"Why not?" I shouldn't push. Why am I pushing?

He takes his time replying. When he answers, he seems surprised. "I wanted you back. You're here now. It's all good."

I struggle to keep my heavy eyelids up. My tongue is thick as I say, "It's not good. At all. You're fucked in the head. As soon as I can, I'm going to run, and this time, you're never going to be able to find me."

He wraps his arms tightly around my trembling torso. "Shh," he whispers in my ear. "You don't have to fight. I'll go back to the way I was. You can go back to pretending everything is fine. You liked it like that. It's over now. You can relax."

He lifts me from the tub and winds me in a thick, white towel. Then he puts me in bed and covers me with a fluffy comforter. I blearily check the clock. It's nearly nine thirty. The New York Stock Exchange is opening.

Dario heads out the door. It shuts with a snick and then there's the unmistakable click of a key turning in a lock.

8

DARIO

I'm soaking wet, hard enough to pound nails, and I stink like flowers and soap.

I grab a change of clothes, rinse off in a guest room shower, and head for my office. I pop my head in the surveillance room and tell Ray to keep an eye on Posy. The lock on the door is flimsy, but all the hallways and the grounds are monitored by CCTV. She can run, but she won't get far.

She was so tired, though. I wanted to play with her, but she wouldn't have been any fun.

I open my trading software and adjust some orders. It's a sluggish day at the end of a slow quarter. I click a few buttons, make a million bucks. I could do this with my eyes closed.

I work for a few hours, but I never get settled. My dick's at half mast, and I've got too much energy. I'd go down to the gym, but I don't want to miss it when she wakes up.

How much sleep does she need anyway? She's got to be up by lunch.

I drum my fingers on the polished desk and then wipe

Chapter 8

the smudges with my cuff. Satisfaction and nerves war in my chest.

I got her back. She ran, I caught her, and she was terrified. I can't stop my lips from curving. She hung up on me, and I stuffed her in my trunk. It's a bit like bringing a gun to a knife fight, but when I win, I do like to go big.

Finding her wasn't a foregone conclusion, either. Before that conversation with her boozy friend, we were on the wrong trail. But as soon as we had the name Nevaeh Ellis, we were golden. We ran her through the system. Her license had been used on a rental application that had been declined. That got us in the right town. The investigator found her in less than a day.

Posy's so bright, but she constantly sabotages herself. She trusts people, longs for affection and acceptance. She gets lonely. She wants to please. She's as vulnerable in this world as a snail without a shell.

Why am I fascinated by her weakness?

I didn't like it when she was gone, and knowing that she's upstairs in my bed is unaccountably...pleasing.

She's going to try and run again; she's not a fool. I can't keep her locked away forever. It's a problem. I'm not that concerned. I like solving problems.

Figuring out how to keep her isn't what's unsettling. It's the change.

The common wisdom, as best as I can tell, is that being raised by Rocco Volpe warped me. Or God just blanked when making me. Who could say? It was an issue when I was younger. I had to learn that hurting people came with consequences—messes that needed cleaning, hush money. My father was always pissed that I was wasting his time with my penchant for inconvenient violence.

It's no wonder Lucca and his crew constantly whaled on

me. I was a strange kid. I get the sense that the older men thought my quirks could be beaten out of me, and they encouraged their boys to put me in my place. A medieval kind of remedy.

It didn't work. I grew stronger. The beatings taught me to fight, and except for Lucca and Tomas, the others learned to fear me. And then I showed an aptitude for making money, and no one concerned themselves with "why" so much anymore.

My messes became acceptable. The cost of doing business.

If I had to guess, I'd say I've always been this way. I can't remember being any different. Until now.

Now, I *want*. I want Posy to wake up. I want to know what she's thinking. I want to pick up what I broke and fit the pieces back together until she's exactly the way she was—but I want her to still see me like she does now. The way I truly am.

It doesn't make sense. Why should everyone else in the world be a Claymation and this one woman is live action?

She's pretty. Bright enough. Her bastard of a father taught her to be obliging. Seen and not heard, that sort of thing. There's nothing *special* about her except that for some reason, her feelings are real to me.

And I don't function well when she's gone.

That makes her my weakness. For the moment. This isn't how I'm made. I'm sure it'll pass. Familiarity will breed contempt. When we first met, she wasn't any different from anyone else except she played chess well. And then, one day, she won a close match, and she screeched, and I *felt* it.

It wasn't novel like a new smell or shade of color. It was like all the air in the world was suddenly tinted pink. Like a glimpse at a new dimension.

I can recognize feelings, but only Posy's are *real*. Only Posy's *matter*.

I click the mouse. One quick trade. Five hundred thousand.

When is Posy waking up?

Did she fall asleep too suddenly? Her head did bounce when it hit the pavement. She was making sense in the tub, but what if she has a head injury? A slow bleed of some kind?

That's highly unlikely. She didn't complain of any pain. She wouldn't though, would she? She's scared. Overwhelmed. Exhausted. She's a feast of feelings, and I'm hungry.

I reach for the phone, but it rings before I can find the number I'm looking for.

It's Renelli.

"Yes." I level my voice to hide my irritation.

He clears his phlegmy throat. "She's back."

Fuck.

How does he know?

Ray cleared the house when we brought her in. I banked on some time before dealing with Renelli. He's going to need handling. He's not going to like rescinding an order.

I grunt.

"You beat me to it," he chuckles. There's no humor in it.

"Of course." I was motivated. His men were not.

He laughs again. "You're an arrogant motherfucker, aren't you?" He doesn't wait for my answer. "But with your skills, you can be."

He's speaking the truth, but he leaves part unsaid. He needs me, and he hates me for it. Without me, he's a dinosaur with a dwindling protection racket, waxing sentimental about the days when he ran the numbers. But my

Midas touch made the Renelli organization relevant again. He's in power because I have no interest in wearing the crown, and he knows it, and it galls him.

I don't respond. It's understood between us.

"The problem is taken care of. You need not concern yourself with it anymore." He's not going to fold and accept that immediately, but I want to be clear.

"It's not that simple, son."

"I think it is."

He lets out a long-suffering sigh. "This isn't a one-man operation. I can't have bitches causing conflict between brothers."

"There's no conflict." Frankie will pay, but I can wait in the interest of smoothing things over for now.

Renelli clicks his cheek. "That Santoro slut is trouble and no mistake. She wastes my time and money. Distracts you from your work. No, my son. She's no good. Listen. Take a week or two. Fuck her a few more times. Get her out of your system. Then get rid of her."

He pauses. Waits for me to show my hand. He thinks he knows me. That I'll get hot because he called her a slut. Maybe I'll lose my temper, and he can flex on me like he's been wanting to do for a while now. He doesn't know me.

"If you don't, I will," he says.

I tap my index finger on the desk and stare out the window at the pool. Before Posy swims, she stands at the edge with her toes curled over. Then she slowly dips a foot in, shivering, hugging her big, beautiful tits. She makes a face, and then all of a sudden, she jumps in and shrieks. Every time.

I love to watch her. The reluctance. The shivers that shake her thin shoulders. The flash of courage as she braces herself and leaps, eyes screwed tight. It makes me hard, and it makes me high.

Posy Santoro isn't *in* my system. She burst into life in my empty shell and made it into something. She *is* my system. Maybe I didn't understand that before I lost her. I'm a man. I can be a cliché. Still, it's true, and I know it now, ever since the moment I caught her. I don't just get off on what she is—I need it.

"Do we have an understanding, son?" Renelli's tone allows for no dissent.

"I understand you."

"We're agreed?" he presses.

"Agreed," I lie. "In a week or two. I'll solve the problem."

"Good. We'll see you Wednesday? For the dinner?"

"Yes. I'll be there." He asks me his usual questions about the portfolios, and then he hangs up. He doesn't speak of Posy again. He cannot fathom that she is going to be his downfall, but if he forces me into a choice—it's simple.

He's the arrogant motherfucker to think he can tell me what to do. To believe the authority he wields is anything but an illusion. Money is power. He's capo because until this moment, I had no other preference.

He thinks to take what's mine? And his rats, scurrying to do his bidding, equally blind to the fact that they continue to exist because I don't prefer otherwise? I think it's time to clean house. Who told him?

Not the housekeeper or the cleaning staff. They came in after Posy was safe in our room, and they stick to the kitchen and their scheduled areas. Today is the gym, the media room, and the east and west parlors. Ray's loyalty is unquestionable. That leaves Ivano and his wandering eyes.

I stand, cracking my neck.

Where's that dirty snitch?

I stride from the office. The door flies into the wall. Maybe I'm a little amped up.

Ray pokes his head from the surveillance room.

"Go get Posy. Bring her to the gym."

An idea is forming in my mind, a smile playing at my lips. I can kill two birds with one stone.

Ray stalks off to do my bidding.

"Be careful of her head," I call after him. "She hit it on the pavement."

I hunt my prey, steps light, an unholy excitement throbbing to life in my veins. I've been stressed these past weeks. This is going to feel amazing.

"Ivano!" I shout.

There's the dashing of feet in the kitchen. The help are making themselves scarce.

Can they hear it in my voice? They must.

I find my quarry buffing his car in front of the garage, hair slicked back, gold chains dangling.

"Hey, boss." He meets my eye, wiping his palms on his tracksuit. Totally unconcerned. Why would he be? He thinks Renelli's the man in charge, and he's been a good little rat.

"I want to spar."

"Now?"

"Now." I can't contain the smile.

Ivano tosses a shoulder. "Sure thing." He tucks his rag into his back pocket and comes along.

How can he not sense it?

He's been with me for a few years now. I know I give very little away, but after all this time, he can't tell?

It always boggles my mind—how people see what they think is there. In school, I always had my nose in a book. I liked computers. I was a nerd to Lucca and the others. They still see me that way, and there's always that flash of surprise when I pull out my knife.

I walk beside Ivano to the basement. He makes conversation about the cars. Oblivious.

By the time we change into shorts and tape our hands, Ray has brought Posy down. There's a mat the size of a regulation boxing ring in the middle of the space, my equipment organized along the walls. Ray fetches a metal folding chair and urges Posy to sit.

She looks like shit. She's pasty white, and her hair's uncombed. She's thrown on a pale blue hoodie and a matching pair of yoga pants. That first day, I had the things I'd bought her boxed, but when my temper cooled, I asked the housekeeper to return them to her drawers. I didn't like the dresser and closet half empty. It felt like a tilted picture frame.

Posy's smart enough not to ask me why she's here. She huddles in the chair, slumped over. The marks on her wrists are red. Are they infected?

Displeasure threatens to overtake my anticipation, but thankfully, Ivano steps onto the mat, slapping his fists together and bouncing on his toes.

"No headgear, boss?" he mumbles through his mouthguard.

I shrug and take my place.

"Here. Ray." Ivano jerks his chin. "Get this off." Ray unstraps his head protection.

I stifle a sigh. Machismo. A vague sense of disappointment dampens my mood. This will be over too soon.

Ivano and I tap gloves.

"Ding, ding," Ray says, taking his place beside Posy. She's woken up a little. Her spine has straightened. She understands me now.

"Take it easy on me, boss," Ivano jokes and swings.

I drive a fist into his nose. Blood sprays. He curses.

"What the fuck?"

"How did Renelli know that Posy's here?" I ask, jabbing.

He ducks. "He called. He asked me what's going on. He's the boss, right?"

"You just called me the boss," I point out. He lands a decent hook. Clears my sinuses.

"You were looking for her, too," he whines around his mouthguard.

"Because she's mine." I force her to meet my eyes. She's blanched even whiter, huddled as small as she can get on the folding chair. "Renelli wants to kill her. You picked the wrong horse, Ivano."

I drive my fist into his kidneys, a quick series of sharp blows. He finally realizes what's happening and throws his whole strength into blocking the blows, but it's too late. His vision is impaired, he's missing easy shots, and although he carries more muscle than me, he doesn't have the instinct.

I slam a left hook into his side, and a rib breaks through the skin. It snaps. He screams. I sweep his leg, and there's another satisfying crunch. He topples, and I stomp the knee, feel it crack like an egg under my heel.

He's begging, bawling, trying to crawl away.

I grab his hair, wet with blood, and drag him off the mat, slamming his face into the hardwood floor until it comes up mashed beyond all recognition.

And then I roll him over and kneel on his chest. I tear off my gloves, rip the tape with my teeth, and take my knife from where I tucked it in my sock. I fish for his snitch tongue, and while he moans with fear, I saw it off. His blood is warm and smells like pennies.

The air is red, and my lungs are clear. I can breathe easy

for the first time in weeks. I roll my shoulders and pound a fist against my chest. I feel amazing.

The room is ringing.

Screams.

Shrill.

Not Ivano. He's not making a sound anymore except a quiet gurgle.

I stand and turn, confused.

It's Posy. She's standing, the chair collapsed on the floor. Ray's arms are around her, pinning her in place. She's struggling, but she's weak. She sags against him.

I don't like that.

"Drop her."

He does, instantly.

She stumbles and catches herself, her screams trailing off as her eyes catch mine. Her pupils are huge. The blue of her irises has almost disappeared.

"Are you going to kill him?" she gasps.

"He's not dead?" I look down at my feet. His chest is still moving. Very slightly. I'm surprised.

"What did he do?" she mumbles.

"He betrayed me." I go to her, push the stringy hair out of her face. It's damp. From tears? There's a rancid smell. I glance down. She was sick.

"I never betrayed you, Dario, I swear," she whimpers, swaying. She's going to pass out. I grab her upper arms.

"I know," I say.

"I never cheated on you." Desperation tinges her voice.

"I believe you."

She moans. If I weren't holding her up, she'd probably fall to her knees. She's looking past me now. She can't tear her eyes from Ivano's mangled body.

"He's gonna die, Dario."

"Probably."

"Why did you do it?"

"He's a rat. He told Renelli that I found you."

"Why am I here?" Her wild gaze flies to my face.

"Because I need you to understand."

"Understand what?" The hysteria is rising in her voice. I don't have much longer before she's useless.

"I killed Giorgio Fusco. Ivano here, barring a miracle, is going to bleed to death on this mat. And this isn't the end. There's going to be a trail of bodies before I'm done."

I grab her chin and force her to look me in the eye. "I do it for you, Posy. You belong to me. You're a very dangerous woman now."

"You're crazy."

I suppose that's true after a fashion.

On the mat, Ivano moans. It gurgles.

"You have to do something," she begs.

"Why?"

Her gaze darts to his twisted, bloody body. I don't like it. I feel better when her eyes search out mine again.

"I never saw a man killed before."

It's a nonsensical explanation, but maybe she's beginning to understand the game we're playing now.

I exhale, and my lips curve. I rest my forehead on hers.

"Are you sure? He wouldn't save you."

"No one can," she breathes, so quiet, it's almost voiceless.

I smile. She's right.

"You're not going to try to run again, are you, Posy?"

"No," she agrees immediately.

"Good girl." I'd kiss her, but she's a mess.

"Ray, call the doctor," I call and then I scoop her up and head for the stairs. She needs a bath, and then she needs to get back in bed. She looks awful. "After he patches up Ivano, send him upstairs. I want him to look at Posy's head."

I'd make Ivano wait if I thought he'd last. If he's still alive by the time Dr. Albano makes his way here from the city, he won't have much time left.

Posy trembles in my arms.

She's probably not going to be up for a game anytime soon.

I need to shower anyway. There's blood splatter all over me.

Maybe after a nap she'll be ready to play again.

9

POSY

When I wake up, Dario's sitting at the table by the window, playing on his phone. He's set up the chess board. My mouth is so dry my tongue sticks to the roof of my mouth.

I can't think about earlier. I can't. I was raised around dangerous men, but they never brought it home. Never made me watch. My stomach lurches, and I swallow it down.

Dario rolls a bishop in his fingers. Rays of late afternoon sun warms his tan skin, and his hair's damp. A stray black lock falls onto his forehead. He's wearing a gray zippered hoodie and black track pants. His feet are bare. He rarely dresses so casually.

He lounges in the leather wing-backed chair, an ankle propped on his knee. He looks so normal. So classically handsome.

There's no trace of the blood that covered him earlier.

I struggle to sit, the sheet falling to my waist. At some point while I slept, I'd stripped down to my white ribbed tank top and panties.

The doctor had come. He'd checked my head and treated and wrapped my wrists. Then he gave me a pill. That's why I'm so groggy.

I rub my eyes as I piece time back together. Is this the same day? Is Ivano dead?

"Good. You're awake. I'm tired of waiting." Dario pushes back the chair across from him with his foot and gestures to the empty seat.

"Come on then," he says.

"You want to play chess?" My voice is a croak.

"We can play Go if you want."

I swing my legs over the side of the bed. My head swims, but it doesn't throb anymore. My bumps and bruises ache, but nothing hurts too bad.

My lips are chapped. There's a carafe of water on the table beside a vase of posies. Nice touch. Carolyn's been busy.

Where are my clothes? I search the floor, but they're gone. Dario probably put them in the hamper. Everything in its place.

I don't have the energy to make it to the closet, so I pad to the table and sink gingerly into a chair. The leather is a shock of cold on the backs of my bare thighs. I fumble with a glass. Dario swats my hand away and pours me some water.

"You go first," he says, nodding toward the board. I guess I'm white.

I move 1 to f3.

He raises an eyebrow. "The Barnes opening?"

I shrug. He counters with d5.

I move my knight to h3.

"Knock it off," he growls. He plucks up my pawn and knight and thumps them back in their original positions.

I move 1 to a4.

He grinds his teeth and leans back, glaring at me. "If you don't want to play, say so."

"I don't want to play." I want another one of those pills. I want to pass out and wake up somewhere else. Anywhere else.

"Well, I do."

"Then play." I can lose in two moves. It'll be a quick round.

He huffs, irritated. "You like to play."

I let my eyelids drift shut. "Not now I don't."

"Why not?"

Does he really not get it? Or is he toying with me? I'm exhausted, and I can't sort it out. He doesn't act at all like the Dario from before. He was cold and self-contained, and I knew he was capable of horrible things, but he pretended, and so did I. Like my mom and my Nonna.

"You made me watch you beat a man to death."

"Ivano's not dead."

I blink. There was so much blood. My brain slides over the memory. I can't think about it and sit here, having a calm conversation with the man who pummeled another person beyond all recognition.

"Aren't you happy?" Dario asks.

"No."

The pulse point in his temple throbs. He's getting angry. My breath quickens. I should watch my mouth. Give him what he wants. What's wrong with me?

He drums his fingers on the table. "What would make you happy, Posy?"

"Let me go." I say it quietly. I don't anticipate an explosion. I should have.

Dario's chair skids back, and I jump, scrambling on the

Chapter 9

soft leather. I get nowhere before he reaches over the table, seizing the front of my tank top and hauling me to my feet.

My hands fly up to protect my face. He spins me, bending me over the table until my abraded cheek hits the cold wood. The board slides. Pieces fall and roll onto the floor.

He shoves my panties down. I don't have a chance to escape. He's between my legs, his chest like a slab of steel against my back, his breath jagged in my ear.

"Knee up on the table," he orders, fumbling with his pants.

I'm frozen. I should struggle, but I can't. I'm too scared. What will he do if I fight him?

I've done it plenty of times when I wasn't in the mood. With him. With other men. It won't last forever. I can think about something else.

I force myself to stop moving. I'm facing the window. The sky's a perfect, cloudless blue. I can look at that, and it'll be over soon.

Dario's hot cock pokes between my legs. I try to relax. It'll hurt more if I tense.

He draws back, and then his cock is replaced by rough fingers.

"Why aren't you wet?" he demands.

A hysterical laugh bubbles from my lips.

"You're usually wet." It's an accusation.

He spits on his hand, rubs himself, and tries again. He forces the tip in, and I bite my cheek, focusing on the pain. I can do this. I don't have a choice. I'll live through the next few minutes, and then it'll be over.

There's a twinge, and I whimper.

"Posy?" It's a question. I don't know the answer.

All of a sudden, he stops. He lets his head fall, resting his forehead between my shoulder blades. I can feel his hot breath through my thin tank top. My breasts are squashed against the table.

He stoops and pulls his pants back up. Then he eases my panties up, too.

"Stand up."

Why? So he can push me over again?

"*Stand up.*"

I don't want to. I can't roll with anymore punches. I want to stay here, folded over a table, until it's over. It has to be over soon, right?

By some miracle, the queen's still upright. I reach out and flick her over. She didn't stand a chance.

Dario grabs my elbow and tugs. I have to stand or he'll yank my arm out of the socket. My legs wobble.

He wraps his arms around me like a lover, hugging me close. We're both facing the window. I'm trembling, and he's strong and steady. A stupid, raw part of me that never wised up clings to the suggestion of security.

"What are you looking at out there?" he asks, leveling his cheek with mine, his beard tickling my jaw.

"Nothing. The sky."

"You're upset." He says it as if he's discovered a secret I've hidden from him, and he's vaguely pleased with himself because of it.

I keep my mouth shut and try to pull myself together. There's no fast forward. I have to live through this moment and the next. I have to figure out how to survive.

Dario breaks the silence. "Why did you let your ex fuck you in ass when you didn't want it?"

I suck in a breath. He asks me this now? And his tone is perfectly nonchalant. He's just making conversation.

"Well?" he prompts.

Jesus. I don't know. "I thought I did at the time." It's the best answer I have.

"Bullshit. I saw your face. You hated it."

Why rehash this now? I test his grip, try to put some space between us, but he tightens his arms.

I huff a sigh. "I don't know, Dario. You tell me."

"Because you're a love-starved people pleaser."

I almost buckle from the blow. How can anything he says still hurt? I don't love him anymore. I don't even know him. And so what if he's right? There are much worse things to be. Like a psychopath and a murderer.

He sighs and rocks me slightly side to side. "He didn't deserve you. There is no way a piece of filth like him could have appreciated what he had. Of course he took advantage."

What?

"But your low self-esteem is a real issue. You get that, don't you, Posy?" He doesn't wait for me to respond. He plows ahead. "You're allowed to say no."

My blood runs cold. It's a lecture I've given myself a hundred times, and if I'd listened, I wouldn't be here.

"Why didn't you tell me no, Posy?"

I did. Didn't I?

Should I have to? He kidnapped me. Hurt me.

"Read the signs, Dario."

He sighs, his breath ruffling my hair. "I'm not good at that."

"Then assume it's a no."

"It never has been before."

Before was different, for fuck's sake. God, I hate him. My muscles bunch. I'm going to rip myself out of his arms if I have to drag him down with my dead weight.

I lurch, but he's already letting me go. He awkwardly pats my shoulder. "It's all right. We'll figure it out."

"You hurt me." I didn't plan on saying it. It seems ridiculous to complain.

He nods. "I'll learn how not to."

I should quit while I'm ahead, but his answer only makes me angrier.

"Why? Because I play games with you? You really couldn't live without your chess buddy?"

I pace toward the bed, narrowing the distance between me and the door. He tracks me with his cold eyes.

"You won't play with me now."

"I'm not in the mood," I throw over my shoulder. The greater the distance I put between us, the more my fear ebbs.

"Being in the mood doesn't matter to you." I know he's talking about sex.

"Yes, it does." I'm surprised by the vehemence in my tone. Maybe I've acted like it doesn't matter in the past, but it always did. Just other things mattered more. Keeping Dario happy. Not causing waves. Not giving him any reason for his eye to wander.

Wonder where I learned that?

I remember Mom taking me to Stansbury Park, and how she'd drag me away at exactly four o'clock—no matter if I was in the middle of a game or not—because she had to get home, put her face on, and get dinner started before Dad got home. She'd tell me on the bus that she was so proud of me but remember to tell Dad we were shopping. He wouldn't want us wasting our day playing chess.

Linda Santoro was a walking contradiction. I guess if we live long enough, we all are.

I inch closer to the door. I know if I run, I won't get far. I feel better by the door, though.

Dario remains by the table. He squats to pick up the chess pieces, his sweats hugging his muscular thighs.

I like him better in a suit. It puts him at a remove. It feels safer.

"You didn't like it when we had sex?" he asks, his attention focused on re-setting the board.

"Sometimes I did. Sometimes—" I shrug.

"I knew that. I figured you're the kind of woman who doesn't cum every time."

"Guess you figured right."

"I like it better when you get off."

My face warms, and I cross my arms in front of my boobs. I don't care. He's crazy, and I'm pretty much a captive at this point. My brain offers up an image from earlier, Ivano desperately trying to push himself up from the floor, his leg bent in the wrong direction, his palms slipping on the bloody mat.

My flush fades as a chill seeps into my chest.

"Why did you do that to Ivano?"

"That's a quick change of conversation." He places the black king on its square.

"What did he do?"

"He's a rat."

"You let a rat live?" That's not how it works. My uncle was a rat. He paid for it with his life, and the rest of us lived with the stink. It was a miracle Renelli didn't kill my father even though he had no idea what his brother was doing. I was in junior high when Renelli caught him skimming. One day, I was popular. I had a boyfriend. I was queen bee. The next I was sitting at the lunch table alone.

"You asked me to."

"You don't do anything you don't want to," I scoff.

He inclines his head. "You need to know your power."

"I have no power."

"To the contrary." His eyes darken. "You decimate my control. If you run again, if you make me angry enough, I could kill you. I might not even mean to."

He offers a chagrined smile as if he's admitting to a minor fault, his expression almost boyish.

"You wanted him alive. And I needed to send Renelli a message." He considers a second. "It'll likely come back and bite me. Hopefully he'll stay in whatever Sicilian backwater they ship him to."

A different smile, sharkish and wide, twists his lips. "If he came back, I could finish him, though. He'll want revenge. He'd be a threat to you." He sounds wistful.

He sighs and taps the table. "Come on, now, Posy. I gave you what you wanted. Give me what I want."

"I don't want to fuck." I hike my chin. "I'm not in the mood."

"Come on." He pats his lap and adjusts the chess board so it's sideways. We've played this way before. It usually ends up with me riding his cock reverse-cowgirl.

He casts a long-suffering glance at the ceiling. "Only chess. I promise."

It's one of the last things I want to do. I need a break. A shower, a nap, a change of clothes. My wrists and the bump on my head are throbbing. I'd like an aspirin or a stiff drink. But the deranged boyfriend wants a rematch, so I guess we play.

I pad over to him and perch on his knee. He scoops me back and tucks me to his chest.

"Since you fucked around, I'm white this time," he says. I can hear his delight.

"Be my guest."

He moves his pawn to e4. Ruy Lopez or the Italian Game. Boring.

I counter by moving my pawn to g5.

He shakes me lightly. "The Borg Defense? Are you still fucking around?"

"Just go."

His body is tense under mine, but as we play, he relaxes. I'm too tired to hold myself stiff, so I let myself slump against his chest.

He's warm. His left arm is wrapped casually around my waist while he moves his pieces with his right. His chin, raspy with five o'clock shadow, nestles in the crook of my neck.

He smells like the soap I buy him, sandalwood and bergamot, and underneath, the musk that's only him. A knot unfurls in my belly. I know I'm not safe, but my body is lowering its defenses, and I don't have the energy to fight.

I take one of his knights. My stomach growls.

He slips his fingers under my tank top and strokes my belly lazily. He takes my bishop.

"What are you up to?" he mutters to himself.

I don't even know. I'm playing on instinct.

My gut gurgles again.

"Why is your stomach making that noise? It's distracting," he complains, moving the wrong pawn. He just opened a huge hole in his defenses. He's going to live to regret that. I sacrifice a bishop to keep him distracted.

"I'm hungry." Isn't it obvious?

"When is the last time you ate?"

I can't remember. His fingers hover over his queen. If he moves her, I win in two. If he doesn't, I lose in three. I can't help but squirm, and his cock stiffens under my butt. I freeze.

He shakes his knee, jostling me. "I asked you a question."

"Oh. I don't know. Yesterday. The night before yesterday?" Time has blurred together. I heated up a microwave burrito at the Gas-and-Go when I started my shift.

"You need to eat."

This is probably the first time he's noticed that. He helps himself when he's hungry, or he asks me to make something. I learned early on when I moved in that I need to help myself, too. He doesn't register other people's needs. I chalked that up to being an absent-minded professor, his mind always on the markets.

I had an excuse for everything, didn't I?

All of a sudden, I want to win. Bad. Why won't he move?

I hardly suppress a groan when his hand falls away from the board. He digs in his pocket for his phone. Oh my god. Move the queen.

He taps and snaps at Ray to have a tray sent up. "You can stop making the noise now," he informs me.

Does he know how stomachs work?

I stifle the smart response as he reaches for the board. Come on. Qd7. Qd7.

He takes the queen by her crown. D7.

I exhale, and my lips curve.

Boom.

"Check," I say.

Boom.

"Checkmate." Over in two. I knock his king over with my queen, and then I stretch, arching my back.

He chuckles and makes a happy hum. "The Borg defense."

"That was a stupid move with your queen," I point out although I'm sure he realized it as soon as he did it.

"Yes," he says. "It was."

The game is over, but he's not letting me go. His hands wander, gentle, questing. He's checking my bumps and bruises.

"You're very delicate," he complains.

"No more than anyone else." An awareness is rising inside of me. Nerves. He doesn't usually touch me like this. He usually goes straight for my tits or ass.

"More than me."

I snort. "No, you're not delicate."

His fingers ghost over a bruise on my thigh. "I didn't even hit you."

"You threw me in a trunk."

He tenses beneath me. "I don't like it."

For a second, I'm confused, but then I realize he's talking about the mark on my leg. "Yeah, well, don't throw me in trunks."

"Don't run away from me again." There's an edge to his voice. A warning.

I don't say anything. Of course, I'll run as soon as I get the chance. I might not have a great sense of self-preservation when it comes to men, but I don't have a death wish. And no matter how Dario smells and feels like the man I fell in love with, he isn't, is he?

I fell in love with a fantasy. My heart aches. I thought I was done mourning, but his presence brings it back. It's unfair that you can grieve a person who never existed, the loss of a love you made up in your head. But then again, life's unfair.

There's a knock on the door. It's the tray. I make to get up, but Dario won't let me go.

"What would it take? To stop you from running again?"

"A time machine."

His hand moves to grip my hair, and he forces my head back so he can stare down into my face. His eyes glint.

"If you run again, when I catch you, I'll hurt you. Worse than this."

My scalp aches, and my eyes water. "I won't run," I gasp.

His lip curls. "You're lying. Don't run again, Posy. I don't want to hurt you."

Then he lifts me and sets me on my feet. "Eat. I want to play again when you're done."

And then he gets on his phone and tunes me out, just like he used to do.

I fetch the tray from the hallway and bring it to the table. There are two plates under silver domes. Club sandwiches, chips, pickles, and sparkling water. I place Dario's plate in front of him, and he grabs a bite without tearing his gaze from his trading app.

Before, I thought he was a workaholic, and he is, but it goes deeper than that. I sit across from him, eating and watching as he scrolls and taps. I've completely disappeared from his world. If I speak now, I'll have to repeat myself a few times before he'll respond, and he'll be pissed.

I only interrupted him a few times before I learned my lesson. Don't speak to him when he's working. Or exercising. Or reading. Or listening to music.

I had to wait for my openings. And I was okay with that. Why?

Because when I had his attention, I had all of it. And he was *fascinated* by me. No one's ever been into my mind, but Dario admired it like a painting. And then, when he was done, he put me away like his laptop, his barbells, his books, or his records.

I was a belonging, and I craved it. Belonging.

It might hurt a little still, but he did me a favor when he kicked me out. He tore off my blinders. I wasn't in love. I was deluded.

I didn't really lose anything at all.

And his hyper-focus—it's an opportunity. It's how I'm going to get out of here again, and this time, I'm not going to look back.

∽

THE NEXT DAY, Ray and I are hanging out in the media room when his phone chirps. He checks it and looks up. "You have to get dressed. You're going to dinner in an hour."

After our strange lunch yesterday, Dario disappeared, presumably to his office, and I didn't see him again. I laid down for a nap which ended up lasting until the morning. Dario never came to bed. When I woke and peeked out the door, Ray was in the hall, propped on a stool. He dogged my heels when I headed downstairs, huffing and bitching under his breath.

I guess I have a babysitter.

It's fine for now. I need time to come up with a plan. Ray can watch this god-awful rom com while I figure out my next move.

I need money. I could have stayed off the grid if I'd had cash. My dad always had a stash, but he was old school. Dario uses credit cards exclusively. Even if I miraculously developed the skill to pick pockets, whatever Ray and the other staff have in their pockets wouldn't get me as far as I need to go.

I need my jewelry. The watch, the earrings, the matching diamond and sapphire set Dario—or rather Carolyn—got me for our six month anniversary. Even at pawn shop valuation, I could get enough to totally disappear for a nice long time.

I bet it would drive Dario crazy to lose me twice. He's clearly knocked off kilter. I should be scared. It sure as hell shouldn't feel even the slightest bit good that I've pushed a monster over the edge. Me. The girl everyone could resist. I can make Dario Volpe crazy.

"Did you hear me?" Ray raises his voice over the surround sound.

"Yeah. Dinner in an hour."

"In town."

Dario's letting me leave the house? So soon? My heart kicks up a notch. He thinks he's got me back in line. I suppose he's right. I'm not going anywhere today. Not with Renelli looming.

I was at a disadvantage when Dario put me out. He had the element of surprise. When I make a break for it, I'm going to have as many ducks in a row as I can.

"Fifty-six minutes," Ray drones from the lounger behind me. I think he's actually watching the movie.

I flip him off as I go upstairs to change. Ray mutters at my back as I go.

Dario hates going into Pyle for work, but about once a week or so, he likes to go downtown for a meal or to check out something he wants to buy before he has it delivered. He rarely takes me to business functions, but he always expects me to go when it's just him.

I thought they were dates, but thinking back—he never asked. Not if I wanted to go out that night, not which restaurant I wanted to go to. We left when he was done, and he never asked if I was tired and wanted to head home.

His decisiveness turned me on.

I'm an idiot.

When I get to the bedroom, I make a beeline for the safe in the closet where Dario had me keep my jewelry. I spin the knob. 13-29-46. The door doesn't budge. I try it a few more times to be sure. He's changed the combination.

I didn't figure it'd be that easy. I grab the first cocktail dress that's handy, a one-sleeved bodycon number that looks like gold sequins from a distance, but it's actually an intricate pattern done with metallic thread. It makes me look like a Bond girl.

Why is this dress in the front? It's not a favorite. I thought I'd buried it in the back. And why are my sweaters on the lower shelves?

Now that I'm noticing, all my clothes are in the wrong places. I had it organized by what I like to wear the most. Someone took all my stuff out and then hung it back up by season and type of garment.

My spine tingles.

Either Dario reorganized my clothes for shits and giggles, or he really was done with me, and then he wasn't. What changed his mind?

What if he changes it back before I have a chance to run?

It's exhausting to try and figure out the workings of a mind like Dario's. Is that why I never looked too deep? It was easier to accept appearances and gloss over the occasional sense that everyone in the house was tiptoeing around a monster?

I don't have time to shower, so I blow out my hair, slip on the dress, and dig out a pair of gold peep-toe stilettos. My foundation does a decent job of covering the scrape on my cheek. I consider chunky bracelets to cover my bandaged wrist, but they chafe too bad. I could change into a dress with two long sleeves, but I can't be bothered. Dario's the one who messed up my wrist. If we get stares, he can deal with it.

By the time Ray knocks on the door, I'm ready to go. He helps me with my coat and escorts me out to the town car. Dario's already in the back, absorbed in his trading app. There's a new man in the passenger seat. Ivano's replacement, I guess. I wonder if he knows what happened to his predecessor.

I shiver.

"Turn the heat up," Dario orders, his gaze never leaving his phone. "She's cold."

This is new. He doesn't notice, well, anything to do with my comfort.

Ray obliges and we pull out. The sun sets as we drive downtown in silence. The new guy is hyperalert, checking the rear and side view mirrors methodically, his posture rigid. It makes me nervous. Is he expecting something?

Ray and Dario don't seem concerned. Dario's oblivious, and Ray's obsessed with people driving too slow in the fast lane or passing on the right. I'm used to him cursing people out under his breath as we drive. The familiarity of it is almost comforting.

"Where are we going?" I call up to Ray.

"La Calomba," Dario answers. This is new, too. Usually if I have a question, Ray's the guy. Dario uses transit time to work.

Dario tucks his phone in his pocket, redirecting his attention to me, raking his flinty eyes down my body. I press my knees together more tightly. The outfit is my usual for a night out. The hem hits high on the thigh. My legs are bare.

It's probably still a little too early in the season for peep toes. My exposed skin is chilly and puckered with goosebumps.

Dario reaches over and strokes from my knee to the hem of the dress, pushing it higher into my lap. I squeeze my thighs.

"What panties are you wearing?" he asks.

I cast a glance to the front seat. Both men are keeping their eyes straight forward, pretending they didn't hear, but there's no way they missed what he said. He didn't even bother to lower his voice.

My face heats. I lift my chin and stare out the side window.

He reaches out as fast as a whip, grabs my jaw, and turns me back to face him. "You don't ignore me."

"*You* ignore *me*." I didn't plan on baiting him. The words just flew out.

"I'm talking to you now."

"We've been in the car for twenty minutes. You haven't said a word to me until you asked me about my panties."

"That bothers you?" He's gentled his grip on my chin, but he hasn't let go.

I shrug. I hadn't intended to complain. I was only being argumentative. "I guess not. I don't care what you do."

"You wanted to talk about something?"

"No."

His eyes narrow like they do when we're playing a game, and he's trying to figure out the method to my madness.

"You want me to talk to you?"

He's not dropping it, and I don't know what to say.

"Before, you talked. All the time." He says it like an accusation—like how dare I change the rules now.

He's right. I was very good at filling the silences with chatter. Just like Mom babbled away at the dinner table while Dad shoveled food in his mouth, interrupting her every so often to ask her to get him another beer.

"Maybe I had more to say then," I toss out.

Dario leans closer to me. His sharp, clean scent teases my nose.

"I like listening to you," he says, his voice cast low.

The way he's turned, he's blocking me from full view from the front seat. I feel small. Pinned in place.

"Why?" I ask.

He smooths his fingers down my throat and slides them to my shoulder. He bends even closer until his mouth is right next to my ear. "It's like listening in on a broadcast from another country. Makes me wonder what it's like."

"Wonder what *what* is like?"

He doesn't answer. "I want to see your panties, Posy."

His hand strokes my thigh. It vaguely registers that we've pulled into a parking garage. A tendril of excitement curls in my belly. It's wrong to be excited, but it's not *crazy*. Dario is a beautiful man. He smells amazing. His voice is gravelly and deep.

It's not messed up to be turned on. It's natural. Not smart, but not crazy.

For some reason, he's abandoned his "take what he wants, when he wants" strategy. He seems to want my cooperation. Maybe I can work this to my advantage.

"You want me to show you my pussy?" I whisper back.

His eyes spark with fire.

"Gentlemen. Out of the car," he barks, his gaze not leaving mine.

There's a quick slamming of doors. I peer around Dario's shoulder. Ray is in front of the car by a low wall, his back to us, staring out over the city skyline. The other guy must be behind us.

"Yes," Dario breathes. He edges back to give me room. I unclick my seat belt.

"Show me," he groans.

Am I going to do this?

Yeah.

I don't say no. I don't know how to play that game where you cling to your pride or your standards or whatever. But this one? Show me? This game I know.

This feels familiar, and familiar feels safe.

I slip my feet out of my shoes. If I rest the stiletto heel on this buttery leather upholstery, I'll rip a hole, no doubt. I wriggle the dress up until it's bunched under my boobs, and Dario can see my white silk bikini briefs. They're nothing special. They don't even match my bra.

Still, he sucks in a breath. Yes. I like that.

"More," he demands.

I swallow. My throat is tight, and the swirling in my belly has spread to become a thrum between my legs.

I prop a foot on the seat he had been sitting in, and I let my knee fall open, canting my hips. I look down, following his gaze.

My panties cover me completely, but he can see the tender crease where my thighs meet my hips. Dario strokes a finger along the line. I smother a gasp. Then he hooks a finger under the elastic, tugging them to the side, revealing my puffy lips, reddened and shiny with my juices.

Dario's breath turns jagged and rough. He's being so gentle, so tentative. He's never like this.

My whole body is on edge. My breasts feel heavy, my stiff nipples chafing against my bra. My skin is hot. Perspiration tickles behind my knee and above my lip. I'm going to sweat out my hairdo.

What am I doing?

I don't know, but I don't want to stop.

Dario's looking at me like he does when we play games. Intent. Curious. Amused.

"Take them off."

My gaze darts out the window where a silver SUV is parked.

"No one but me will see. Sal's back there."

"Is Sal the new guy?"

"You don't need to give a fuck who Sal is," he growls. "Take your panties off."

A little spasm causes flutters deep inside me. He's being a dick, but I don't care. I want this. I want to be the center of his world.

I shimmy the scrap of fabric down, leaving it ringed around an ankle. I prop my foot back up on the seat.

"Good girl," he exhales, reaching out, parting my pussy with his rough fingers. Cool air hits my hot folds, and my core clenches. My swollen clit has popped from its hood.

"Show me how you play with yourself," he demands.

We've never done this before. Dario's pretty much a penis in vagina kind of guy. He's into all sorts of positions, but he's not really into appetizers. He goes straight for the main course.

But if he wants me to handle this growing ache? I guess I don't mind.

I circle my clit, slow and light. My knees tremble. I check Dario's face. Should I finger myself? Flick it? He's going to get bored watching me get off like I actually do.

But then, what do I care? He asked. I settle back, get comfortable.

He takes my foot and rests it on his chest, opening me even more to his scrutiny. And he is scrutinizing. It's like he's trying to memorize my pussy.

Chapter 9

I keep circling, gradually applying more pressure, edging closer and closer to the puckered bud. My excitement builds, shoving my constant thoughts and worries further and further out of my head.

This feels good. His eyes on me are like another touch, his silent approval an accelerant. He's really into this. He's entranced. I draw back the hood of my clit, really show him the slick, hardened nub.

He cradles the top of the foot pressed to his pec. I press the ball of my foot into the muscle as I lift my hips. There's no give. He's so strong. So solid.

I'm actually getting close, panting, licking my dry lips. I slip my finger to my slit, gather some wetness, and return to drawing circles, faster, rougher.

It feels so good. I'm coiled tight, getting tighter, but I want more. I cup my breast, and it stokes the wanting higher, but it doesn't push me over. I'm teetering on the edge. I want to plunge over, I *need* to, but I can't. I'm stuck.

I'm whining now. The sound fills the car.

"What's wrong, Posy?" he asks. "What do you need?"

I don't know. My gaze flies to his, and he's so calm and cool and in control. I'm a mess. My pussy juices are dripping down my crack onto the seat, and he's watching me like a documentary. That shouldn't turn me on, but the tension inside me ratchets tighter. I need to cum.

I stifle a sob. I need it so bad.

"Dario." It's a plea.

His brows spear down. He doesn't know what I need either.

But then his hand is on his belt. There's a zip, a tug, and then his cock springs free, thick and ruddy and veined.

"Hold this." He passes me the leg he'd propped against his chest. Then he spreads my pussy lips and jerks his cock, firm, from root to tip. He works quickly up to speed, racing to the finish. His hot head glances against my folds as he works himself.

I buck. I want him inside me. I'm empty, and I want him to fill me up.

"I'm going to cum all over your pretty pussy. And you're not gonna touch it. You're gonna wear my cum tonight because you belong to me, don't you Posy? This pussy is mine. You're mine."

His grip on himself is harsh, his strokes almost painful to watch.

He grabs my hair with his free hand and tugs. Little pricks of pleasure-pain erupt across my scalp. "Say you're mine, Posy. This pussy is mine."

"It's yours, Dario." I'm hurtling over, almost there, almost there. I couldn't stop now if I wanted to.

"Say it again." His grasp tightens. I whine. It hurts.

"This pussy is yours, Dario."

"You're going to cum now. Understand, Posy?"

"Yes," I pant.

"Watch," he demands, forcing my neck to bend. Cum shoots from his pulsing cock, lashing across my flushed, wet pussy, and I come, harder than I can ever remember, pure ecstasy ripping through me, shocking my system and muting my mind. My thighs tremble, and I instinctually clench them together.

Dario shakes the last drop of cum onto my quivering belly.

He exhales, as if in great relief. He reaches down to the floor, finds my panties, and eases them back up my legs. Then he grabs my chin, lifts my drooping head to meet his gaze.

"When we get inside, you don't wash it off. You wear my cum tonight, understand?"

I don't, really, but I'm too pleasure-dumb to argue. "Okay."

He studies me for a long moment, brow knit. Finally, he presses a perfunctory kiss to my lips.

"You look beautiful," he says as he helps me out of the car. It's an obvious lie. I try desperately to smooth my rumpled dress and repair the disaster that is my hair.

He grabs my wrist. "Stop. I want them all to know."

"Them all?"

Oh, shit. We're having dinner with other people? I guess that yet again, this isn't a date. And I have to make nice with mobsters while wearing soaking panties and reeking of cum.

∽

THE HOSTESS SHOWS us to a large private room at the back of the restaurant. La Calomba is one of my favorite places on the Promenade. It's luxe and done in a monochrome palette with geometric glass doves hanging from the ceilings like postmodern mobiles.

From the boozy volume and the fact that entrees are being served, I gather we're late. Dario guides me to the table and pulls out my seat like a gentleman. Two dozen people stare. Half of them snicker. A few of the classier wives and girlfriends studiously avoid looking in our direction.

My stomach drops—they've all seen the video. I knew that, but with everything that's happened, it wasn't at the top of my mind.

It sure as shit is at the top of everyone else's. Frankie

Bianco's leaning back with his arm on the back of Jen Amato's chair, smirking like a bitch. Jen's tittering behind her hand to her sidekick Dita.

The only people not staring—or pretending not to stare—are four older guys in suits. They must be from some other outfit. I've never seen them before.

"Dario, you finally grace us with your presence," Renelli calls from the head of the table. His gaze slides over my face. There's no acknowledgement. The hairs on the back of my neck stand on end. The message is clear. I'm nothing.

Renelli elbows one of the unfamiliar men. "That's the moneymaker. My cousin Perla's boy."

"It's nice to be surrounded with family," the man says in a thick European accent, raising his glass.

The whole table takes Renelli's lead and pretends I'm invisible. That might be better than the alternative, the laughter. How could Dario bring me here?

My face flames. I refuse to feel ashamed. The video was a stupid thing to do, but I wasn't the one who shared it. The sinking, hollow feeling sure as hell *feels* like shame, but it's not. I won't let it be.

"I'll drink to that," Renelli answers. "Here I've got my sister Sara's boy." He toasts Frankie. "And over there I have my sister Rosario's boy." He gestures across the table to Lucca.

"You're blessed," the man intones, clinking his glass to Renelli's and drinking.

"I am. Cousins as close as brothers. They have their petty squabbles, but at the end of the day—" Renelli thumps his chest with a fist. "Loyal to the bone."

There's a wave of nodding and murmured agreement. I shift in my seat. Under the table, Dario stills my squirming with a heavy hand on my knee, but his focus doesn't waver from his plate. He's spearing his steak, chowing down, appearing to blithely ignore the conversation.

"Isn't that so, Dario?" Renelli calls down the table.

Dario blinks as if he hadn't been listening. He was, though. I can tell. Now that I've seen him without his mask, when he wears it, he's obvious.

"I'm sorry." Dario raises a befuddled eyebrow.

Renelli repeats himself between forkfuls of branzino. "I said you and your cousins. You're as close as brothers."

Dario lifts a shoulder, finishes chewing, and swallows his meat. "Business is business."

"Now that's how we Russians see it," another of the guests, a rugged, bald man, says. "Family is one thing. Business is another. You Italians always mix it up, eh?" He slaps Renelli on the back.

Renelli smiles, but it doesn't reach his eyes. "Family first," he says.

Frankie interjects. "Dario's always seen things a little differently than the rest of us. He doesn't do family. And he doesn't really care if his business gets around, eh?"

Renelli's face hardens, but he doesn't give Frankie a discouraging look. He stares down the table at Dario, waiting for a reaction. Dario's eyes are on his plate.

He's not touching my thigh anymore, but I'm frozen in place. There is no way I can eat. I'd choke.

"Isn't that right, Dario?" Frankie repeats, mocking. There's a smattering of drunken laughter, but some men—Lucca, Carlo the accountant, Miles the bookkeeper—they fall silent.

"What's this about?" the guy with the thick accent asks. He wants in on the joke. I'm going to puke.

"Let me tell you, man. No, better yet, let me show you—"

Frankie says, reaching in his pocket. There is a simultaneous buzz and hush.

This isn't happening. I stare at the white fabric napkin in my lap, my chest tight.

"Posy," Dario says, low and even, so softly I doubt anyone else can hear him. "Excuse yourself and go to the ladies room."

He doesn't have to ask me twice. I mumble something and flee, forgetting the napkin. It flutters to the floor.

I head down the hall to the restrooms. It's in the back by the exit. I could run. For once, Ray is nowhere to be seen.

I hesitate at the ladies room door. Escape is less than ten feet away.

How far would I get? My purse is back at the table. I have no money, no phone. In this restaurant, I'm chic, but put me on the street, I look like a hooker, and my panties are still wet with cum.

Besides—

What's Dario doing?

He sent me off on my own. He has to know I'm a flight risk.

Is he beating Frankie like he did Ivano?

I don't think so—I think if Dario did that, he'd want me to watch. Honestly, there is no doubt in my mind that Dario will kill Frankie one day. Maybe not soon. He can't. Not without causing a war. But I know now that it will happen.

Everyone knows that Lucca is favored by the men, but Frankie is Renelli's favorite and chosen one. There is always speculation about what will happen when Renelli finally loses his edge. Who becomes capo? Lucca or Frankie?

Neither man will play second to the other. Dario is the goose that lays the golden eggs, but even he can't get away with killing the heir apparent while Renelli lives.

Chapter 9

So what is Dario doing in there?

And why doesn't he want me to see?

I sit on the toilet, but I don't have to pee. My panties are a sloppy mess. There's a sink in the large stall. I could rinse them out. Or just toss them. Dario would be pissed, but I don't think he'd be surprised.

He won't expect me to leave it be. I kind of want to see what happens when he realizes I did what he asks.

I go to the mirror, wash my hands, and try to fix myself. It still looks like I was rolling around in bed. I'm running wet fingers through my hair when the door swings open.

Jen Amato strolls in swinging a small crystal purse from her thin wrist.

"Hi, porn star," she says, sidling up to the sink beside me. "Is your asshole still gaping?" She purses her lips at me in the mirror.

"Fuck off."

There was a time—a long, long time ago—that Jen Amato and I had sleepovers at her Nonna's house. We'd watch cartoons and make marshmallow crispy treats. That was before Uncle Marco and the skimming. Before a lot of things.

I want to ask her what's going on out there, but I've got some pride left. Precious little, but some.

"What's it like knowing that all the men in a room have jerked it while watching you cry?"

I can't help it. I gasp from the blow, and the sound echoes off the tile.

Jen rounds her eyes. "I mean, *I* would be absolutely humiliated. I could never show my face again. But you always would sink a little lower than everyone else, wouldn't you? It's that Santoro blood."

I don't have to stand here and listen to this. I stride for the door, but she steps in front of me and blocks it.

"Bad enough that you threw yourself at my boyfriend—" she says.

"—You and Frankie were split."

"We were on a *break*. But that didn't bother you. Nothing does, does it? You'll do anything."

"Get out of my way."

Jen widens her eyes even more and flashes a carnivorous smile. "Do you get off on it? Being with a man who killed his own stepmother? You sick, sick bitch."

What? My brain flips through old memories. My family was cut off from the social scene after Uncle Marco, but we still went to Saint Celestine's with everyone else, and my mom still visited her friends in their kitchens. There just were no more lunches or spa days.

I vaguely remember when Rosario Volpe passed. She wasn't killed. It was cancer.

"You're talking out your ass." If Jen doesn't move, I'm gonna shove her.

"Oh my god. You didn't know?" Her voices oozes delight. "You didn't know that your twisted boyfriend did his own stepmother? No one told you?" She turns down her lower lip. "Maybe if you weren't such a dumb slut someone would have cared enough to warn you."

"Move, or I'm going to move you."

"How do you sleep next to him, knowing he could murder you in your sleep?"

I'm speechless. Reeling. What she says—it has the ring of truth. It explains why the others don't chase Dario like they do Lucca, Frankie, and Tomas. And I've had a front row seat to what Dario is capable of doing.

I don't fool myself. I was born into a circle of violent

men. In the room I just came from, no one has clean hands. But this—it's unspeakable.

Hold up. No. He *couldn't* have done it. I always forget but Lucca Corso is Dario's stepbrother. Lucca lived with his dad—they weren't a family or anything. Regardless, Lucca wouldn't sit across the table from the man who killed his mother. There's no way.

Jen's full of shit, spreading old rumors like a ghost story around a campfire, trying to get in my head. And succeeding.

I need to be done with this bitch.

"I sleep like a baby," I answer her question. "How do you sleep knowing your boyfriend liked watching me so much he had to share it with all his friends?"

She snorts. "He was doing everyone a favor, letting them know what a dirty skank you are."

Her lips are moving, but my brain is off. The whole video scandal is rearranging itself in my mind. We're not in high school anymore. There are millions of dollars at stake in the other room. Jen Amato doesn't follow me to the bathroom to play mean girl for shits and giggles.

Something's going on here.

The pieces are sliding together, forming a shape. This wasn't another tragic episode of Santoro misfortune.

I don't think leaking that video was about me at all.

No one in the organization actually cares about Posy Santoro. Except Dario Volpe. He's the power behind the throne. He doesn't interest himself in the gossip and machinations that my dad would drone on and on about. All he wants to do is be left alone to make money. But that doesn't mean everyone else is equally disinterested in him.

Whoever has Dario controls the money. Money is power. And Dominic Renelli is getting old.

I can almost see it. The outline is there, but I can't quite make it out.

Whatever the game is and whoever is playing, they think I'm a key piece.

It's not out of casual maliciousness or jealousy that Jen Amato is trying to mind fuck me in the ladies room. It's strategy. I bet Frankie knows she's here. I bet he sent her. Does Dario know?

Of course he does. He has more information than I do, and he knows this particular game better than I ever will.

Is he using me as some kind of sacrificial pawn? Set me up as if I'm important to him to distract his adversaries?

My head throbs. I'm hungry, and I can't bring myself to eat surrounded by sharks. And this bathroom smells like bleach. I'm done with this.

"Move."

Jen opens her mouth, no doubt to drop another bomb, but I'm at the end of my patience. I slam an elbow into her side and shove her as hard as I can into the sink. Her heels are even higher than mine. She staggers and trips like a drunk baby deer. I duck past her and head out.

The emergency door beckons, but nothing has changed. I'm still broke, and Dario's no more of a monster than he was when I walked into the bathroom.

I have no choice but to head back to the piranha tank. Before I step through the doorway, I stiffen my spine and plaster a bland look on my face. Frankie is going to expect me to walk in looking shaken, and I really want to disappoint him. I put an extra sway in my hips as I rejoin Dario. He's furiously tapping on his phone, and he doesn't even look up when I sit.

Everyone is drunk and having a good time. There's no awkwardness. No broken chairs. I guess part of me thought

Dario sent me to the bathroom so he could have it out with them—defend my honor—but from the sly and smirking glances I'm getting, that didn't happen.

Why did Dario send me to the bathroom?

Maybe he was disgusted. Maybe he thought if I left for a while, everyone would move on, but the video is too juicy. People aren't even bothering to lower their voices anymore. Jen's sister Rina is cackling so loud over a joke I can hear her halfway down the table.

I hate this. I hate them.

"I want to leave," I mutter into my lap. Dario either ignores me, or he's so absorbed by his phone he doesn't realize I spoke.

"So afterwards, we get to see a live version of the entertainment?" the man with the accent calls out. Oh god. While I was gone, someone showed him the video.

I'm going to puke. I shift to stand, but Dario grips my knee and squeezes. "No. Wait."

For what? For me to disappear into the ground in a puddle of humiliation. Is Dario getting off on this? Is this my punishment for embarrassing him?

I shove at his hand, but he's too strong. I can't budge him.

And then there's a ding. And another ding. Then a few more phone alerts like a tornado warning or a flood watch. Carlo and Miles check their phones. So do Lucca and Tomas. Miles rises from the table, almost tipping his chair over, and stalks from the room. Carlo's face blanches and he follows.

What's going on?

Miles and Carlo are money guys. If they're freaking, it's something to do with the markets. Why isn't Dario even looking at his phone? He's set it face down on the table beside his plate.

He tops off my wine glass.

"Drink," he tells me. "You look pale."

There's a panicked muttering among the men at the table. They're showing each other their phones. Tony has gotten up to whisper in Renelli's ear. The Russian guests are obviously confused. So am I.

Only Lucca Corso is relaxed in his chair. He's watching Dario, a sardonic smile playing at his lips.

"You have something to say, brother?" Lucca asks.

I can pick some words out of the whispers now. Five million. Loss.

Hands are moving to hover at waistbands and tucked under jackets. My stomach clenches. Shit. What's going down? An air of expectancy fills the room, and conversation peters away until there's silence.

Everyone's looking at me. No. They're looking at Dario.

"You have our attention now," Lucca says.

Dario finishes chewing his last bite of steak, swallows, and takes a sip of wine. The room feels as if it could erupt in gunfire with a word. We're hanging on some kind of precipice, and Dario's fastidiously placing his knife just so across the top of his dinner plate.

"If you have that video on your phone, delete it. If you feel the urge to bring it up, don't." His voice is unaffected, matter-of-fact. He glances over at me. His hand is still heavy on my thigh. "If anyone mentions that shit in your hearing, Posy, you tell me."

What's happening?

A raspy throat clears at the top of the table. As one, everyone's gaze turns to Dominic Renelli. His craggy face is inscrutable. Everything seems to balance on the head of a pin.

"You heard the man," Renelli says. "Get rid of it."

Hands dig into pockets and purses. Fingers fly. My stomach lurches. That video was on literally everyone's phone.

Renelli wheezes a strained laugh. "It was a bad joke." Renelli stares down the table at Dario, daring him to disagree. "A stupid prank. Maybe now my nephew sees it's unwise to joke with a man who has no sense of humor."

Dario waits for a long moment before he drops the slightest nod. "I joke, too."

It's an obvious lie. No one laughs.

Dario flips his phone and taps it a few times. An oblivious waiter rolls in the cart with dessert. A minute later, dings fill the room again. Hushed voices raise, marveling. Laughter booms.

Tony Graziano claps Dario's back. "You crazy motherfucker. Ten million. Holy shit. Champagne! We need champagne!"

There's an explosion of conversation. Dario finally takes his hand off my leg to select a cannoli. He slides it in front of me. Chocolate-dipped. My favorite.

I sneak a peek at his face. It's impassive. Almost bored.

"What did you do?"

"Sold all our shares in Micron Tech at a loss."

The five million. He lost five million dollars while I was in the bathroom. On purpose.

"And then?"

"I sold their competitor short."

The ten million. He made ten million in seconds.

"Isn't that illegal?"

His lip quirks up in the barest hint of a smile. "We're criminals, Posy."

"Why did you send me to the bathroom?"

"You were upset. It distracted me. I needed to focus." He nudges my plate. "Eat. You haven't had anything."

I do, although I can't taste a bite. The pieces are all jumbled in my head again. It doesn't make sense.

What Dario did? In essence, he stole from the organization. Right in front of them. Renelli doesn't tolerate thieves or rats. I know that better than most.

But the rules are different for Dario, the man who can make ten million with the snap of his fingers.

If it were any other man, I'd say he did it out of damaged pride. When he kicked me out, I figured that was why. His male ego couldn't handle another man touching his property and everyone else knowing. It wasn't because he loved me. I know now that he's not capable of love.

But I distract him.

It shouldn't mean anything. And I'm sure it's because of my daddy issues or whatever, but I like that more than I should. I like it a lot.

I always thought falling for the wrong man would be my downfall—like it was for my mom.

Maybe it's worse if the wrong man falls for you.

∽

The rest of the dinner is uneventful. The champagne flows. I have two glasses, and since my stomach is mostly empty, it goes straight to my head. I lean on Dario when it's time to go.

I expect him to go back to usual, obsessed with his phone, but he keeps it tucked away. Instead, during the ride home, he alternates between staring out the window and staring at me. It makes me squirm. My panties are still damp with his cum.

He's going to want sex when we get home. His cock is already tenting his slacks.

I don't know what to do. Or how to feel.

I shouldn't want it. He's hurt me. A lot. And there's no pretending this is normal. Or okay. It's more fucked up than my relationship with Frankie. After Frankie popped me one, he bought me flowers and said he was sorry. Dario shoved me in a trunk, and I'm fairly sure he still sees nothing wrong with that.

I should want better for myself. I should want what I thought I had with Dario, a healthy relationship where I'm treated like a princess and my man works in an office all day while I shop and garden and cook him dinner.

I do want that. But I also want this.

No one has ever wanted me before. My dad was disappointed I wasn't a boy. I was useless to him.

Every boyfriend I ever had has gone on about how pretty I am, but that didn't stop them from fucking other women or treating me like shit. And I took it. Because at least I was wanted for something. Because I knew what it was like to lose all your friends and get pushed to the outside, and if I was with a man, I was in. Home free. At least for however long it lasted.

It's a sad fucking history.

But with Dario—now—it's different.

He wants more than my body. I don't know why. Boredom. A quirk of his genius. I bet even he couldn't say. But I have what he wants.

That's power. And maybe it makes me a bad person, but it's heady, heady stuff.

His eyes are on me now. It's dark in the car. His face is cast in shadows, but there's a glint. Sal's still vigilant, but Ray's dragging. He yawns like a walrus as he fiddles with the radio, probably searching for the baseball game.

I lean over and whisper in Dario's ear. "You want to fuck me, don't you?"

"Yes." He doesn't hesitate.

The excitement from earlier springs back to life inside me as if it's on tap. No foreplay needed. This is so different.

I rest my head on Dario's shoulder. "I don't know if I should let you," I murmur.

It's a silly thing to say. He can obviously take what he wants. It's not a matter of me *letting* him do anything.

"What do you need?" he asks. I glance up. He's serious.

"A ring," I joke. "And a house with a white picket fence. And a dog. And lots and lots of therapy. For you." I think a second. "And me, too."

"I bought you a ring."

I sit back up. I didn't expect him to admit it. "You did?"

"I was going to propose."

"You wanted to get married?" Obviously, but it's just so hard to believe. Before, I was happy to delude myself that we were in love. Marriage was the next chapter in my own personal fairy tale. I know better now. This isn't Cinderella. It's Little Red Riding Hood, the messed-up version where she gets eaten.

"I didn't return it. I'll give it to you when we get home."

"Like a proposal?"

"Yes."

"I can't marry you."

"There's nothing stopping you." He slides me a glance. His muscles have tensed.

"Only common sense and self-preservation."

"You would have said yes before. Nothing's changed."

"*Everything* has changed."

"I'm the same man. You just know me better now. The facts are the same. I have money. We're compatible."

"What does money have to do with it?"

"It's why you're with me, isn't it?" His voice is matter-of-fact. Completely unoffended.

I'd slap him if I weren't so gob smacked by the turn of the entire conversation. "No. I wasn't with you for your money. I told you when I moved in that I wanted to keep my job."

"Maybe money was the wrong word. I should say influence. Security. You like not being the reject. You like the respect you get from being with me. Having a place you belong. Being taken care of."

Chills shoot down my spine. How can someone incapable of human feeling see other people so clearly?

"You think you know me so well."

"I know you perfectly well."

"You don't seem to like me very much." I don't like the hurt audible in my voice.

"What do you mean?"

"According to you, I'm needy. I'm a clinger," I snipe. It might be true enough, but he's an asshole for saying it, and in the grand scheme of things, my shortcomings are nothing to his unrepentant psychopathy.

"I like that you need me. It drove me crazy when you didn't anymore."

My breath catches. How can he be so honest? As if it doesn't cost him anything?

"How could you think I cheated on you if you knew I needed you so much?" The question kind of slips out. In the dark, whispering, slightly buzzed, I can be honest, too.

"I should have known it was bullshit right away. The doctoring was piss poor. It took Miles a split second to see the timestamp was photoshopped."

Dario sounds like he's still baffled by the fact that he could be duped at all. That must have been a blow to that rock solid ego.

"Maybe you wanted to believe it," I say without thinking. "It gave you an excuse to bail."

"I didn't want to bail."

I shrug. Men get bored, and they ditch you, cheat, or push you away. That's how it goes. If you're lucky, you see it coming, and you go first. If you're not, a guy dumps you and your suitcase on a sidewalk downtown.

"I chased you down," he points out.

"Hurt pride," I suggest.

He laughs softly. "Do you really think anyone can hurt my pride, Posy?"

I picture him at the table, calmly chewing his steak as people laugh at him for being with the accidental porn star. No, I guess not.

"What would you have done if Renelli got pissed at that stunt?"

Dario barks a laugh. "Oh, he's definitely pissed."

"You're not worried?"

"I'm as concerned as I ought to be."

"What does that mean?"

Ray is pulling up in front of the house, engaging the emergency brake with a zip. Sal gets out with alacrity, scanning the yard, hand resting on his piece.

Dario reaches over, takes my chin gently, and then lightly strokes his fingers down my jawline.

"Renelli has already threatened what matters most to me. It's just a matter of time now."

"Until what?" I ask, breathless, belly clenching from the completely novel tenderness.

"Until it's him or me."

"What is he threatening?" Renelli would be a fool to take him from his work. Tonight proved that if he didn't already know.

"You." His lips curve and his brow creases in a mystified smile. Then he shrugs and disembarks from the car, pulling me behind him as Sal falls in at our backs. A frisson of fear shoots down my spine as Dario draws me inside.

∽

We play speed chess for an hour or so, and then a gratuitously complicated game about public utilities with so many little wooden pieces that I spend the second half of the game building small towers and knocking them over. I still win. Dario was experimenting with strategy, having a grand old time, and I just wanted to be done.

We don't talk much. He's in his element, and my brain's replaying the conversation from the car. If I'm still in Renelli's crosshairs, getting gone has developed a new urgency. I had been thinking I wasn't a loose thread anymore now that I'm back, but that's not what it sounds like.

I need money. Now. I don't have the luxury of time.

I could ask for my jewelry back, but that would be obvious as hell. I could wait, work it more naturally into a conversation. I'll have to do that. Unless—

"Were you serious about proposing?"

Dario is methodically replacing the pieces of our last board game. He loves putting everything back in its place. I swear it's almost sexual for him.

His hand stills for a second.

"Yes."

He continues what he's doing.

"Okay. You can put a ring on it."

His gaze flies to mine. "Just like that?"

"Just like that."

"Why?"

"I figure I'll live longer if I'm wearing your ring." It's the stone-cold truth.

He nods. It doesn't make me feel any better that he's acknowledging that I'm right. He eases the lid on the game, and a change comes over his face. The corners of his lips turn ever-so-slightly up, and his eyes flash like they do when he wins a particularly hard-fought game.

"Take your clothes off and get in bed," he growls.

The thought makes me shudder. "I want to take a shower. I'm dirty. From earlier."

A full-blown grin breaks across his face. "Show me."

My cheeks heat. "No. I'm filthy."

"Yes," he flings back. "Do it now, Posy."

I roll my eyes. It's undignified, but if that ring is still on the table, I'm going to humor him. I stand, my bare feet sinking into the carpet. Except for kicking off my shoes, I haven't changed from dinner. I hike the dress to my waist and slide the panties off. They're utterly ruined.

There are traces of his dried cum on my belly and the triangle of blonde curls I leave when I wax.

He hums his appreciation. He's still sitting, one leg extended, utterly relaxed, the king of the world.

"Come here," he beckons, grabbing my wrists when I come close enough, drawing me to stand between his legs, shoving my dress even higher until it's above my breasts. He smooths his rough hands over my hips, my back, my thighs, exhaling, his hooded eyelids drifting lower until there's only the narrowest slit of chocolate brown.

He strokes down my obliques, my muscles twitching under his light touch. A swirl springs to life low in my belly.

He never takes his time like this. I keep waiting for him to get bored, position me how he wants me, speed things up so I don't have to make the choice to stand still, and I can just go along with what he's doing. But instead, he sits there, exploring every inch of me that he can reach, lost in his own head.

I don't think he's trying to turn me on. I think he's actually interested in feeling me, testing the suppleness of my ass by kneading and lifting, measuring the breadth of my hips by tracing the bones.

"What are you doing?" I ask, quiet, for some reason afraid to disturb him.

"I couldn't touch you when you weren't here."

"So it's a case of don't know what you've got 'til it's gone?" I stiffen. It's dumb to feel hurt at this point, but my heart is its own creature. "You never touched me like this before."

"I didn't want to."

There's a stupid twinge in my chest. I go to step back, but he seizes me around the waist and presses his scratchy cheek to my belly right below my breasts. His lips move on my skin, his breath hot.

"I thought you'd figure it out."

"Figure what out?"

"That I'm not normal. You'd get scared. I didn't want you scared."

"You don't care if I'm scared now. You *want me* scared. Isn't that why you beat Ivano in front of me?"

He nods, and his stubble scrapes me like sandpaper.

"You can't run again, Posy. I can't protect you if you're not with me. I can hardly protect you in my own house. You understand that Ivano was a threat to you?"

"He was?"

"He told Renelli I'd found you." Dario tightens his arms wound around my upper thighs. As if he cares. As if I'm precious to him.

I raise a trembling hand and lightly stroke Dario's thick black hair. It whispers through my fingers like silk.

"Is Renelli going to kill me?" I ask, voice low.

"I won't let him."

"How can you stop him?"

"Trust me."

"How can I possibly do that?"

I brace myself for irritation. Or maybe a wry shrug. Instead, he straightens, and before I can react, shoves his hand between my legs, grabbing my messy pussy in a punishing grip.

"This is mine." He squeezes almost to the point of pain, and I rise to my tiptoes, trying to escape the cruel fingers. "*You* are mine. No one will take you away from me. Not Renelli. Not you. Do you understand?"

He glares, shaking the hand that cups me, rough and demanding, and despite the biting grip, the vulnerability, the fear—I get wet.

"Yes," I whine, shame burning my cheeks.

"Go clean this up with a washcloth." He gives me one last shake. "I want to make you dirty again."

He releases me, and I step backwards so fast I nearly trip, but I can't tear my eyes from his face. He raises his hand to his mouth, darting out his tongue to lick the tip of a finger, his gaze turning pitch black, a raw sound like a deep purr vibrating from the back of his throat.

He doesn't move. He lounges, the lord of his castle, observing me.

As if I'm fascinating. As if he can't wait to see what I do next. My body floods with awareness, every nerve ending sensitized, ready, on fire.

I'm disconnecting from my thinking brain, completely willing, letting myself fall into the intensity of his expression, the ravenous hunger, the obsession.

He wants me, craves me, and I've never had that before so how could I know that *that's* my drug, my weakness, the switch that controls my mind.

I'm his, not by my choice, but because he wants me so damn bad.

He has all the power, but I win. I'm the player still standing. It's better than a rush, purer than a hit. It feels so damn *good*.

I want more. I want to *play*.

I free myself of the dress, finally, drop it on the floor, and I saunter off to the bathroom, swishing my hips, prickles dancing up and down my spine.

He's watching. I know he is.

I take my time in the bathroom. I get the tap water steaming and slide the washcloth under my arms, over my tits and belly, then between my legs, breaking out in goosebumps as the chill air caresses my damp skin. My nipples stiffen and my pussy throbs. The woman in the mirror is a mess, blonde hair tangled, face flushed.

It's not me. I can't tear my eyes away. She looks wild. Alive. Voracious.

What am I going to walk into when I go back out there?

The cold, inscrutable mask? Or the Dario who turns me into this?

Frissons of fear mix with the lust and nerves. Only one

way to find out. I wring out the washcloth, hang it up, and head back out to whatever is waiting for me.

Dario is not in the chair anymore. He's standing at the window, his back to the room. He's taken off his shirt and pants, leaving only his black boxer briefs. He has the body of a swimmer, broad shoulders and tapered torso. He really is an exquisitely beautiful man.

When he turns, I see the box from his sock drawer clutched in one hand. Oh, no way. He was serious?

Something loosens in my chest, competing with the conflicted feelings already running riot in my brain. Relief or incredulity—I'm not sure which.

"Get on the bed. Prop yourself up on the pillows. Legs spread." It's a demand, but it's not cold. Far from it. He's not hiding anything. His face blazes with a ferocity I've never seen before, a raw hunger so intense it triggers a primitive instinct inside me—run, fight, or submit.

Heat bursts through me in waves. I want this. Now.

I follow his orders. I crawl up the bed on my hands and knees, flashing him my swollen, wet pussy, and settle myself on the pile of fluffy pillows in crisp white linen.

"Like this?" I've got my legs straight.

"Knees bent."

I comply. I don't know what to do with my hands. I clasp them at my waist, but that feels wrong, so I rest them at my sides.

"Reach behind you. Hold on to the headboard."

Yes. I do what he says, reveling in the stretch as my back arches and thrusts my swollen breasts up. I'm an offering, a willing victim. He caught me. Now he gets to feast.

Dario stalks to me as if drawn by a magnet, stopping at the foot of the bed to devour me with his eyes. There's no other way to describe it. He licks his full lips, and it's not a practiced move. I doubt he's aware he did it. He's as intent on my body as he's ever been during a game or sparring in the gym or at his computer, clicking the buttons that win and lose millions in seconds.

More. Much more. I knew he was capable of uncommon intensity, but this is another level. Superhuman. Molten. Insane.

I did this to him. Me. Posy Santoro.

Another wave of heat crashes through me, curling my toes. The feather comforter is too warm underneath me. I want cool cotton against my clammy, bare skin. I want air. I want him. Now.

I drop my knees to the side, thrust my hips, dig my heels into the mattress.

"Dario," I whine.

He doesn't mock me, doesn't tease. He knows I'm hurting—I'm losing my mind—but he's going to make it feel better. He shoves his boxers down, his cock springing out, fully hard, jutting and thick and ruddy.

Dario kneels on the mattress, level with my feet, sitting back on his heels. He's taking me in, not just my bared pussy, but my taut nipples, my clenched belly, my flushed face. His gaze lingers there.

"Dario, I want it," I beg, no embarrassment. I don't want to play it cool with him anymore. We've both left all that behind like a shell. No more roles. No more pretend.

If he's what he is, I can be whatever I am, too.

"Gimme your left hand first," he says.

I thrust it forward. He flips open the box revealing a diamond big enough to distract me from the simmering under my skin. My breath catches. I lean forward, close my thighs, tuck my knees to my chest. He holds it up so the dozens of facets catch the light.

I've spent hours on wedding sites on the internet, wasting time and daydreaming like a girl doodling her crush's last name in a notebook. I know the four "Cs" of cut, clarity, color, and carat, and this ring is ridiculous.

In the back of my mind, my last brain cell points out it won't be easy to hock. The rest of me is entranced, floating from arousal to whatever magical mystery land I've stumbled into now. Handsome princes, diamonds, dreams made real.

Dario slips the ring on my finger. It actually has heft.

His eyes are caught like mine, marveling. Does this feel as surreal to him as it does to me? It should mean nothing at all, a gesture as empty as all the bouquets and jewelry Carolyn ordered, but somehow, the moment shines.

"Did you pick it yourself?"

He nods. "I told them I wanted a big one."

A giddy laugh flies from my lips. "They sure delivered."

"Do you like it?"

I hold up my hand, rotating my wrist until the lamplight catches the stone and it glitters. Do I like it? It shouldn't be a hard question. It's a beautiful ring. It's my ticket out of here.

I'm cooling off by the second now, my brain coming back online, anxiety and memory grinding back into motion like rusty gears. There's an aftertaste of heartbreak in my mouth. Before everything fell apart, this ring would have been everything I'd dreamed of since I was a girl. I would have screeched yes at the top of my lungs. Thrown my arms around him. Overdosed on my delusion.

His eyes are narrowing. He's waiting for me to say something.

"You bought it in New York?" I ask, even though I know.

"Before Christmas."

"But you didn't give it to me."

"I was waiting."

"For what?"

"To be sure," he says.

"Guess you were happy you waited when you got that video." I force a laugh.

"No. That's when I knew I should have done it sooner. When you moved in. You wouldn't have fucked around if you had a ring. That's what you wanted."

"I didn't fuck around."

"I know that now."

"But you thought I could."

"Of course you could. You want what I can't give you."

Love. Neither of us say it. It's obvious, isn't it? My history with men. My willful blindness with him.

"I wouldn't have cheated on you." I'm not that kind of girl. I'm the one who clings to the wreck as it sinks, not the one who jumps ship. Even with Frankie, I held on way past the point a normal woman would have lost the stars in her eyes.

He waves a hand. "I didn't mean I was waiting to be sure about you. I meant sure that you'd say yes."

"You know I would have."

"The odds were good, but it wasn't a sure thing."

My brow crinkles, and I buy time by examining the glittering ring. This is all so intense. He's so close. We're so naked. And there's no pretense between us. No polite fictions. The slut and the psychopath. The predator and his prey.

"Bullshit," I finally sigh. "You read me like a book."

"Sometimes."

I raise my gaze to meet his. "Now?"

His lip quirks. "Yeah. You're thinking about how you're going to hock that ring and run."

On instinct, I tuck my hand to my side, curling my fingers into a loose fist. His smile becomes bemused.

"It's yours to keep, Posy, but that's the wrong choice. If you're not here, I can't protect you." There's a glint in his eye that makes me think maybe he'd like that. If I ran, he could catch me again.

"If I'm here, I'm in danger." On so many fronts. Renelli. Dario. My own crazy heart and utter inability to learn from my mistakes.

"I won't let anything hurt you."

"*You'll* hurt me."

He lifts a sculpted shoulder ever so slightly. "You'll survive."

"What happens when you get tired of me? Do you throw me to Renelli, let him take out the trash?"

It's a crazy question, a hundred percent hypothetical. I'm not going to be here to find out. But I want the words. *Never. I want you. Everything will be okay.*

And what's wrong with me that I crave consolation and reassurance like an addict, like a love-starved, orphaned child? And I'm asking for it from Dario Volpe? It's like asking for mouth-to-mouth resuscitation from a fish.

Still, I listen for his answer, rapt, my thin arms wrapped around my bare knees, shivering.

He runs his thumb over the ring. "I've been playing chess since I was four years old. I'm not tired of it yet."

"So I'm a game to you?" It's not an accusation; it's a clarification.

"No, not a game. You're the one."

"Which one?"

"The only one in the world." He slips his fingers down my shin and brushes lightly across the top of my foot, the merest dusting of a touch, as if I'm dangerously delicate, liable to crumble with any pressure at all. "Everyone else is a piece. A pawn, a knight, a king. Not you."

I snort softly. "Let me guess. I'm the queen?"

"Nope. You're the one on the other side of the board." And then his eyes take on a wicked glint. "Spread these again." He urges my knees apart. "Hands back on the headboard."

"I didn't say yes," I point out, but I do what he says.

"I didn't ask you anything."

His gaze dips to my pussy, and instantly, I'm wet again, thrumming with want, as if time sped up, and I'm spinning, disoriented, rocked by a wave of want.

He shifts forward, braces over me, and watches as his fingers delve between my folds, find my clit, and circle slowly, careful not to touch the throbbing bud. My stiff nipples brush his hard chest, and it feels so good, so I arch and do it again, raking my tits through his smattering of chest hair as I try to drop my knees lower, expose more of myself to his infuriatingly patient, methodical petting.

He's doing exactly what I did in the car. Same tempo. Same everything. And he's scrutinizing my face for my reaction. I'm panting, mouth open, laid out for him, losing myself like I never have before.

"Does this feel good?" He circles closer, rougher. Perfect.

"Yes," I gasp.

His hands leave me to drag me flat, my grasp pulled loose from the headboard.

No. I was getting there, and with only his touch.

Then he's up on his knees, and he's notching the head of his cock inside me and stroking in, filling me, hot and hard, and his finger is back, circling, faster and faster. I moan.

"Do you need more?" he asks.

"Yes!" My nails scrabble at his chest, but he doesn't come

closer, he looms over me, sober and intent, watching his own cock as he drives into me, banging the spot deep inside that makes my inner thighs go completely weak.

I love this. I don't want it to stop, but I'm hurtling towards release, my hands for once unoccupied, free to roam Dario's tensed muscles, grip his powerful thighs as they rise with each thrust.

"You like this?"

"Yes."

"You're going to come?"

"Yes!"

He flicks my clit and slams home, over and over. "Do it, Posy. Come on my cock. Do it now."

And I do. I spasm, my stomach crunching without volition, and hot delicious pleasure spills through me in a rushing torrent, disconnecting body from mind. I scream, my eyes screwed shut, held tight, an arm like a vise clutching me to a sweat-slick chest as Dario finishes inside me, pounding my pussy so hard my arms flop like a ragdoll.

I'm boneless, mind obliterated, squished under Dario's heavy upper body as he gulps down air.

Now he'll hop up. Check his phone. Maybe pat my haunch as he heads off for a shower. I keep my eyes closed so I can linger in this daze a little longer.

But he doesn't bolt. He rolls onto his back, not touching me, but close. I can feel his heat radiating along my side. He's still and quiet for a long moment. Another brittle piece of my heart cracks open.

"We're going to get married, Posy. You'll have my babies. You'll be happy." He pauses, pensive. "It's what you wanted. Right?"

I don't say anything.

He knows the answer's yes.

Just like he has to know the answer is "no" now.

It would be insane to marry a man who hunted you down. Threw you in a trunk. Made you watch him almost beat a man to death. A woman who could do that could have no self-respect, no survival instinct at all.

To fall in love with a man like that?

It would be signing your own death warrant, wouldn't it?

10

DARIO

Posy is still asleep. I told Sal to wait in the hallway outside our room and phone me when she stirs. It's nearly noon, and no call. She must be exhausted. I woke her up three times last night to make her come. The last time she fussed like a drowsy kitten, mewling at me to leave her be until she got into it and wrapped her slender fingers around my wrist and held me in place.

I monitor the markets, idly flipping my attention from screen to screen. Everything is behaving as expected.

Well, everything except me.

I don't care about other people's feelings. It's not a philosophy. It's a biological fact. It's generally expedient to pretend that I do, so I've learned how to fake it, but ultimately, unless it pertains to a project or work, I don't consider what's happening inside the other meat sacks in the room.

Maybe that's why I've become fascinated with Posy. She's an interesting aberration, the one person in the world whose feelings have life to me.

It's a convenient explanation, but it doesn't quite meet

the facts. I don't need her for anything. She's actually causing me a great deal of consternation. And I don't just wonder what's going on in that twisty little brain of hers, I want her to—

I grit my teeth until my jaw aches.

I want her to stay, and so she has to believe she's safe, and worse, she has to be happy.

My nails bite into my palm. I had her exactly where I wanted her, smiling, teasing, willing. I was the center of her world.

And then that damn video. Why didn't I ignore it? Even if she was fucking around, why did I care? If I didn't like it, I could've put Ray on her, found the guy, slit his throat. An easy solution and an effective deterrent.

But I lost my shit, and I needed her to hurt. I know her so well; I knew exactly what words to use. She's always thought of herself as a whore. All I had to do to break her was confirm her worst suspicions.

But she didn't break, and it turns out I didn't want her to, either. By the time I figured that out, I'd shown my hand and fucked everything up. And now, I have a new obsession. I can't make her smile anymore, but I can make her come. It's not hard. Simple mechanics: rate, pressure, friction. Once she showed me, I could do it without looking.

As long as I rub her clit the right way, I can do whatever I want, and she falls to pieces. I took her from behind, had her ride me, and the last time, I spooned her as she tried to wiggle away and conk out on me again. Each time, I felt the tell-tale spasm of her pussy gripping my cock, and she softened a little more, letting it go a few minutes longer before her face shuttered with resolve.

She thinks running is the smart move, and it makes sense that she would come to that conclusion. In a dog-eat-dog world, staying to fight is a losing strategy for a woman like her. She's prey. She was raised to be—the barely-tolerated daughter of a disgraced family who escaped that ignominy by becoming a party girl passed from bed to bed. Flight is generally the better bet for a woman in her position.

Things are different now, though. She's not defenseless anymore. She has me.

I don't know why she's the only one. Maybe it's a biochemical coincidence, the universe flashing a giant arrow over her sweet pussy to point out that we'd make superior offspring. No doubt that we would. She's as bright as I am in her own way.

An image of her round with my child flashes behind my eyes. She'd be fiercely protective, lavishing them with all the love and protection she's been deprived of over the years. Would that make her happy?

I shove back from my desk in frustration. Why does it matter? As long as I have her with me, why do I care how she feels?

It's bullshit—God or whatever flipping the script on me this late in life. Why her? Why is she the only person out of billions who matters?

If we had children, would I care about them?

I take care of what belongs to me—just look at my cars. But would this glitch in my brain for Posy extend to our babies? If it didn't, she'd know. She wouldn't like it.

I huff a sigh. I'm getting ahead of myself, and I'm distracted. It's not like when she was gone. I'm trading on autopilot, doing pretty well considering the piss poor jobs report that released yesterday. The Fed is going to act, and I'm well-positioned. I can see how it'll unfold, but it doesn't give me the usual satisfaction.

Chapter 10

I'm bored with the market.

Is Posy going to sleep all fucking day?

I'm grabbing for my phone when there's a sheepish knock at the door. Ray. He's probably going to slump around the office, working up the courage to ask about his precious Posy. His attachment runs deep—some misplaced sense of responsibility due to the daughter he walked out on back in Sicily when he was young and ambitious. The little girl died in a car crash with her drunk mother before Ray could establish himself and send for them.

I don't begrudge Ray his infatuation. It's an opportune weakness. He'll protect her—even from me. Even though he doesn't move as quickly as he once did, that makes him valuable. I guess I can tolerate him sighing and rustling the damn newspaper for a bit.

"Enter."

As expected, Ray pushes open the door. But then he stands to the side. Lucca Corso strolls in, jacket unbuttoned, silk scarf dangling from his neck, the picture of a roaring twenties playboy from a novel they make you read in high school.

He flashes a smile and sinks into the chair across my desk. "Can I get an espresso, Ray?"

Ray grunts and shoots me a look. I jerk my chin, dismissing him. He shuffles off. Lucca had better not be holding his breath for the drink. The odds are not good that Ray remembers to pass on the request before he wanders off to find a quiet corner to listen to the game.

"To what do I owe this visit?" I shut my laptop and cross my leg at the knee. I can guess. I'm not getting away scot-free with the stunt at last night's dinner, not when I rubbed their faces in how easily I can crush the entire organization.

Lucca shrugs off his jacket and folds it carefully over his lap.

"Please. Take off your coat. Make yourself comfortable. Can I get you anything? An espresso?" I raise an eyebrow.

Lucca chuckles. "Touché."

"Did Renelli send you?" I cut to the chase.

Lucca nods. "That was a stupid move last night."

I lift a shoulder. "I achieved my objective."

"You looked like a man being led by his dick."

"Do I?" I lean back and smirk. "Do I look like a man being led by his dick?" It's a fascinating idea. Almost quaint. Am I supposed to be bothered by the idea?

"That's Renelli's read."

"And what's his remedy?"

"The woman has to go. Posy Santoro's time is up. That's a quote. You get rid of her now—today—or he will."

Tension bunches my muscles. "And he sent you to pass on the message?"

"I volunteered."

Now that actually surprises me. "I didn't know you enjoyed playing the heavy."

Even when he was brawling and cracking skulls at Saint Celestine's, he was never a bully. More like a charming villain. Frankie was the asshole. Tomas—we all figured his grandma would get her way, and he'd go into the church.

And what was I?

The alien. A sentient machine.

Lucca's casual smile doesn't waver. "Do you remember school?"

It's an abrupt change of topic and oddly coincidental. "Of course."

"I hardly remember you being around. You were always hanging out in Father Andrew's classroom."

Chapter 10

"He taught me how to trade."

"Father Andrew?"

"He was a stockbroker before he was ordained."

"No shit." Lucca's eyebrows raise. "That's where you picked it up."

I lift a shoulder. Father Andrew taught me the basics. I learned a little more at college, a whole lot on my own when I turned twenty-one and got access to the nest egg my mother put aside for me in a trust. Almost as if she'd known she wouldn't make it with my father long enough to see me grown.

"Do you remember the day behind the bleachers?" Lucca asks. So that's where this walk down memory lane is going.

He doesn't have to specify which day. It was in March. Tomas had found me in the library, told me that Lucca was waiting for me. He wanted a word.

Lucca was cupping a cigarette as chill gusts of wind blew across the football field, the kind of blustery weather that ends in a torrential downpour.

Just the day before, Lucca had been to our house for the first time to visit his mother, my stepmother. She'd started life Rosario Renelli, cosseted mafia princess. She'd been married off to Guiseppe Corso at sixteen, had Lucca at seventeen, and by eighteen, Corso had thrown her out, accusing her of whoring herself to my father. Renelli turned a blind eye.

I doubt she acted on it, but she was madly in love with my father. Who knows what she saw in him? He was a cruel man, and he treated everyone beneath him like shit. Rosario Renelli got lucky though.

When Corso put her out, my mother had just passed, and my father needed a mother for his infant son. Unsurprisingly, Rosario never took to me, but she was never unkind. Just distant.

If my father hadn't been in desperate straits—and if she hadn't been a Renelli—my father would never have married Guiseppe Corso's castoff.

He never let her forget her fall from grace. She could visit Lucca, but she couldn't bring him in the house. And she was to keep herself out of trouble and out of the way. She was a specter in our house, the creak in the upstairs hall, the muffled cough in a room with the door closed.

She didn't tell anyone when she found the lump in her breast. Or when the rash spread. By the time she passed out in the front hall, the cancer had spread to her lymph nodes and her bones.

Everyone thought she would go quickly, that she had nothing to live for after all, but she lingered in horrible pain that the medication barely touched.

Behind the bleachers that day in March, Lucca had asked if she showed any signs of letting go. I was the only one who spent time with her besides her nurses. In her delirium, she spilled secrets, all the stories from her generation that had been long buried. It was fascinating shit.

I told him she was much the same. He asked me to kill her. He didn't put it that way, of course. He spoke in euphemisms, his voice cracking, as weak as I'd ever seen him—then or since. He said if I did it, he'd owe me a favor.

When I got home from school, I gave her all that was left of her morphine, and when she fell into a peaceful sleep, I snapped her neck. It was my father's fault everyone found out what I did. He was indiscreet in his shock—more at what I'd done than that he'd lost his wife.

It's always boggled my mind how few people actually realize what I am—even when forced to face it head on.

Posy knows, and I don't think it turns her off. That must scare the hell out of her.

In front of me, Lucca clears his throat. He's been patient while I was lost in memories. I'll give him that.

"I remember that you owe me a favor," I say. "I never collected, did I? Is that what this is? You give me a heads up, and we're even?"

He flicks an invisible piece of lint from his immaculate, unwrinkled shirt. "No. I was wondering if you'd be interested in me owing you another favor."

Now this—this I did not expect. "There's nothing you have that I want."

It's not an insult, it's a statement of fact, and Lucca takes it as such. "But you have something you want to keep."

Posy. My fingers curl around the smooth metal arm rests. "It would be a catastrophic mistake if anyone were to try and take her from me."

I knew this day was coming. I'd hoped Renelli would see sense, but it seems like he's going to cling to his pride, and I'm going to have to burn this organization to the ground.

"I understand that," Lucca says. "Renelli does not."

"What is it you want me to do?"

"Nothing you aren't already planning. I just ask you to adjust to my timeline."

With that slight tip of his cards, what he must be planning unfolds in my brain, each step leading inextricably to the next, as clear as if he drew me a picture. We're not brothers, but we aren't unalike. He's a devious motherfucker.

"You can ensure that Posy is safe?"

"You have my word."

"If anyone harms a hair on her head, I will bring it all down. There will be nothing left."

He inclines his head. "Understood." He narrows his eyes.

"You know, Renelli is starting to believe you're too dangerous to let live. Too erratic. This thing with Posy is a test. If you've slipped the reins, he's decided to put you down, too. He's been looking for an excuse since you maimed his little rat Ivano."

"And you? Do you think I'm too erratic?"

He crosses his legs and flashes his blinding white veneers. "Not at all. You've become very predictable. Almost *domesticated*." He casts a glance at the door. "I don't think I'm getting my espresso."

"I don't think you are," I affirm, rising to my feet. He follows suit, slipping on his jacket.

"We understand each other?" he asks.

"We do."

"Give my regards to Posy."

I'm not going to do that. I open the door, catching sight of Sal hovering a few feet down the hall, tense as hell. That man really wants to shoot someone.

"What is it, Volpe?" he asks as he adjusts his scarf. "Why Posy Santoro?"

I shrug, and I take a shot in the dark. "I don't know. Why Tomas Sacco?"

Fire flares deep in his dead eyes. A direct hit. Interesting.

Too late, he schools his expression, flips me off, and saunters through the hall. The only thing missing is the 80s soundtrack and the popped collar.

~

I RETREAT TO MY DESK, wrap up some business, think about how the next part will unfold. Renelli won't move right away. He'll want me to fall in line of my own volition, prove to everyone that he's the puppet master, and despite the creaking knees, he still commands fear and respect. I have at least a day. Maybe a few.

If I send Posy away with Ray, she'd manage to ditch him in hours. She's safer here.

Is she really sleeping this late? I bet she's lying there, plotting. She can do that down here with me as easily as up there.

It feels good to abandon self-discipline and mount the stairs two at a time. I've got a picture in my head of her still under the covers, gasping and struggling into a seated position when I walk in, trying to hide her naughty fingers, slick with her own cream.

I throw open the bedroom door.

"Damn, Dario," she snipes. "Where's the fire?"

She's sitting cross legged at the table, shoveling scrambled eggs in her mouth and reading a crumpled newspaper. I see that Ray's been by.

"What are you doing?" It's obvious, but I can't think of what else to say. She's supposed to blush. Stammer breathlessly. React *somehow* to what I did to her last night. I figured her out, damn it. I played her like a violin.

She shrugs, gesturing at the table with her fork and blinks her bright blue eyes. "Plotting your downfall. Eating protein."

Cheeky little brat. I force my lips not to twitch as I take the seat across from her.

"You slept late. I exhausted you." No matter how she's acting, that's a fact. I smirk as I select the cribbage set from the low shelf under the picture window. Since we're both here, we may as well play a round.

She huffs. "I'm not in the mood."

"Then get back in bed. Take off—that—" What is she wearing? It's some kind of thin cotton dress. I can see the hard points of her dusky nipples. Is it a nightgown? A sundress? Hell if I know, but she's not wearing it out of this room.

"I'm only good for sex or cribbage, is that it?" She's playing it cool, teasing, but I know she believes this. I'm not going to indulge it.

"Most women are mediocre at both. You should be proud."

"Just because you finally give a shit about my needs in bed, it doesn't mean I like you. I think I hate you more."

My hands freeze on the game board. She's not being a smartass now. She's trying to conceal it, but there's real hurt in her voice. I didn't appreciate what I was going to be walking into this morning. She's—upset.

"Why?" I ask.

"Because if you care now, you could have cared then, but you didn't bother. I was a sure thing. No effort needed on your part."

"I made an effort. You were happy." Her face was softer then. Not open. Never open. But she smiled all the time. She skipped around the house. It was annoying as hell, her sneakers squeaking on the marble.

"*Carolyn* made an effort. She swept me off my feet. Best relationship I've ever had." Posy folds her arms, squishing those ripe tits to her chest. "She knew my taste better than I know myself." She hikes that adorable, wobbly chin. "You lived in your office and brought me out to play with when you got bored."

My temper flares. I should ignore it. She's here. I'm not letting her go. She's not actively fighting me. Why do I care if she comforts herself with a little petulance? If it soothes her hurt pride, why not let her nurse her hurt feelings?

"I had a net loss of three million the first month we were

together." The words are out of my mouth before I realize I'm saying them.

She stiffens. She thinks I'm blaming her. In fairness, with the men she's chosen, it's a reasonable assumption. Weak men blame women for their shortcomings. My gut sours. I don't like what her past has taught her.

"It was my fault," I explain. "I thought Miles was capable of taking the reins, and he wasn't. Obviously, I wasn't going to give up time with you—"

"The games weren't going to play themselves," she snarks.

I arch an eyebrow. She lifts a shoulder and tries to look acerbic. Her vulnerability slams me in the chest. She's as fragile as spun glass. She can run, and as weak as she is, she can take blow after blow. But her feelings—they're so tender, so easily bruised. She allows herself to be crushed, over and over again.

Is it masochism? Whatever, it's the irony of my life. The only person whose feelings I care about, and she's the equivalent of an emotional eggshell.

"I developed a system. Trained Miles. I figured out a method that accounted for his relative lack of expertise and ameliorated the risk."

She's staring at me. She doesn't understand what I'm saying.

"The month that I hardly saw you? I built a trading system. When I decide to take it to market, it'll make me a billionaire."

She rolls her damn eyes. "Congratulations?"

"It was an *effort*." I enunciate the word.

"You figured out a way to get what *you* wanted."

"Yes." I'm getting bored with the self-pity. It's destructive. She'll be happier when she allows herself to let it go. Maybe

I should give her a nudge. Or a shove. "Why did you suck my cock until you gagged?"

She freezes, her face blanching as if she was struck.

"You did it so many times. I didn't even have to ask. You fell on your knees and let me fuck your face until you cried. Why, Posy? Did you like almost puking on my cock?"

Her mouth is gasping on air.

"And why did you let me take your ass whenever I wanted? You hated it. You breathed through like fuckin' Lamaze class. But if I told you to get on all fours, you always did. Or remember on the sofa, facing the mirror? I told you to bounce up and down on my cock so I could watch, and you did, and you couldn't sit the next day."

Her face isn't frozen anymore. It's contorted, her lips drawn back in a horrified grimace. There's a sharp pain in my chest. Weird.

"Why did you let me use you like a whore, Posy?" I give her time to answer, but she can't seem to find words. "It's because *you* figured out a way to get what *you* wanted. You just want to be loved, and you'll do anything for it. Does it even matter to you who's giving you your fix?"

It's an interesting thought. I rub my chest. The pain is more like a burn. My breakfast must be disagreeing with me.

I think she gets my point, but just in case, I drive it home. "You played porn star for that loser boyfriend. You played whore for me. Does it matter who's giving it to you, Posy, as long as you can pretend that you're in love?"

She couldn't possibly have loved me. She didn't know me. I don't fault her for that. I'm careful to conceal what I really am, and with her, I was meticulous.

The burn is spreading to my guts. I need an antacid, and I don't think Posy's up for a round of cribbage. I stand and pat her stiff shoulder. She jerks from my touch. My stomach turns.

"Don't worry about it. I pretend, too. And if it makes you happy to believe that I love you, you can."

I walk out, heading for the kitchen. When I reach for the pink bottle in the corner cabinet, my hands have the slightest tremor. I don't know why.

11

POSY

I race to the bathroom, and kneel over the toilet, retching. By some miracle, the eggs stay down. The tears come, though. I'd held them back—I have no idea how, but sitting on the bamboo bath mat, slumped against the tub, they stream down my cheeks.

This is my own damn fault.

If you pet a vicious dog, and it bites you, you shouldn't be surprised.

And Dario was right about that, wasn't he? Time after time, I put myself in this position. I see the pit, and I walk into it. What's wrong with me?

A bleak darkness cracks open inside me. Threatening. Tantalizing. I want to throw myself into it; I want to soothe all the heartache with self-loathing. It'll make it all go away. Better than any drug. I never run out. I never have too much.

It's right there, but for some reason, for once in my life, I can't fling myself into it. I'm stuck.

I'm stuck on *why*.

Why did I let Giorgio Fusco take that video? Yeah, I was young and stupid, but I've let most of my boyfriends record us if they asked. Hell, I sent videos to Vincent Ricci when he was down at the shore for the summer.

Why did I let Dario do whatever he wanted? Why did I let any man who called me his girlfriend use me however he liked?

I didn't just take it. I volunteered. I was an enthusiastic partner in whatever they wanted. I never stopped to consider whether I wanted it. Of course I wanted it—if it made them happy.

I don't hate myself. It's not some kind of self-flagellation. Is Dario right? Am I so desperate for what seems like love that I'll do anything?

And how fucked am I because I have no idea how to *not* want to be loved.

So why am I beating myself up about it? Because Dario ripped me up for it? He's a dick. If it bothered his principles so much, he could have turned me down. This is bullshit.

I struggle to my feet. This is a trap. *This* is the pit I walk into. I let people make me feel like trash for doing exactly what they want me to do.

It's so obvious when you think about it. It's brilliant, really, and so messed up. A man dangles love. The girl leaps. She does what he wants. He castigates her for it. And then he dangles love again. How much higher will she leap? Because she has no other choice, right? If she wants what he's offering?

There are only two choices. Accept being unloved. Or try harder. I'm a scrapper. Of course I wasn't giving up.

Every relationship I've ever had flips through my mind, the pattern so glaringly obvious. The flowers and dinners at the beginning devolving into the sordid shit at the end as every jerk in Pyle tried to see how low I would go.

How low? So low Dario didn't even have to ask me to get

on my knees. So low I got down on the floor myself and begged him to choke me harder.

But like a dream come true, the flowers and dinners never stopped. And the jewelry.

The ring.

I'm not wearing it right now. It kept snagging on the sheet as I slept. It's on the nightstand. Dario didn't mention it. Maybe he's already having second thoughts. How could I possibly know? I don't know how lizards think.

What even happened just now? I was eating a late breakfast, riding the high from last night, and then he showed up. I didn't feel like playing cribbage, and all of a sudden, he decided it's time to burn the witch.

I haul myself up to the sink and splash some cold water on my face, trying to reconstruct the conversation. He was being smug, like he deserved a cookie for finally figuring out how my clit works. And then he was talking about business and how he figured out something so he could spend time with me, and I accused him of doing it because it was what *he* wanted, and—

He got angry. He lashed out at me. He hit me where he knew it would leave a mark.

I grip the smooth edges of the vanity, letting water drip down my cheeks into the sink.

Why did he get angry?

He understands other people's feelings. He can manipulate them if he wants. His issue isn't that he can't comprehend emotions, it's that they don't affect him. He proved that to me beyond a shadow of a doubt that day in his office, and he confirmed it with Ivano in the basement.

But he got pissed just now. He wanted to hurt me. Because I pricked his manly pride? Because I wasn't duly impressed by his prowess? That can't be it. He sat at that

Chapter 11

table at La Calomba and didn't bat an eyelash while everyone yukked it up over my sex tape.

So why come at me so hard?

He knows I won't play with him when I'm upset, and he plowed ahead against his own interest. The man who must have paid Carolyn a fortune to keep me placated with bouquets and diamonds, who strutted into this room like the cat who ate the cream, scored a goal on himself like he meant to do it.

It doesn't make sense.

And you know what? I want answers. And if he doesn't have any, if he's got such an issue with how I fucked him, I am more than happy for him to fuck himself from now on and leave me the hell out of it.

I pat my face dry with the fluffy towel, change into a pale pink T-shirt dress, and head off to his office. He'll be in there click-clacking on his damn computer, ice cold and unperturbed, enjoying his inability to feel empathy.

Asshole.

As I stalk through the hall, there's not a soul in sight. I could slip out the back door. Grab the keys to his Range Rover. I'm sure he's changed the gate code, but if I took a lap around the house, I could get up enough speed to batter through the metal. Maybe.

Or I could climb over the fence in the back. It's only ten feet high or so. I wouldn't break a leg on my way down. And I could totally scale it in the first place. If I brought a step ladder. And I had time.

I am not made for spy shit. Besides, I'm sure that in the security office, someone's monitoring the CCTV. I wouldn't get past the pool house.

Back to plan A. I storm into Dario's office. His chair is empty. Miles is in some kind of conference call with his feet on his desk, tossing a stress ball over his head. He startles and straightens. I wave at him and retreat.

Where did Dario go? Did he have a meeting? I didn't hear a car in the drive, but I wasn't listening, either. I wander back toward the stairs and pop my head into Ray's usual hidey-hole. He's reclining in his chair, dozing off. The cramped surveillance room is as new as the rest of the house, but it smells like stale coffee and old man.

"Hey." I rap on the door. Ray sniffs and rouses himself like a sleepy dog. Or a sea lion.

"Yeah, yeah," he mutters.

"Sorry to interrupt your very important nap."

"You don't sound sorry," Ray grumbles, scrubbing his face.

"I'm looking for Dario."

"He's not in his office?"

"Nope."

The wrinkles in Ray's brow deepen, and he squints at the bank of monitors. "There he is." He pokes the screen. That's gonna leave a smudge. Dario would lose his mind if he saw.

I sidle closer. In black and white, it's clear the house isn't as empty as it sounds. The housekeeper and her help are in the kitchen. Sal is walking the perimeter. A maid is clearing up my dishes in the master bedroom.

And Dario's in a guest room closet.

"He's getting into the safe room?"

Ray shrugs. "He doesn't ask my permission to do shit. He ask yours?"

"You're really grumpy when you get woken up from your nap, you know that?"

"I'm not the one making the boss crazy."

"He's not my boss," I sass, sweetening it with a smack on

his leathery cheek. I go to flounce off, but his voice stops me mid-stride.

"No. You're his." The words are a tired joke. A thing that people say. But the tone—there's a warning in it.

"Sure thing, Ray." I turn again to leave, fully expecting him to grunt and settle back into his swivel chair.

Instead, he stops me in my tracks. "Your dad was Al Santoro, right?"

I haven't heard his name in a while. It still fills my mouth with a bitter taste. "Yeah. You knew him?"

"Everyone in this town knows everyone else. You were his only kid?"

"Yeah. He wanted a boy. Of course."

"There's no 'of course.'" Ray spins slowly until he's facing me. I linger in the doorway. This is not our usual repartee. "Al got elbowed out after Marco turned rat, yeah?"

"Yeah." Is there a reason we're recounting old history?

Ray sniffs. "Those were the days. Any stronzo could skim from the take. It was the numbers, then. Protection. Women. Loans. Fuckin' simpler times."

That's not how I remember it. I remember that we were living in a big house on the bluffs, and my phone was constantly blowing up—I had friends, I went to parties, I was invited on holidays to the beach—and then one day, I was invisible. Worse than that. Toxic.

"Where you goin' with this, Ray?" I think his timing's a little off, too. Lotto was legal when I was growing up. My dad didn't run the numbers. He was in collections. When I was a kid, everyone's dad was in collections.

"Renelli was small time back then. Pyle is a mid-sized city. He was a big fish in a small pond. And then Dario Volpe comes back from school. The whiz kid. He sees an angle, and he works it. In an illegal cash business, the laundryman is king, right? And he gets how everything works now—the internet, the markets, cryptocurrency. Bitcoin. What is that shit?"

Ray sighs and shakes his head. Where's he going with this?

"Anyway, he changes everything. All of a sudden, New York, Las Vegas, the cartels, the Russians—they want what Renelli can do for them. Pyle is on the map. All because of this nerdy kid who ain't quite right in the head."

"What does this have to do with me, Ray?"

"Dario is the kingmaker. And you're his woman. Do you know what that makes you?"

I shake my head.

"Powerful."

I huff a bitter sigh. "Bullshit. I'm a prisoner."

"You want to run? Where you wanna go so bad, Posy?"

"You'll take me?"

He chuckles. "I work for the boss. He works for you. Get him to take you where you wanna go."

"You've got it all wrong, Ray."

"Wouldn't be the first time." He raises a hand to me in dismissal and turns his attention to a half-filled coffee mug, sniffling and wincing before he gulps it down.

I take my cue and head off. That was by far the longest conversation Ray and I have ever had. I never would've pegged him for having such a romantic worldview.

I'm not Dario Volpe's queen. And that's a dumb thing to be intrigued by anyway. So I ran to nowhere last time. When I get a second chance, I'm gonna make it count. The world's my oyster. Next time I get my chance, I'm going to Paris. Or Austin. Or Santa Fe.

I'll figure out a dream, and it'll become my passion, and I'll never think about Pyle, Pennsylvania or Dario Volpe ever again. The idea feels like work, but I'm sure that next time I fly free, I won't end up lost and lonely and clerking at a convenience store.

I don't even remember why exactly I'm looking for Dario now. To tell him off, but my heart's not in it anymore. I'm dragging. My body's weirdly flushed and sensitive from last night, and what sleep I did get was broken by dreams of running and falling.

I have half a mind to go back to bed, but when I pass the guest room, I wander in. It's an unremarkable room across from the master suite, tastefully decorated in cream and royal blue by—I imagine—Carolyn's preferred interior designer. The panic room is through the walk-in closet.

Ray showed it to me when I first moved in. It's not Hollywood quality. There's no furniture, only a bunch of guns hanging on the wall, a hook up to the CCTV system, a trunk with food and water, a satellite phone, batteries, those kinds of things. It creeps me out.

I clear my throat as I come through the closet. I don't want to surprise the man in the room full of guns. When I come to the open door, I linger. It's wild how the outside looks like a painted wall, and underneath, it's a bank vault.

Dario has his back to me. He's laid out three guns on the metal shelf that runs the length of the far wall, and he seems to be deeply considering them. He hears me. I'm not being stealthy. He doesn't acknowledge me, though. His back is stiff.

Is he still pissed? Is he picking out which gun to shoot me with?

It strikes me then—like the earthquake we had when I was a little girl, the only one in memory in this part of the state. I was in our kitchen, helping my mother with the dishes. All of a sudden, the floor shook, and my legs turned to jelly, but there was no rumbling, no crack of thunder, no warning. Not until my mom's painting of Jesus in the Garden of Gethsemane fell off the wall.

I'm not really scared of Dario Volpe anymore.

I know he's not going to shoot me.

All my delusions have been ripped away, and I know that what he feels for me isn't love, but it's real and huge and powerful, all the same.

I'm his exception. So what does that make *him* to *me*?

"What are you doing?" I ask.

His shoulders square, and he picks up a silver revolver as he turns to face me. I don't bother to try and read his expression. It's the default, the steely, implacable gaze, oozing arrogance.

"You need a gun." He crosses the few feet between us and presses the metal into my palm. "What do you think of the weight?"

"Is this loaded?"

"Of course not."

I snort. "Figures. You wouldn't make it that easy for me."

He gazes down at me, and it's only because I have a sense of him now that I know something's going on behind those cold eyes. He cracks his jaw and stalks back to where he's laid out his selection. He crouches and opens a safe tucked under the counter, retrieving a small rectangular box.

"These are hollow point. You know to aim for the torso, right? The torso presents the biggest target."

He thumbs open the round cylinder and loads the gun. Then he comes over and offers it to me, butt first. I'm not stupid. I take it.

I'm no expert, but I've shot off a few rounds over the years. Guys like going to the range. It turns them on. I know

Chapter 11

the basics. I keep my finger off the trigger and the muzzle pointed down. It's light.

Dario takes a few steps back and stands, staring at me, waiting. For what?

My breath shallows. My hands tremble.

"Why do I need a gun?"

"Personal protection."

I bark a laugh. "You're joking."

"You know I'm not."

"I could shoot you right now. I could blow your head off."

He lifts a shoulder ever so slightly. "Do you want to try the semi-automatic?"

"Is your head that thick?"

That earns me the ghost of a smile. "Sometimes, yes."

"Why were you so nasty earlier?" I hate that my voice wavers. "Do you get off on hurting me?"

"No." It's a simple statement of fact. "I lost control."

I don't know what to say. I was expecting—something else.

He pivots until he's in profile, picking up another gun and ejecting the magazine. If he were another man, I'd think he was avoiding meeting my eyes.

"You were a real dick." It's an understatement.

"I know."

"I don't throw your issues in your face."

"My issues aren't self-destructive." He draws back the slide and peers into the gun's chamber.

"I didn't see you worried about my self-destructive tendencies when your cock was in my mouth."

"I didn't fully understand then."

"Understand what?"

"That it bothers me when you're unhappy." His jaw

tightens, not like he's embarrassed by the admission, but more in reaction to the idea itself.

He doesn't like the thought of me being unhappy. My mind doesn't quite know what to do with this information. It explains some things and makes other things even more nonsensical.

"If you don't want to make me unhappy, why did you kidnap me?"

"It bothers me more when *I'm* unhappy."

It's the obvious answer, but it still feels like a slap. I want to wrap my arms around my middle, protect myself somehow, but I've got this damn gun.

"And Renelli would have found you eventually," he goes on. "You weren't safe. And you were miserable in that shitty little town."

"I'm clearly not safe here, either. Not if I need a gun."

"Here you have me." He finally turns to face me again, to skewer me with his cold brown eyes. "I can't love you, Posy, but I can destroy anyone who threatens you. I can give you anything you want. I can make you feel good."

He falls silent. It feels like he's waiting for an answer, but it wasn't a question.

"You're cruel to me."

He says nothing, but then again, what could he say?

"I should want more for myself."

The muscles in his throat tense.

"What's the difference between degrading myself for some crumbs of affections and whatever this is that you're offering me?"

Silence.

I stare at him. He could play the devil in a Hollywood blockbuster. He has the swarthy complexion, the hooded eyes, the chiseled bulk and electrifying presence that makes your pussy tingle although you know he's the definition of unattainable.

His clothes drape perfectly. Not a scuff on his shoes. The edges of his beard are razor sharp. He's unreal. This whole thing is unreal.

And then he closes the space between us, easing the pistol gently from my grasp. He bends and brushes a kiss across my forehead, and then slips the semi-automatic into my hand.

"Aim for the torso," he says, voice low and silky. "And if you shoot, don't stop until the magazine is empty."

I raise the gun like Giorgio Fusco taught me way back when, wrapping my left hand around my right, aligning the dots, and squeezing my left eye shut. I aim for his head. He's so close, it's a big enough target.

"Give me your wallet and the passcode for your debit card."

"No." He doesn't move. I relax my elbows to try and stop my hands from shaking. My throat is bone dry.

"I'll do it," I warn, adjusting my sweaty grip.

"You won't."

Shit, shit, shit. I don't think I can. Why can't I? Why am I so weak? My nose tickles and my eyes pool with unshed tears.

I take a step forward, stick the muzzle into his chest, right above his heart.

"Say you're sorry." My voice wavers.

"I'm sorry," he says. No hesitation. No reaction.

"What for?" I demand.

"Everything."

"Then give me money and let me go."

But I don't want to go. I don't want the power. I don't want to make the decision because I pick wrong, every single time, and I want Dario Volpe. I don't even want things to go back the way they were. I want him like this—unapologetic and cold and obsessed.

"No," he says, his voice a gritty whisper.

Our eyes are magnets. I step forward, inch by inch, until we've reversed positions, a slow-motion dance. I don't know what I'm doing, and then I'm doing it. I set the gun down next to the others, and I lean back against the ledge. I grab the sides of my cotton dress with my sweaty palms, and I watch him watch me draw it up.

I lick my lips. He exhales so very softly. Sparkles dance in irises gone as pitch black as his pupils. If you didn't know him, it'd read as emotion, but it's not. It's impulse, as primitive as hunger.

I show him my pink panties with the little white bow. They're damp in the middle.

"Yes," he exhales in a hiss.

He drops to his knees.

He's beautiful, strong, powerful, hard thighs straining his finely tailored gray slacks, his crisp dress shirt as white as fresh snow. Every line so elegant, every button, belt loop, and seam so exquisitely wrought there can be no doubt it's bespoke.

He's money, and he's danger, and he's at my feet.

Yearning and mistrust swirl in my belly, stoking my nerves, sensitizing every inch of my skin. He hooks his thumbs in the waistband and drags my panties to my ankles.

"Step out."

I do. He tosses them away, stroking rough palms up the back of my legs, lingering behind my knees, then molding and kneading my ass. Shivers fly in the wake of his touch. I heat for him. The swirling becomes a throbbing.

He wraps his finger around my ankle and tugs up. "Put

this on my shoulder," he urges, guiding my foot to rest in the crook of his neck.

I forget to breathe. He's never done this for me before. I thought he was like a lot of the guys in our circle who think oral's demeaning. He doesn't seem the least bit reluctant, though. He does seem out of his element.

He parts my folds, exposing my hot core to the chilly air, and he considers my pussy, his head cocked the slightest bit to the side.

Oh my god, I've seen this look—when he's learning a new game.

"Have you ever done this before?"

"No."

There's no hint of embarrassment, only impatience. Because I'm disturbing his focus? I smother a hysterical giggle. The fog of lust is clearing, my brain beginning to creak into gear again. I don't want second thoughts. I want to make a bad decision.

"Do you want directions?" It comes out snarkier than I intended.

"No," he says, completely unoffended, and begins to circle my clit. He's peering closely. He must see the little bundle of flesh peek from its hood. It's clinical, but still—it feels good. I close my eyes and try to sink back into sensation.

I jerk when his hot tongue replaces his finger, same tempo, same pressure. A tension inside me uncoils. He's going to make me feel good. He's figured out if his technique works one way, it'll work another. I settle in, propping myself on the counter to take some weight off my foot.

And then he inhales, and he moans. It's a hungry sound, as if he'd been starving, and in an instant, everything changes. He's not licking me in methodical, concentric circles anymore—he's *eating* me.

He burrows his nose inside my slit, then he captures a swollen fold in his hot mouth. He sucks and nips, spearing his tongue into my dripping center and then lapping my cream as if he needs to consume every drop.

His fingers grip my ass so hard it hurts, holding me steady so he can feast. He's wild, and he's breathing deep, moaning that gravelly, desperate moan each time he draws in my musky scent. I can smell myself, too, earthy, tangy, and the sounds—he's a messy eater, slurping, smacking.

I wail, my face burning, the leg I'm propped on wobbling, and he's bearing most of my weight effortlessly as he goes wild on my pussy like the spoiled kids in the movie when they first see the chocolate factory.

Now he's plunging his long, thick fingers inside me, seeming to delight in the squelching sound because he thrusts harder, makes it louder, wetter. I balance on the counter, lean back, and let him please himself.

The pleasure comes in waves. He'll happen onto a rhythm, and I surge toward the cliff, and then he'll get distracted, explore something new, and I'll go back five spaces, miss a turn. I buck my hips in frustration, but I also don't want it to ever end.

I like this game. I like playing with him. There's something wrong with me, but my mess fits perfectly against the jagged piece that's missing from him. I'm needy, he's heartless, and by some magical alchemy, this—this creature we become together—solves us both.

He flattens his tongue and swipes from my clit to my asshole and back again. A wave crashes and recedes.

"I want to cum," I sob, driving my fingers through his thick black hair, forcing him to stay in place, right where I want him. He takes the hint, sucking my clit into his demanding mouth, and I explode, dissolve, sway and tilt, and then he's laying me on the carpet, driving his cock into me, and I'm spasming again, every ounce of ecstasy wrung from my body until I'm limp and useless on the floor.

Dario comes with a short shout, slamming into me, grinding his pelvis into my hip bones as if he can get any closer, as if we aren't already glued together with sweat and saliva, cum and cream.

He pushes up on his elbows and brushes a damp lock of hair off my forehead. "I like how you taste," he says.

"Like milk and honey," I joke, still catching my breath, my brain fighting to come back online after being short-circuited again and again.

"Like raw pussy. You're swollen from last night."

I blush which is silly since we've done crazier things, and even if it was his first time eating out a woman, I'm not new to the whole business.

His eyes narrow. "What do you want after?"

"Huh?" I can't follow.

"After sex. What do you want? Do you want me to hold you?"

"Not on this carpet." It's scratchy, the fluorescent lights suck, and with all the guns hanging on the peg boards—it's a whole mood, but not really a postcoital one.

He grunts and hops to his feet. How can he move like that? My muscles are jelly.

He zips and buttons his pants, tucking the semiautomatic into his waistband at the back. I have to rock a few times to get myself into a sitting position. I tug my wrinkled T-shirt dress down as far as it'll go, and I grab my panties. I can't put these back on. They're filthy.

"Come on." Dario offers me a hand. I take it, and he hauls me to my feet.

He leads me through the guest room to our master suite, guiding me straight to the bed. The maid's been through, so it's perfectly made, the silver brocade decorative pillows arranged just so. Honestly, I'd rather lay on the safe room carpet than those pillows. They itch.

Dario urges me to lie down. He must want more. I'm tired and achy, my thigh muscles in particular are complaining, but I'm too bemused to turn him down. I guess my man has discovered he likes eating pussy?

My man? My brain is more burnt than I thought.

Dario sets the gun on the night table and lowers himself next to me. We're both on our sides, facing each other, a hand's length between us. My eyelids are drooping. He watches me, serious, intent. What is he waiting for me to do? Declare my undying love like I used to after a good dicking?

I yawn. I'm too slow to cover my mouth.

"What are we doing?" I mumble, laying my cheek on my extended arm. I can't muster the strength to keep my head up.

"Cuddling."

My snort is soft and sleepy. "You don't cuddle."

"I watch TV, Posy. I know women like to be held after sex."

"You're not touching me," I point out. He's not a snuggler. I accepted that early on in our relationship. I'd accepted it from men before. Some guys want to spoon; some want to shower and eat. I was cool with whatever.

Well, not really, but I didn't think I could insist on my preference.

Why not? The men I've been with had no compunction about insisting on theirs.

"Do you want that?" Dario presses. "Do you want me to hold you?"

Why is he pushing this now? My brain is mush. I roll onto my back and stare at the ceiling. "I want a nap."

He's quiet for a moment. I let my eyes drift close. He'll head off to his office any minute. If I've learned anything dating Dario Volpe it's that there's a market about to open somewhere in the world at any given time.

I almost drift off, and then I'm being lifted, manhandled up and onto his chest. I yelp, jerking awake. He wraps his arms around me, a firm hand cradling my head, the other pressed to the small of my back. His shirt buttons dig into my chest, but he smells—soapy and musky and good.

"What are you doing now?" My complaint is muffled by cotton and muscle.

"What the fuck does it seem like, Posy?" he says, grouchy as hell. "Cuddling." He slaps my ass. Hard. "Shut up and take it."

Despite the sting, I giggle, and eventually, when I realize he's dozing off, I let myself relax into him, nestling my nose in the crook of his neck, enjoying the scratch of his beard on my cheek.

This isn't love, but how can you tell the difference?

It feels like love. More than it ever has with any man before.

Is my stupid heart going to say "good enough?"

Has it already?

～

DARIO IS HOVERING. For the rest of the day, he makes me hang out in his office, and when it's time for his workout, he tries to drag me with him to the gym. I balk at the top of the stairs. The last time I was down there, he was cutting out Ivano's tongue. He assures me that Ray got the blood stains out of the mat, and then he gets pissy when that doesn't make a damn difference to me.

He makes me run the perimeter of the property with him about a dozen times, and then he wants me to provide an anchor for all these exercises with resistance bands. I've been told my ass is thick before, but never that it's the perfect counterbalance weight.

When we go to bed, he's insatiable. He makes me come over and over. Around three in the morning, I've had enough, and when he sidles up to me for another round, I try to shove him onto the floor. I only get his torso half off the bed, but he takes the hint.

The next day, it's more of the same. We eat breakfast in his office, and then I play on my phone, curled on the sofa while he works. It's all very calm and domestic, but there's something wrong.

His exterior is as ice-cold as ever, but there's a mania to him. He raps off orders to Miles in bursts, and then clacks away on his keyboard before falling into brooding silence. Then he begins the cycle over again. Every so often, he calls Ray or Sal to check in. What's he checking on?

It's impossible to focus on anything, so I scroll through social media. I'd be a nervous wreck if I wasn't totally worn out from mind-altering sex.

I'm so limp and muzzy from last night's marathon that when the knock comes, I don't even jerk, even though it's a staccato banging, clearly not Ray, clearly not good news.

My gaze flies to Dario. He stands and adjusts the sleeves of his suit jacket as if he's been expecting a visit. Maybe he has been. He doesn't tell me his business. I wish he did. I would have worn something else. I'm wearing pink booty shorts, a matching raglan belly shirt, and white canvas sneakers. I look like a sorority girl in a porn mag.

Dario's lips press together in a thin line as the door swings open and a half dozen of Renelli's men swarm into the room. One has Ray by the upper arm. Finally, my body reacts. My heart jumps, adrenaline surges through me as I scramble upright.

The men have guns. They're aiming them at Miles. At Dario. At me.

A whimper escapes my lips, and Dario's jaw tenses, but otherwise, he's unperturbed.

"Gentlemen," he says. A smile plays at his lips. Is this exciting him?

My pulse races. Why doesn't he reach for the gun under his desk? Why don't I have the gun he gave me? It's in the nightstand drawer because I didn't know what to do with it, and when I said we'd better put it back in the safe, Dario said, "What good is it going to do you there?"

I had a gun, and I left it somewhere else because why? Because I felt safe? Why the fuck did I feel safe?

What's happening here? Is this payback for what Dario did at the dinner? Is this about me?

Is he going to let them take me?

My brain sputters, and my hands ball into fists, fingernails cutting into the skin.

"Mr. Renelli wants to see you," Vittorio Amato intones, the casual threat so obviously well-practiced.

Vittorio was only a made man, not sottocapo, when he beat the hell out of my father for the crime of being related to the rat Marco Santoro. Until the day he died, my father would spit whenever he heard his name.

Dario inclines his head.

"And her," he adds when Dario has come around his

desk, the pause between requests intentional, for effect or to flush Dario out into the middle of the room, I don't know. My heart slams against my chest, and my blood pounds in my ears.

Renelli wants me. The loose end. He's going to put a bullet in my brain.

Dario's blank expression doesn't change.

"Come," he says to me.

He's going to hand me over. I have to run. There are too many men. Too many guns. There's no way out.

Dario steps over and seizes my clammy hand. "Come," he repeats, stern, unruffled.

He pulls me in his wake, and I have no choice but to follow him through the silent hall, out into the blinding sunshine, surrounded by men in suits and the crunch of their hard-soled shoes in the gravel.

There are three cars out front. Vittorio Amato gestures Dario into one while another man, Tommy Vanzetti, a cousin of an ex, hustles me off to another. I squeeze Dario's hand with all my strength, but he draws his away, and my palm is so sweaty, it slides free.

"Go with him," Dario says. "And Posy—" He waits until I meet his eyes. "Don't try to run."

Oh god. Oh god. Another man, Joey Zito, helps Tommy wrangle me into the back of a town car. I'm not resisting, but my body won't move willingly. They shove, and I move, and my brain spins.

Dario is handing me over to Renelli. I'm going to die.

But it doesn't make sense.

Why would Dario make that point at the dinner with the Russians if he was just going to give me up to Renelli? And why would he come along? Does he want to see me die?

If he wanted me gone, why wouldn't he do it himself?

Chapter 11

And all the guns—Dario is in trouble, too. Are they going to kill him? Why not do it in Dario's office then? Why the trouble of dragging us to a second location? Because they take you to a second location when they kill you. Everyone knows that.

My stomach sloshes from the fear and the jerky driving of the man behind the wheel. It's Nicky Biancolli, one of Lucca Corso's hang arounds. He's blasting the radio so loud my head pounds, and Joey sits across from me leering at my tits while Tommy plays on his phone.

They've stuck me in between two guys, and they jostle me every time Nicky takes a corner too quick and tight. Joey sits across from me and gawks as my tits bounce. I'm not wearing a bra. I was too sensitive this morning from the abrasions left by Dario's beard as he suckled me for hours, experimenting, as obsessed with mastering my body as he's ever been with any game.

My heart lurches. Is Dario okay in the car up ahead?

Is he betraying me?

Should I try to escape? I could lunge for the door at a stop light. I'm not buckled; Tommy's beefy ass is sitting on the belt. I'd never make it past the guys even if by some miracle the child lock isn't engaged. But I have to do something, right? I can't go willingly to my death. I'll wait for an opening.

Or I'll tell myself that so I don't lose my mind to the rising panic that's clutching my chest tighter and tighter.

"I saw you get fucked in the ass," Joey bellows over the music, leering, licking his thick lips.

He's exactly the type I used to go for. Good looking, gelled hair, immaculate sneakers, and the swagger that comes with being an unrepentant asshole. Compared to Dario, he looks like a little boy.

I don't dignify his shit with a response.

"Didn't look like you were into it." He smirks. What did I see in guys like this? Too much body spray, loud tracksuit, gawdy pinky ring—he looks like the dude pushing thirty who'd crash house parties back in high school.

I'm not listening to this guy.

My silence obviously pisses him off. His smile turns mean.

"If you say pretty please, I'll get Nicky up there to take a detour. You can give us a repeat performance. We'll make it feel good." He cups his dick and sort of mashes it around in his sweatpants. "Don't you want to go one last time before you meet your maker? A slut like you, you wanna go out with cum in all your holes, don't you?"

Sick bastard.

The other men keep their mouths shut and won't meet my eyes. A sudden weakness seeps down my limbs, like in a dream when you want to run but you can't move your body. They're going to kill me. That's the plan. I'm a warning or a loose end or a message, I don't know, but this ends with my body in the river.

My breath gets stuck in my lungs.

I don't want to die.

I should have never stopped running. I should have never looked back.

"What I don't get is why Volpe put a ring on it," Joey yammers on. "You that good? You didn't look that good in the video. Looked like fucking a corpse." He laughs. "Bet Volpe would be into that, though."

We drive for about ten more minutes, and he runs his filthy mouth the whole time. Are these the last things I'm going to hear? This terrible house music and Joey Zito's big mouth? I don't know which is worse.

My temples throb. I thought we were heading downtown, but at some point, we got on the beltway and took an exit I'd only ever driven past. We're in a rundown industrial area now. Low buildings with loading docks and lots surrounded by barbed wire. We pass more recent construction until the streets become pocked with potholes and the buildings get older—dilapidated, windowless brick boxes from back when Pyle was synonymous with steel.

There's no traffic back here. No parked cars.

Nicky the driver turns off, passing an abandoned guard shack. We follow the car carrying Dario to a parking lot behind a three-story warehouse, its few windows covered in plywood, graffiti covering the brick as far up as a person can reach.

I have to run.

As soon as they let me out.

It's my only play.

Dario's words echo in my ears. *Don't try to run.*

Why would I listen to him? Why would I trust him?

I twist my ring around my finger, scanning the area I can see from the window. Past the buildings is a rusted metal fence, collapsed flat in places. Several acres away, beyond fields of knee-high weeds, the Luckahannock winds, sluggish and shallow. In the far distance, an overpass arches high above the river on thick concrete pillars.

If I run, they'd catch me in seconds. There's nowhere to go. Nowhere to hide.

The emergency brake zips and the car doors click as they unlock. The men spill out. Now. This is my moment.

"You first," Joey says. He cops a feel as I exit ahead of him, digging his fingers into my pussy so hard it hurts.

I jerk away, lunge forward, but the other guys fall around

me instantly, herding me to an open metal door. I don't even have a second. No chance at all.

Fear crests through me again. Where's Dario? I can't see him.

I stumble, and Nicky grabs my elbow, forcing me forward through a narrow hall into a wide-open factory floor filled with men. The dim light filtering down from the high windows is yellow from the smoky discolored glass.

There's no equipment, only holes from the bolts and oil stains. A catwalk rings the room, and high above, something's dripping. I can hear water ping against metal. The space is cold, and despite the number of people, it's silent.

Everyone is standing in a loose circle, facing one man who rests a veined hand on an ivory cane. Dominic Renelli.

His consigliere and his sottocapo have taken position at his left and right, feet hip-width apart, hands clasped at their backs.

Dario stands in the middle, unbowed, his gaze never wavering from Renelli's. He could be standing in line at the movies for all he seems affected; he wears that same expression of patient boredom.

I recognize every man here from Saint Celestine's and L'Alba and the clubs. Some of the older guys I recognize from when I was little and my parents threw parties at Christmas and Mardi Gras and the Fourth of July. They tousled my hair and said I was a pretty little girl and gave me peppermints from their pockets.

Some of them were in class with me. Some of them are distant cousins.

I know all their names. Lucca Corso. Tomas Sacco. Tony Graziano. Vittorio Amato.

I've been with more than a few of them. Frankie Bianco. Danny Ricci. Hunter Vanzetti. Dario Volpe.

I gave pieces of myself to all of them. Tried to make them happy. Tried to make them love me.

And they're going to kill me, and I'm going to bleed out on this filthy concrete floor. And no one will care.

Will Dario?

Nicky never let my elbow go, and now with a glance from Renelli, he twists my arm behind my back. I cry out, and it echoes in the quiet. Dario doesn't even turn to look at me.

Renelli gestures for Nicky to bring me forward. He forces me to walk until I'm even with Dario.

Dario still ignores me. He's totally at ease, arms loose by his sides, back straight but not stiff.

The silence swells until it almost presses against my ear drums.

Finally, Renelli clears his throat. "So, Dario, my son—" He pauses, letting the endearment linger. "You have a choice to make it seems. No man here would deny what you've done for our family, but we have come to a crossroads."

He stops as if he expects Dario to respond. He doesn't.

Renelli's lips dart downward for a brief moment, the Italian equivalent of a shrug.

"We are a family, yes?" he goes on. "A band of brothers. Our loyalty is to each other. To this thing of ours, no?"

There's a general murmuring of assent.

"And this—" He waves a dismissive hand at me. "This *Santoro* slut. I mean, she's been passed around more than the collection plate at church, right?" There's sparse laughter, quickly dissipating in the emptiness of the huge space.

"You've lost your head, Dario. I never thought I'd see the day. I didn't think you were—" He seems to search for words. "*Susceptible*. But it ends now. I can no longer allow her disruptive influence in our business."

He's made his declaration, and he shifts back on his heels, expectant, dark eyes sunken in his wrinkled brow. Still, Dario says nothing.

Those eyes flash with rage. "So I give you a choice," he says, projecting his voice so it booms. "Do her like you did Rosario—make it quick, put her out of her misery. Or I let everyone have another turn with her for old times' sake, and if she lives through that, we bash her beautiful face against this floor until there's no chance anyone can identify her when they pull her out of the river."

I stifle a scream and sag; my shoulder socket burns as my weight falls against Nicky's unfaltering grip. Panic floods my system, and I fight, throwing my head back and kicking, bucking, but I'm not strong enough. They're laughing at me, caustic, hateful.

What did I do to deserve this? I gave them whatever they wanted, and I'm nothing to them—I'm entertainment.

I renew my struggles, even though it's useless, even though I'm trapped.

And then Dario reaches over and seizes my jaw, digging his fingers in, grinding skin into bone. He forces me to look at him.

"Stop," he says, and then his grasp loosens, but he doesn't let go.

I can hardly think. The terror is too loud.

He strokes my cheek, exquisitely gentle, almost tender. "D4. D5. C4," he recites very quietly, almost under his breath. Those are chess moves. Why is he telling me chess moves?

Some animal part of my brain gloms onto his words, repeats them on loop.

D4. D5. C4. D4. D5. C4. D4. D5. C4.

There's nothing but fear, and then a synapse fires. *D4. D5. C4.*

That's the Queen's Gambit.

Dario smiles. "Don't fight, Posy. Don't try to run."

What is he doing?

I go still. I can't escape. I can't even get free of one man, let alone twenty. I shake, and I try to remember my prayers, but it's been so long, and I'm so scared that I can't get past "hail Mary, full of grace, the Lord is with thee."

Why the Queen's Gambit? Is it a ploy to calm me down? What did he do to Rosario? Renelli must have meant his stepmother, the woman Jen Amato said he killed. Oh god. Is Dario going to kill me?

D4. D5. C4.

The Queen's Gambit. Sacrifice a pawn. Secure control of the center of the board. It's a common move. Predictable. Give up something worth little to gain an advantage. Is that what he's telling me? One last dig to remind me how expendable I am?

"Well, son?" Renelli prompts. "Did you see enough in that dirty video or would you like the live action version?"

Dario lets his cool fingers fall from my face, and every muscle in my body tenses.

I wait, and in the end, it isn't Dario who answers him.

"You use my mother's name," Lucca Corso speaks from our left, crossing himself, Tomas Sacco at his side as always. It's jarring, a man as pretty as Lucca, so impeccably dressed and affable, casually hanging out in this shithole, in this hellish moment that won't end.

Lucca flashes his perfect white teeth.

Renelli offers a wry smile back. "No offense intended, of course. My sister was a good woman; may she rest in peace."

"Was she?" Lucca arches an eyebrow. "My father called her a whore."

Renelli lifts his bony shoulders. "Water under the bridge."

Lucca steps forward, his dress shoes clicking on the concrete, Tomas on his heels. He comes to a stop, his gaze slowly swinging between Dario and me and the cluster of made men surrounding Renelli.

"Is it?" Lucca cocks his head ever so slightly. "Dario, how much did my mother weigh when you snapped her neck?"

Dario glances at the ceiling as if consulting his memory. "Eighty pounds maybe."

"She was in pain," Lucca says.

Dario nods.

"Alone," Lucca adds.

"Except for me and the hospice worker—" Dario nods again.

Around us, men are shifting, a restlessness moving through the ranks.

"Why this walk down memory lane, Lucca?" Renelli sniffs and wipes his nose. "You want to do the honors 'cause of what he did to your mother?"

Lucca ignores him, training his gaze on Dario. "Did she tell you what I promised her that last time I saw her?"

"That you would kill the bastard."

Lucca closes his eyes, tilting his head to the sky as if in prayer. "That I would murder the bastard who could have protected her but instead decided to use her as a wedge between the two men he saw as his greatest threat—your father. And mine."

"You don't know what you're talking about," Renelli scoffs.

"You whispered in my father's ear that my mother was a

no-good whore, when she was a *child* thrown to the fucking *wolves*." His voice rises with each word, along with an accompanying tension, twitching fingers, darting gazes.

Lucca's eyelids fly open.

"Another favor, my brother?" he says to Dario.

"Yes," Dario agrees and the world explodes in slow motion.

Nicky the driver throws me to the ground and curves his body around mine.

At the same moment, Dario stretches an arm and Nicky slides a gun into his palm.

Dario and Lucca turn, a Flamenco dance, until they're back-to-back, Tomas on one knee in front of me, pistol propped on his wrist.

Gunfire erupts, echoes against the metal roof, deafening. Vittorio Amato hits the floor, blood so dark its black gushing from the chunk taken out of his skull.

I'm crouching, arms wrapped around my head, Nicky on my back, eye level with the carnage. Tony Graziano and Tommy Vanzetti collapse in a tangled pile of arms and legs. I glance up, and looming over me, Dario calmly aims and fires.

Frankie Bianco jerks back, arms flying wide as the impact yanks him off his feet, and then he crumples. There's one, two, three more shots, and then silence except for Frankie's moaning. Somehow, he's still alive, huddled on the floor.

And so is Renelli. He's cradling a bloody hand, his pistol and his ivory cane at his feet. Lucca strides forward until he's eye to eye with the old man. He's swaying on his feet, and his craggy face is blanched white, but there's no surrender in his eyes.

"So this is how it ends, nephew?" Renelli rasps.

"You could call it an end. Or a new beginning." A smile plays at Lucca's lips.

Renelli laughs. "You think you're strong enough to keep that psychopath in line?" He's talking about Dario. "The first time you turn your back, he's going to do you like you're doing me. That monster killed your mother. He knows no loyalty. He's a rabid dog, and you don't have the balls to keep him in line."

Lucca glances over his shoulder, and for a second, his eyes meet Dario's. A current runs between them, an unspoken question and a voiceless answer.

Then Lucca turns back to Renelli. "Dario killed my mother out of mercy. Because I asked him."

There's a gasp from behind us, and a moment when even Renelli is struck silent. He recovers quickly. "Dario Volpe has no mercy."

Lucca lifts his shoulder, the slightest acknowledgement. "No mercy. No loyalty. Almost sounds like the only use you have for the man is his ability to make you money."

It's Renelli's turn to shrug.

Lucca shakes his head. "You think small. You have a man who can spin gold, and you've got him working for the Russians and the cartels. It's like you have a Ferrari, and you're so proud of how quickly you can pick up your dry cleaning. That's what's wrong with the criminal mind. Limited."

"You think you know fuckin' everything 'cause you have the gun." Renelli spits.

Lucca glances at the pistol in the hand dangling at his side. "No. Not everything. But I know more than you."

Renelli snorts.

"I know the difference between a rabid dog and a man

with something to lose. You don't. And so you die." Lucca flashes a brilliant smile and raises his gun.

He meets Dario's eyes, and without looking down, he squeezes off a single shot. The top of Renelli's head explodes, spraying Lucca's face, staining those perfect white teeth. Lucca laughs, and Renelli's body slumps to the ground like a puppet with its strings cut.

Behind me, there's a retching. I turn, and that's when I see Frankie. He's dragging himself toward the exit using his elbows, his knee a bloody, pulpy mess. Dario's black eyes pivot to track him, and it's his turn to smile.

"Where are you going, Frankie?" Dario stalks over and crouches beside him.

Sweat is dripping down Frankie's face. Lucca's returned to his usual place next to Tomas, and he's watching the tableau with a detached interest.

Dario prods Frankie's mangled knee with his gun. Frankie's screams ricochet off the corrugated metal ceiling.

Dario cocks his head. "It must be awful. Here you are—weaker than me. I can do whatever I want, and you have to take it. Are you scared?" Dario grins in delight. "You're scared, aren't you?"

Frankie doesn't answer. He grunts as he keeps trying to pull himself away, even though it's hopeless. I can't help the pity. We were good together once. It's a blur now, but there were nights at the club, the customary flowers and sweet talk before he figured out how genuinely easy I was. How he could use his hands, and I'd cry and sulk, but I wouldn't go anywhere.

"Posy." Dario's voice is gentle. It flows across the space. "Where did he hit you?"

My brain can't make sense of the question.

"At his apartment?"

"In the face? Ribs?"

How can he be asking me this now? That's a locked box. I got out of it, and I never looked back. Unlike this moment that stretches on and on.

"Posy?"

"My stomach." If he was sober, he didn't like to mess up my face.

Dario prods the gun into Frankie's belly, and he shoots. Just like that. A muffled pop. Frankie screams, clutching his guts. The blubbery shrieks fill the spaces between the silent men.

This has to be the end. It can't keep going.

"You fucking madman," Frankie spits.

"Where else?" Dario demands, his eyes glowing. He doesn't sound cold and detached now. He's—aroused.

"Where else?" he repeats, and so help me, I'm scared.

"He slapped me."

Dario whips his gun against Frankie's face, slamming his head into the floor.

"What else, Posy?" Dario's gathered Frankie by the collar, holding him up. He's still alive, still whimpering, but he's fading. "Posy!" The order rings out.

"He p-punched me when he got drunk."

"In the face?"

"Yeah."

"That's how you got that black eye?"

He remembers? It was so long ago. We didn't speak back then.

"Yeah."

I want to look away. I want to crawl inside myself and shut my eyes tight until it's over. But I don't.

I watch while Dario digs the muzzle of his gun into the soft skin under Frankie's left eye.

"I'm sorry," Frankie cries, his gaze searching me out for the first time. "I'm sorry. Make him stop. P-please, Posy."

"I can't." I don't control Dario Volpe. No one does.

"I'm sorry, goddamn it," Frankie says.

"Did he say that before? After he hit you?" Dario asks like he's asking for the time.

I don't even think before I answer. "No." He pretended it never happened, and I did, too.

Dario squeezes the trigger, and the left side of Frankie's head explodes, chunks of skull and brain flying into the air and then raining onto the concrete with moist splats.

I shove a fist into my mouth to stifle the scream, my teeth biting into my knuckles, and all around me, men loom, still and silent, stinking of fear and blood and gunfire.

There's so much blood. Dark pools. Bodies frozen, arms and legs akimbo, lax and unmoving. I huddle into myself, eyes bugging, swallowing against the puke in my throat.

There are seven dead bodies I can see, and how much time has passed? Two minutes? Three?

I mash my lips against the moan I can't stop from climbing up my throat. It's a massacre.

Above me, Dario has come to his feet. Lucca approaches him and slaps him on the back.

"Capo," Dario says to him with a slight bow, lips curved.

"Consigliere," Lucca replies.

Nicky and Tomas have risen, too, and there's a general shuffling and murmuring as the men left alive survey the scene, scrubbing at their necks, glancing warily at the two men in the middle of the ring of blood and bodies.

I can't move. I'm nothing but a ball of horror, rocking, willing myself to disappear, to turn off like a machine.

"Come on, Posy." Dario strides over, grabs me, and hoists me to my feet. When I pitch forward, he winds an arm around my middle, pinning me to his side. "You're fine."

He bends over and nestles his nose in my hair, inhaling, and then he brushes his temple against mine. For some reason, this seems to relax him.

"Did anyone touch you?" he asks as he urges me to step forward, through a rivulet of blood, toward the hall that leads outside.

My brain is numb. I can't even make words.

"Joey grabbed her pussy," Nicky pipes up from behind.

Dario drops a kiss on my forehead, and then he casually turns, aims his gun, and squeezes off a round into Joey's throat. Joey had been helping drag a body into a pile, and he kind of pitches forward and lands in the heap with a heavy thump.

And I finally run.

I sprint down the corridor, out the door, between the cars, through the glass strewn, weed-eaten parking lot, arms pumping. I scramble over the fence where it sags almost parallel to the ground, the barb wire biting at my legs. If there's shouting, I can't hear over the blood roaring in my ears.

I race through the field, tall grass whipping against my skin, and I stumble, but my forward motion propels me on, and my lungs scream, and my thighs burn, but I can't stop.

And then, when I'm almost to the river, I can't go on anymore. The stitch in my side is becoming a cramp, and I'm jogging, and then I'm only stumbling and trying to suck down air.

I have to keep going. I can't stop. If I stop, it'll all catch up to me.

I'm too beat to even react when I realize I'm not alone. Dario is right behind me. He lopes forward, grabs me, lifts me off my feet. I flail, my hand connecting with his iron jaw, my foot nailing his shin. He hisses, tightening his arms, and I fight harder with everything I have. My skull glances off his, and my nose prickles with the impact. My ears ring.

Mindless panic beats in my veins like a drum. I scream, "Let me go."

And he kind of throws me from him, not violently. Almost—carefully.

He raises his hands in surrender.

"Okay. Okay." He's panting, but nowhere near as winded as I am. He rolls his shoulders and catches his breath, cracking his neck and pacing like he's having a nice post-workout stretch. He eyes me warily.

Somehow, I landed on my feet. My gaze darts wildly from the field to the river to the overpass in the distance. I'm cornered.

"Don't jump in the fucking river, Posy. It's disgusting. We'll catch tetanus."

You can't catch tetanus from swimming. I don't think. I wheeze, lungs burning. I can't go any further.

We stand a little while as I suck down air. He hovers a few feet away. Not too close, but close enough.

"Can we go back now?" he finally asks.

"No." It's all I can manage. I'm leaning over, bracing myself on my thighs. Sweat trickles in my eyes.

"All right." He checks his watch. "We probably have a few more minutes until the bodies are handled."

My stomach lurches at the reminder. I glance up. He shrugs.

"It was—that was—that was a *bloodbath*." My voice breaks.

He widens his eyes, as if encouraging me to go ahead and make my point. A hysterical giggle flies from my lips.

He's utterly unaffected by what just happened. By what he *did*.

"So Lucca's capo now? And you're his consigliere?"

Dario nods.

"And everyone's fine with that?"

He shrugs. "Or dead, yeah."

"This was a setup. You knew."

"The broad strokes," he allows. "Not the specifics."

"You used me as bait."

"You were already marked. I killed two birds with one stone."

"Two?"

He actually smirks. "Maybe more than two."

"I could have been killed."

"I had Tomas covering your front and Nicky on your back."

"It was a goddamn pinball machine of gunfire in there, Dario."

He scrubs the back of his neck, exasperated. "It was the only way. You can't run forever. You can't hide. No one can hurt you now." His lips curve, a look of satisfaction crossing his dark angel's face.

"And you feel nothing? Another day at the office?" I can hear the hysteria creeping into my voice.

"Oh, no, Posy. This is a good day." He grins. An actual, honest to God grin. "I've waited a long time to kill Frankie Bianco."

"Because he sent that video." Of course. Psychopath that he is, Dario still has his pride.

"Because of the video," Dario concurs. "And because he's fucked you. And he slapped you around."

"You knew about that?" He never mentioned it. Not once.

Chapter 11

He rolls his eyes. "You were always 'running into doors' and shit when you dated that asshole. Everyone knew he was using you as a punching bag."

My face flames and a sour taste fills my mouth. Dario isn't the only one with pride. I tell myself it was no big deal. I got out. That's what counts. I can't look too closely at why I stayed so long. I push it all back into a cobwebby corner of my memory. If revenge helps, I have it now. Dario gave it to me.

What was it he said after he cut out Ivano's tongue? *I do it for you, Posy. You belong to me. You're a very dangerous woman now.*

Chills race down my spine.

"You noticed me back then?" I thought I wasn't on his radar until I came onto him in the club.

"I've always noticed you."

"Why didn't you talk to me?"

He raises an eyebrow. Fair enough. I did all the heavy lifting when we first got together. He doesn't exactly have game.

"But you noticed me." Even after everything that happened today, I can't stretch my brain to wrap around the idea.

"You're the person," he says like it's an explanation.

"What do you mean?"

He scans the river, and when he speaks, he's as casual as if he's talking about the weather. "You know the difference between a psychopath and a sociopath?"

"I have no idea."

"People talk about levels of aggression, mimicry, those sorts of things. But if you read about it, ultimately, it comes down to whether you can care about another person. Until I met you, I was a psychopath. And then I was a sociopath."

"That's better?"

He laughs. "I think it's more a distinction without a difference."

"So you care about me?"

"I'd die for you. Kill for you."

"You love me?"

"I don't know what that is."

"It's like floating." That's how it was with him at the beginning. Everything was perfect. Magical. *Right*.

"Then, no, I don't love you."

My heart, still thumping double time from my mad dash through the overgrown lot, crunches in my chest. Why? I'm not floating anymore. I haven't since the day he made me watch the video in his office.

My head's not in the clouds. Blood is soaked into my canvas shoes. I'm complicit. I'm Dario Volpe's willing whore.

And what do I care if he can't love me? I've been in love a dozen times. This is deeper than that. I feel closer to him than any person alive. He trickles through my veins. He's seeped into my bones.

He stands there, wary of me, hovering—close but not too close—because I'm the center of his world. He's proved that. I know it like I know my name.

He belongs to me. His ugliness. His twisted brain. His heartlessness, and his savagery. It's all mine. It's not love, either, but it's what I feel.

Dario's waiting, expectant. What for?

"Sometimes, I guess, love is more like the person is yours," I say. "No matter if they feel the same way or not. They belong to you. And that's that."

Dario inhales and nods in recognition. "Then I love you, Posy. Does that make you happy?"

The question is genuine. Almost vulnerable.

Chapter 11

I open my mouth to deny it, but the words won't come. So I take a step forward, closing the distance between us. I stare up at his bearded jaw, his sharp cheekbones. His perfect face. There's doubt there. A dark longing that if you squint and tilt your head just so—looks like hope.

I slip my small hand into his much larger, colder one.

"I'll never break your heart again," he vows. "You can trust me. It can be like it was before."

I squeeze his hand. "I don't think so, Dario."

"Then it can be different. It can be anything you want."

"Because I'm your one person." I can't help but say it again. It melts in my mouth and surges into my bloodstream, a hit, a rush, a miracle.

I'm sure it's wrong to want a love like this, but I am greedy to my soul, and I'm going to take it and never, never let it go.

Dario tightens his grip on my hand and draws me back toward the factory. I follow, and I guess I was wrong, because my feet don't quite touch the ground.

"I belong to you?" I ask as we trek back through the tall grass that we trampled flat.

"Yes."

He rushes me, and I have to trot to keep up. He picks me up in his arms like a bride to get back over the collapsed fence that cut my calf.

Dario's face is impassive again, his mouth turned down.

"And you belong to me?" I press, gazing up, letting him carry me to one of the idling cars.

"Yes." It's clear his mind is on something else—the murder scene we fled, no doubt—but there's no impatience in his tone.

"And you would kill for me? And die for me?"

"Yes." He drops me to my feet without warning so he can

open the car door for me. The impact jolts me back into reality a little.

"And I'm supposed to trust you?"

He guides me into the back seat, reaching across my chest to buckle me in. His forearm grazes my breasts, and heat springs to life in my belly.

He shrugs and taps the back of the driver's headrest. It's Nicky.

"Yeah, boss," he says.

"Home," Dario orders.

We pull away, and Dario unbuttons his dress shirt. I'm vaguely aware that my teeth are chattering, and my hands are fluttering as if I've been electrocuted. Dario prods me until I let him thread my arms through the sleeves.

"You're in shock," he says.

"I'm in shock?" I repeat.

"Yes. And yes, you're supposed to trust me. And yes to all the other questions." He leans over, nestles his nose behind my ears, and draws in a jagged breath. "For you, always yes."

"Always?"

"Yes," he exhales, gently cupping my neck and pressing his lips to mine, softly, as if I'm the only woman in the world for him, and all his words are true.

12

DARIO

Even three months later, there's still wariness in Posy's eyes. She's settled in, back to lounging around the house and nagging Ray or Sal to drive her to the mall. She knows she's not allowed anywhere without protection.

Everyone in the organization has fallen in line, but that doesn't mean there aren't knives being sharpened. The mantle of power has passed, and for some, it's been an opportunity, but for others, it's the end of an era they're not willing to let go of.

Maybe that's why Posy's still holding back, the sense that the sword of Damocles is hanging over our heads. Lucca wants to lure his enemies into the open and finish them with a hail of gunfire. For as sophisticated as he is in terms of style, his notions about wielding power are basic as hell.

I pointed out that when the cash keeps flowing undisturbed, feelings will inevitably be soothed, and loyalties should realign themselves with reality. Already, the surviving Biancos and Amatos have kissed the ring. The

Grazianos were always hot headed, but the sons are too young to commit to a vendetta.

Still, I'm sure there will be another bump or two in the road. Nothing Posy needs to worry about. I tell her this, and she says she believes me.

But she tests me constantly.

Every morning, she makes me tell her I love her. And after we fuck. And before she falls asleep. And whenever she's bored she texts, and if I don't respond quickly enough, she calls.

She never says "I love you" back. She smirks and sashays off, usually to go rummage in the fridge. If I didn't make her workout with me, she'd be as big as a house. As it is, her waist's filling out. I like it. Her tits are a little bigger, too, and the extra padding has made them more sensitive. When I graze my teeth over her nipples, she shrieks and contorts like a fish dangling from a line. It's cute as hell, and so much fun to catch her and hold her steady enough to slip inside.

And then there are the drive-bys like what she's doing now. It's ten in the morning, Miles and I are working, and she strolls into the office in a stretchy white mini skirt and skintight matching shirt. Hair in a messy bun. No shoes. She looks like a drunk hooker, and if Miles looks up from his desk, I'm gonna blind him with a letter opener.

She saunters to my desk and leans over, propping herself on her elbows with her arms squeezing her tits until they almost spill out of her top. It's wasted effort. You can't miss them. She's obviously not wearing a bra, and her nipples are visible through the fabric.

"Want to play Monopoly?" she asks, popping the "p."

"I'm working." I finish the trade I was working on, keeping half an eye on those luscious tits. I feel like her nipples have gotten darker recently. Maybe it has to do with the weather.

"How about chess?"

"Later."

"Wanna fuck?"

I exhale and shut my laptop. Yes, I want to fuck. Constantly, now that I know what it feels like to make Posy cum—like solving a Rubik's Cube, but a million times better.

But Posy isn't the one walking around the house in a constant state of painful arousal. That's me since I don't take her whenever I want anymore. I've eased back, tried to encourage her to come to me when she wants it. That means we have less sex, but she's more present when we do.

And she reaches for me now, sometimes, at night when we're in our bed. Especially if we've watched a sappy movie, or if she's beaten me soundly at whatever game we played after dinner. But she's still not aggressive sexually. Definitely not in the middle of the day.

This is another test that I can't understand and can't seem to win.

"Do you wanna fuck, Posy?" I throw back at her.

"Sure."

She hops onto my desk and peels her top off without a second thought.

"Miles, get out."

The door clicks shut so quickly, he must have already been on his way.

"Well?" She's arranged herself on my desk, knees bent, feet curved over the edge, skirt rucked up to her waist. No panties. Her tits strain for the ceiling, the nipples definitely a duskier color than usual. Maybe because of the chill in the air.

She lets her thighs fall further apart and flashes me her pretty pink pussy, already slick with cream. I was hard when she walked in the room. I'm throbbing now. I unbuckle my belt, unzip my pants, let them fall, and I'm stroking my aching cock up and down her wet slit when it occurs to me.

I'm missing something.

"Dario?" She struggles to her elbows so she can glare at me. "Do you need foreplay or something?"

I don't. She usually does. That's one thing wrong with this picture.

"What's wrong?" I demand.

"You won't give me the dick for some reason."

"Why are you being so vulgar?"

"Why the twenty questions, Dario?"

Her chest flushes. She's getting mad. Did I not tell her that I love her enough times today? Did someone say something to upset her? Is it that fucking video?

If it's that video, whoever shared it, I will kill them, and then I'll skull fuck the pulp of their brains.

"I love you," I try.

"Hell of a way to show it."

Enough is enough. I scoop her up and sit in my chair, cuddling her to my chest. She's warm and soft and grumpy as hell. I give her a little shake. "What's wrong with you?"

She mumbles into my shirt.

"What?"

She rears back. "I'm pregnant! How did you not notice?"

"You're pregnant?"

"I've gained fifteen pounds! None of my bras fit! I make Ray hang his jacket out in the garage because it smells weird!"

"Like coffee grounds." I've noticed.

"Like dirty mop water."

I disagree, but it seems like the wrong time to do so out loud.

"Aren't you going to say anything?" She scowls at me with those beautiful blue eyes. Fucking shame about genetics. Our child will most likely have my plain brown eyes.

Our child...

A rush roars through my veins.

"Will you love it if it's like me?" It's the first question in my mind.

The nature versus nurture argument is never settled, but it'd be naïve to pretend that I might not create an aberration like myself. I've got control over myself now, more or less, but when I was younger—well, I've never been surprised that my father doesn't care for me. I've always been grateful he never threw his hands up and had me put down.

"If *he's* like you," she corrects.

"You know already it's a boy?"

"Or *her*," she goes on. "And yes, I will love him or her. I already do."

She rests her forehead on mine, and I revel in the feel of her sweet breath on my face.

"Will you love the baby? Like you do me?"

There's a tremble in her voice. I don't know, but the truth won't comfort her. Good thing I have no compunction about lying.

"Yes," I say.

"Always yes?" she whispers, her uncertainty and fear clear in the wavering words.

"Yes," I murmur as I kiss her, and I wonder what it will take for her to trust me—and what happens when, of course, she can't.

13

POSY

I'm as roly poly as a pot-bellied pig, but I'm happy. Ish.

I'm married. Dario and I flew to Vegas and got married by Elvis in a chapel. We almost got kicked out of the casino for counting cards, which Dario was totally doing, and maybe I was, too, but not as obviously as he was.

We're going to have a baby, and I spend my days decorating the nursery and bugging my husband to ditch work and play board games. It's a snowy winter, but the temperatures aren't too bitter, and there's no reason for me to be so unsettled.

Dario loves me. I've made him tell me over and over until the words are mundane. I thought that would make them feel real. It didn't work.

It's a real bummer because I love him. Madly. Irredeemably. Idiotically.

And despite some of my life choices, I'm a bright woman, and I know I'm building a house of cards. Of course, I couldn't stop if I tried.

I'm his queen. There's no doubt about that. I can read it on every face when I walk into a party or a restaurant on his arm. There's nothing but respect. Deferential smiles. Dario pays it no mind, but I do. Sometimes I lean a little too close to another man so I can watch the guy tug at his collar and try to take an inconspicuous step back. No one wants a bullet in the throat.

I know Dario has been bracing for blowback from Lucca's coup, but so far, it's been quiet. The laughter at parties has less of an edge now, and everyone is settling into a new normal.

Maybe I'll finally believe in my happily ever after when the baby's born. Or maybe I'll always have this little voice in the back of my head, telling me I'd better run, while my heart digs her nails into love like a desperate bitch.

I plop the last spoonful of noodles from the pot into the serving dish. I made spaghetti and meatballs tonight. Nothing fancy. Dario's already sitting at the table, on his phone, even though I've told him a hundred times no trading during dinner.

I waddle over and set the bowl down on a hot plate, scanning the table. I've got the bread, butter, and salt. Once I sit, I'm not getting back up.

I sigh when I finally lower myself into the chair next to Dario. I kick off my shoes under the table. After the first hour or so I'm up, my feet ache all day, and my toes look like puffy little white sausages. I don't know how I'm going to do nine more weeks.

I snatch Dario's phone and set it face down next to his plate. Without skipping a beat, he reaches for the salad and heaps a serving on my plate. He thinks I'm not eating enough fruits and vegetables. I think he'd better mind his own damn business if he knows what's good for him.

"You should have Maria stay and do dinner," he says,

passing me the Italian dressing. It's homemade, my mother's recipe.

"I like cooking."

"You're tired. You sound like a leaky balloon every time you sit down."

"Sorry to bother you."

"It doesn't bother me." His jaw twitches. Dario cannot handle me when I'm cranky. He tries to reason with me, and it always blows up in his face. "It's just, you don't have to do this."

"Do what?"

"Play the good wife."

My temper flares. "I'm not *playing*."

He scrubs his neck. "I know. It's just this—" He gestures at the table I've set and the food I've made. "You don't have to do it. This isn't the fifties. I don't expect it."

"Then you don't have to eat it." I spear a meatball and plonk it onto my plate.

Now it's his turn to sigh. He focuses on his dinner. I shove the salad to one side and rip off a huge hunk of crusty warm bread.

"Pass the butter?"

He narrows his eyes at my bread. Judging. I reach right past him for the butter dish.

"You need to eat more leafy greens."

"You need to crawl out of my ass." I haven't put on more weight than I'm supposed to, and even if there's a little more of me to love these days, he doesn't seem to mind. If I show the slightest interest, he's all over me. He's downright obsessed with how my boobs have changed.

Dario sets his knife and fork down on the table with a thump and skewers me with a glare. "What is making you unhappy?"

"You."

"Because I didn't pass the butter?"

I shove my plate away. The spaghetti is sticking to the meatballs, and the sauce is clumpy, and it's just gross. "Yes, Dario. I am pissed as hell because you didn't pass me the fucking butter."

He glares up at the ceiling like he's asking the Lord for strength, and now I want to hit him. In the face. In his cold, unfeeling, unconcerned, unconflicted *face*.

"You need to eat better. The bigger it grows, the more the baby is depleting your nutrient reserves." He says this very slowly as if he's speaking to a child. "You need iron. You need vitamin B."

With any other man, I'd flip him off—or bite his head off—but not Dario. I don't take what he says lightly. Not now that he's honest with me.

Unease robs me of the rest of my appetite and puts a damper on my hormonal peevishness.

"The baby isn't hurting me."

He tosses a shoulder. "It would hurt you less if you ate a salad once in a while." He narrows his eyes and his lips turn down. "I'm not upset with the baby. It's just biological fact."

"Okay." I take a slow slip of water.

He exhales. "You're never going to be how you were before, are you?"

"Like how?"

"Happy."

"I'm happy."

He arches an eyebrow. I have my arms crossed, and I'm doing everything in my power not to make eye contact with the red-splattered lump lolling on top of my spaghetti.

I roll my eyes. "I'm pregnant and hormonal. That's all."

"Why won't you look at your plate?"

"The meatball."

He waits as if that isn't explanation enough.

"It's disgusting."

"Didn't you make them?"

"Things were different then."

"An hour and a half ago?"

"Are you trying to start a fight?" I level a glare at him. The sleeves of his white button-down shirt are rolled to his elbows, but everything else about him is unperturbed. His face is a glass lake, not a black hair out of place, his beard a straight edge slashing across his hard jaw.

He still scares me sometimes. Like walking past a tiger at the zoo, the kind of exhibit where they use ledges and moats instead of bars to keep the animals inside. You believe it can't hurt you, but you can't see what's stopping it, either.

"No." He silently considers me for a moment. Then he stands, his dinner uneaten, too. He offers me his hand. "Let's go play a game."

"That's your answer to everything," I spit peevishly, but I'm already hauling myself upright. Anything to get away from the stench of garlic.

He leads me upstairs to our bedroom. The chess board is already set out on our table in the nook overlooking the garden. He must have been hankering to play. I've been getting tired in the evenings, and sometimes lately I don't want to spend hours kicking his ass. Other times, like tonight, I need it. When this thing we have doesn't feel real, the games do. They're the closest we can get to each other, the only wavelength we really share.

I go to take my seat opposite him, but he holds me back. He sinks into his leather wingback chair and pulls me onto his lap.

"I'm too heavy." I squirm, but he has an arm wrapped

underneath my big belly. This is like that horrible day in his office. I tense and strain against his grasp.

"Relax."

"It's uncomfortable. You're too hard."

"Not yet." I can hear the smirk in his voice. He tugs the board close enough for me to reach and moves the white pawn to e4.

"So you're white?"

"I won last time."

"How do you even remember?"

"You were pissy then, too." He says it as if he's recalling the weather. My moods don't faze him in the least. It's a small blessing of being married to a psychopath.

I bring my queenside bishop pawn to c5.

He sighs happily, and we settle in to play. The tension slowly ebbs from my spine, and I curve against his warm chest. He begins to jiggle his knee gently like he does when he thinks he's got something up his sleeve, and it feels oddly soothing. He's clearly going for a variation of the Jerome Gambit. Clever, but I can see it coming a mile away.

Six moves later, he's in check. Then mate. I tilt my head back and rest it in the crook of his neck. "Better luck next time." I nuzzle the spot under his ear. It smells faintly of cologne. The first scent today that didn't turn my stomach.

He's already setting up the board again. "That should have worked." He drops a kiss on the top of my head.

"On an idiot maybe."

He chuckles. "I've been working on that for days."

"Waste of time." I blow air on my nails and polish them on my top. "You should concede now so we can watch TV. It sucks watching you embarrass yourself over and over again."

A low laugh reverberates against my back. He loves it

when I smack talk. The fog of irritation I've been smothered by today lightens a little. I exhale and wind my fingers through his, tilt his hand until he's cradling my belly. She's pretty active. Maybe he'll feel her. Maybe he'll stop forgetting and calling her *it*.

"What was that?" he asks, hand paused above a bishop.

"What was what?"

"You were relaxing, and then you tensed again."

"Dark thoughts."

"You don't have dark thoughts."

"So you read my mind now?"

"Close to."

"Then how come I keep whupping your ass at chess?"

"You only win about forty percent of the time."

"You keep track?"

He doesn't answer. I bet he does. I bet he has a spreadsheet, or maybe he's made an app that runs the odds. My lip twitches. He's such a strange man.

"What dark thoughts?"

I guess he's decided that he might be wrong, considering he is about forty percent of the time.

With my mind half on the game, and half on a hundred other things, I reach for a nothing kind of answer, and instead, I say, "What if all of this is a terrible mistake?"

The hand hovering above a knight drops to the arm of the chair. Now he's tense.

"What do you mean?"

I exhale, and unbidden, all the poison comes out on that breath, tainting the air, burning the scales from my eyes until I can see this is a showroom, I'm a mannequin, this whole life is a fake designed to please a man who can never feel for me like I *feel* for him.

"This is all going to fall apart. You don't love me. I'm not a person to you. I'm the thing that plays games with you. And that isn't love. It *isn't*. And the baby won't know how to play games. You won't care about her at all, and I'm not going to make dinner and smile and make myself pretty, night after night, while you don't even notice her. I won't do it. I *won't*."

It's more truth than I knew I had inside me. It gusts out, and in the aftermath, everything is still. Dario's phone pings a notification. His breath is calm and even, ghosting warm across my cheek.

He takes a hand and rests it on the mound of my belly, so lightly I wouldn't know if I didn't see it there.

"I wish I had met you when we were younger."

I don't know what I was expecting him to say, but it wasn't that.

"If I had known you when that business with your uncle happened, no one would have dared turn their back on you."

"How do you know about that?"

"I know everything about you. I know your father wanted a boy. I know all your friends dumped you when he was forced out. I know you tried to fuck your way back into the inner circle."

I jerk and hiss. He wraps his arms around me, light and gentle, but with no give.

"I know what you've done so you could feel like you were worth something to someone. What you've taken." His beard scratches my jaw. "Don't you think that scares the shit out of me?"

I don't understand. I try to turn and meet his eyes, but his chin is tucked in the crook of my neck.

"Are you cooking dinner and smiling and making yourself pretty because I'm better than no one? Are you *taking* this? Like you took it with Giorgio and Frankie and whoever else?"

He splays his fingers over my bump. "And when this baby comes, and she loves you, and you love her?"

What do I need him for? That's the part he leaves unsaid. My foolish, sappy heart rushes to reassure him, but wasn't I the one who just said this isn't love?

I look at his hands, feel his strength surrounding me. I've never been this close to anyone. The irony is as sharp as a knife.

Eventually, he sighs. "It's late. I have work I want to do before bed."

"Okay." My voice is small. I push up, but he's already bracing an arm under my knees, rising to his feet as if my weight is inconsequential. He lays me carefully on our bed, and then he hands me the remote.

"I'll be back up in an hour or so."

I nod. He smooths down my shirt where it's crept up and lets his palm linger on the curve below my belly button. It's a nanosecond. An afterthought.

It's gentle and common, so ordinary a gesture that he's already gone when it hits me. He cares.

And he doesn't know if I do. He's flying as blind as I am. The idea is so big that I can't swallow it all at once. I settle back, click on the TV, and every so often, I take it out and nibble it—Dario is as uncertain of me as I am of him. I'm not the victim. He's not the villain. Not anymore. We're—something else.

After three episodes of *House Mavens*, I start to get restless. My hip joints ache. I stick a pillow between my legs, try to relieve the pressure, but it's coming from inside my body, and no position really helps.

Where is Dario? He said he'd only be a little while. Is he

brooding? He never has before, but I guess there's a first time for everything.

The house is silent. There are no footsteps echoing from the entrance hall or the crunch of tires in the drive. The day staff have all left. It's not that late, but the sun sets around five these days, so it's been dark for hours. Sal's probably walking the perimeter, bored off his gourd, while Ray's watching hockey in the media room.

I can't relax, and I have to pee again. I haul my ass up, run to the bathroom, and then go to the window and open the blinds. There's a crescent moon, but it's bright, casting a bluish glow over the snow. It's a peaceful scene, and my nerves finally start to chill.

It's a great yard. Much better than the neighborhood park I had to play in growing up. As soon as the snow thaws, I want to get it ready for the baby, too. Buy one of those Amish-made playsets.

Dario says he'll build one himself, and I have no doubt that he could, but he'd be hell to live with while he's doing it. Dario doesn't appreciate directions telling him what to do. I never appreciated that fact before I saw him put together an assemble-at-home baby jumper.

I think I'll put the playset by the bed of posies, right next to the—what is that?

There's a black blob in the snow, half obscured by the shadow of a maple tree. It's not moving. Maybe a garbage bag flew over the fence? Or a tarp?

I sigh. I'm sick of waiting. I'll go see what's holding Dario up, and I'll mention the bag to Ray. I slide into my old lady slippers and check myself out in the mirror. I'm a bombshell. Gray terry sweatshirt dress. With pockets. Preggo yoga pants. How is Dario not rushing back to do this?

I shrug off the hormones and waddle off downstairs.

The overhead lights are out; the wall sconces dimmed. I love the house like this, quiet and mysterious. It's a delicious thrill to sneak through the empty halls and freak myself out when the floor squeaks, and then the "all home free" feeling when I tumble into bed and crawl under the covers—it's as much a thrill now as when I was a little girl, creeping around the big house we lost after Uncle Marco.

Dario has offered to buy a new house if I want to pick one, but I'd rather make this one my own. I'm making inroads, room by room. There's a deacon's bench in the entrance hall now, and throw pillows on all the sofas and chairs in the house. I like to walk into an immaculately, professionally decorated room and see the incongruity of the painting I hung or the rug I bought.

There's a metaphor in there somewhere for Dario and me. He shelters me. I fill his emptiness. I don't know exactly but the thought soothes more of the lingering hurt from our conversation.

I'll feel even better when I see him. When he looks at me like he always does after I lose my shit—as if nothing's happened and everything is the way it ought to be. I've never known anyone who can reset to default quicker than Dario. It's creepy, but it does mean we never fight any longer than I want to.

I reach his office and turn the knob, fully expecting to sashay on in. It's locked. That's weird. He never locks his office. I didn't realize he could.

Is this some kind of message?

I knock. No answer. I knock again. Hard. "Dario!"

I have to bang several times before the door swings open. Dario's already heading back for his desk. He lowers himself slowly to sit rigidly in his chair, eyes directed at me but unfocused. Unreadable.

Chapter 13

What the hell is going on?

His laptop is closed. He wasn't watching porn. And I highly doubt he'd care if I busted him.

And he looks so strange. He's resting his hands on the clear desk top. His face is a mask. The room is dark; the only light comes from the standing lamp in the corner. Icy fingers trip up my spine. Something is very wrong.

"Why did you lock the door?"

He answers immediately. "Go back upstairs, Posy. I'll join you in a minute."

"What's wrong?"

"Nothing. Go on. I'll just be a minute."

"You can't tell me nothing's wrong. You're sitting here in the dark with the door locked."

"It was an accident."

"Bullshit."

"Your hormones are talking again. Go back to bed. I'll be there soon."

His voice is calm, no different than always, but it pings a memory. This room. Early spring. The same even voice asking me to sit on his lap and watch a video. Is he thinking about that, too?

Is he sitting here in the dark stewing on it? On my past and what I've done and how can he tell that what we have is any different?

That's the thing about Dario—there is no way to know what's going on in his head. Not for sure. You can't even accuse him of wearing a mask, really. He *is* a mask.

Something's really wrong. He said he'd only be an hour or so. He keeps his word, or he lets me know.

Unless he's having second thoughts.

I pad a little further into the room. "What's going on? Are you still upset about earlier?" I absently rub my belly.

"Posy," his voice hardens. "*Go*."

Once upon a time, I would have scurried off, but he doesn't scare me anymore.

"No." I plop down in the leather chair across from his desk, not appreciating how far I sink in the overstuffed seat. "Talk to me. Tell me what's going on."

He hasn't moved at all. His hands are still resting on either side of his closed laptop, his posture straight. A vein pulsing in his temple is the only sign I'm getting to him.

"We'll talk about it later."

"We can talk about it now. Are you worried about the baby?" I never answered him when he said that about me loving the baby. Is that what's eating him? My heart aches.

His nostrils flare. "Fine, Posy. I'm worried about the baby."

My insides melt. He's worried that when the baby comes, I won't need him anymore, but I'll need him more than ever. He's the one that will keep her safe. Who will teach her that she's priceless. Who'll never let the world chew her up like it did to me.

"There's nothing to worry about. The baby will make us stronger than ever."

For a second, he seems lost, his gaze flickering, but then something happens, and his face blanks. His lips contort and his eyes narrow. A voice comes out of his mouth that I haven't heard in months. Not since that day in this office when he asked for the watch and the earrings.

"That's not what's on my mind, Posy." He sneers my name. "I'm sitting here wondering what I'll do if she comes out, and she's not mine." He cocks his head slightly to the side. "I don't *think* I'd care, but I shouldn't have cared about that video of you taking it up the ass either."

It comes from nowhere, and it slams into my chest like a train.

What is he saying? This makes no sense. Did someone accuse me of something? Is this history repeating, not even bothering to change the set or the plot?

My brain can't patch it together, but my body understands. All the blood in my body rushes to my feet, leaving my heart thudding in an empty cavity. My fingernails cut into the armrests.

"What?" It's a breathless whisper.

"I mean, the odds are good that it's mine. You're always watched outside of the house. But with your track record— It'd be downright stupid not to account for the possibility that she's Sal's. Or Ray's."

I'm shaking my head. He can't believe this. He knows me. Better than anyone ever has or could. "You—"

He plows ahead. "And if it's not mine, and for some reason I do care, what do I do with it?" His brow furrows. "I guess if I throw it out, you go with it, eh?"

Hot tears are streaming down my face. Where is this coming from? Or has this been in his head all along, and our conversation upstairs somehow busted open the floodgates?

This is the truth. He doesn't lie to me. He doesn't see any reason to.

"How can you say this?" I push up on the arms of the chair, struggle to my feet. "How can you even *think* it? What's wrong with you?"

"You know what's wrong with me," he says, an odd smile playing at his lips. "It's okay. You can run away. Shut the door after yourself."

I can't run. I'm too fucking big. But I rush as fast as I can, slam the damn door, hurtle toward the stairs, half-blinded by tears.

This is what it feels like when the other shoe drops.

Like a self-inflicted wound.

I should have known.

I did know. Oh god.

I burst into our bedroom. No, not *ours*. *His*. Let's be clear about what belongs to whom. His house, his stuff, his psychological condition.

My baby.

I stand in the middle of the room, chest heaving, clutching my belly and trying to make my brain think about my next move. I catch the Othello board from the corner of my eye, its smooth, round, black and white pieces laid precisely in the middle of the board, ready for when we get bored with chess.

Othello is a peaceful game because the moves are so predictable. Mathematical. Like tic-tac-toe. If you're evenly matched, the winner's more or less determined by whoever goes first. It's not a contest, it's a dance, each move a reaction to your partner.

Dario didn't come upstairs in an hour or so like he said he would.

So I went to him.

He told me to leave.

I sat in a chair.

He said horrible things.

He said run.

There's something in the backyard that doesn't belong. Something black in the snow. A bag? A tarp?

A body?

I stop thinking. I dash to the night table, fumble open the drawer, tap in the code, and take my gun from its safe. I kick off my slippers and creep back the way I just came.

The silence isn't eerily thrilling anymore. It's oppressive.

My hands are shaking, and I can't muffle my heavy breathing. The baby's pressing too close to my lungs. I'm in control, though, and my mind is crystal clear.

All the pieces have finally fallen into place, all the garbage in my head finally swept away.

This is my house.

My husband.

My life. My choice. My family.

This is what I want, and no one—*no one*—can take it from me.

A few feet from the closed office door, I hear the muffled voices. An angry man, ranting, his words strangely slurred, interspersed with Dario's cool, even bass.

I can't make out what they're saying, but they both sound as if they're on the far side of the room.

If I'm wrong, if this is some kind of late-night business meeting that got heated—

No. I'm not wrong. Dario lives to make me happy. He'd never hurt me without a reason. He drove me away.

He'd kill for me. He'd die for me. I *believe* that.

I suck in a deep breath.

I'm not going to get a second shot. When I fire, I'm going to empty the magazine.

I pat my belly for luck and throw open the door.

Ivano. But different. No gelled hair and storefront tan. His eyes are sunken hollows, his tracksuit hanging from him like a scarecrow.

In the same instant I take him in, he turns, swinging his gun from Dario's head toward me.

Dario leaps into motion, lunging for Ivano's arm as he

thrusts his body between Ivano and me, but his chair is stuck, and he can't quite block my shot.

I squeeze the trigger. One, two, three, four, five, six, seven. Ivano explodes in chunks. His shoulder. His chest. His head. Blood splatters on Dario, the desk, the painting of a schooner.

And then Ivano—or what's left of him—hits the wall and slides down into a heap on the red, soaked carpet.

"You almost got in the way," I say, my ears ringing so badly I can't hear Dario's reply.

I stare a few more beats at the grisly tableau, and then I lower my weapon. "What did he want?"

"Revenge."

"And he wanted to talk it out first?"

Dario shrugs as he grabs the gun taped under his desk, disengages the safety, and puts one last bullet in between Ivano's eyes.

"He was dead," I point out, my stomach beginning to heave. The baby's going crazy. I stroke my belly and hush her.

And Dario's face transforms. He stalks to me, grabs me by the upper arms, squeezing, lifting me nearly to my toes. His eyes shoot sparks, lips peeled back. He's furious.

"Don't shake me."

"I would *never* shake you!" he roars.

He swings me into his arms, takes five steps, and lays me carefully on the sofa.

"Stay," he barks, dialing his phone.

"Oh, god, where's Ray?"

"He's at the game. I gave him the night off."

"Sal?"

"He's not answering." Dario's back is to me, his gun aimed at the door. He makes another call. "We'll have backup in ten," he says and tosses the phone next to me. "If something happens, call Lucca."

"Wasn't Ivano alone?"

"I think so. I don't know." Dario's positioned himself with legs apart, shoulders squared. No one is getting through him to us.

"What the *fuck* were you thinking?" Dario rages, his gaze never wavering from the door.

"I thought you were trying to get rid of me. And I was right."

Despite the shock settling in, and the horror show on the floor behind the desk, I feel a twinge of satisfaction. Maybe I'm twisted, too, in ways I didn't know. I'm not sorry I did it. Ivano told Renelli I was back. He betrayed me, and he was going to kill my husband.

Fury flares in my chest again. Dario's mine. No one touches what's mine.

"If you ever pull a stunt like that again, you're gonna regret it, do you understand me?" Dario doesn't give me any time to respond. "*Do you understand me?*"

I realize Dario's been reading me the riot act this whole time.

"You could have been killed. The baby could have been killed. Do you get that?"

My hand goes to cradle my belly. "What do you think Ivano would've done after he'd killed you? I'm pretty sure Sal's dead in the backyard. You think Ivano would've waltzed off without checking for witnesses?"

"You should have *run*, Posy. Goddamn it!"

"That never works out as well as you think it will, Dario!"

"Don't you ever do something like this again." He bites out each syllable. That's the final word.

"You're mine, Dario Volpe, and I'll damn well save your life if I want to. My baby needs her daddy. *I* need you. Don't you know that? You know me inside out. You have to know that."

"I do," he says, low and gentle and sure.

We're both silent a moment. The house *feels* empty. I don't think Ivano brought anyone on his doomed mission.

Dario coughs to clear his throat, his back still to me. "Earlier—I didn't mean any of it."

"I realize that."

"I know the baby's mine, but even if she wasn't, I'd love her as much as her mother."

"How do you know?"

I know he would. Deep in my heart where all the truths —horrible and lovely—live, I know that. But how does *he* know?

"Because I love you for what you are. Everything you are is perfect. The baby will be perfect. You made her."

"You do, don't you? You love me just the way I am."

"You didn't come any other way," he says. I guess that's true enough.

And as we sit in the shadows, waiting for more dangerous men in suits to come, I curl in the corner of the sofa, and watch Dario's strong back and proud spine.

He doesn't love me despite my checkered past, my weaknesses, my mess and my desperation. He loves me *with* them.

He loves what I am, in my entirety, and I know he'll love our little girl the same.

We might be broken, Dario and I, but we live in a broken world. And that makes what we have—perfect.

EPILOGUE
DARIO

I'm sitting in the hospital waiting room like it's 1965, and I'm gonna pass out cigars when Posy presents me with a nice, cleaned up baby wrapped up like a present.

I want to kill someone. Or at least beat someone bloody.

I don't want to be camped out in this sagging chair, knees to my goddamn chin, watching my ninth hour of home improvement television because I can't focus on work, and my risk tolerance does not run to losing millions the day my daughter is born.

Fuck.

I need to be with Posy. She's in pain, and they're just letting it happen. I thought I was a psychopath, but this *midwife* and the goddamn *doula*, whatever the hell she's supposed to do besides be a pain in my ass, keep telling her to "embrace the experience."

She needs drugs.

I need drugs.

How are they going to know if something's really wrong? 'Cause when Posy kicked me out? It sounded like something was really, really wrong. Posy was sweating bullets and lowing like a cow, and the machine kept beeping. They said it was fine, but none of them have "doctor" next to their name.

I can't believe I let Posy talk me into a "birthing center." She wanted to do it in a pool, but that's where I draw the line. She's not drowning my kid because Karen the doula says a water birth is "transcendent." You know what's transcendent? Surviving childbirth.

I'm going back there. Something has to be wrong. There's no way this should be taking this long. The baby only has to go—like—five inches. She's stuck. She has to be.

I push up on the miniature chair, and Ray coughs from his seat across from me.

"Better not, boss," he says.

I arch an eyebrow. Is my driver telling me what to do now?

He holds up his hands. "Do what you want, but lookin' like that, you're gonna freak those women out again. You want their hands steady if they need to, uh—do something."

"Do what?" I narrow my eyes. Did he hear something?

Ray kind of gapes at me. "I don't know. Tongs, or whatever."

"They're called forceps." Oh god. What if the baby really is stuck? What if Posy is being ripped apart? She wouldn't say anything. She's conditioned to take all manner of shit in stride—she's married to me.

I can't let this happen. I only left because Posy said to go before I made the doula cry, but Posy doesn't make the right choices. Obviously.

She loves me.

She barged into an execution, guns blazing, six months pregnant with my child, and I'm still not over it.

She cannot be trusted to look out for herself. I've got to get her to a real hospital with a real doctor.

Decision made, I lope down the carpeted, low-ceilinged hall—it's like the place was proportioned for all the small women gliding around in drawstring pants and sensible shoes—and I force myself to stop, take a second, and open the door slowly and gently.

I brace myself. Whatever is happening, I will fix it. Everything will be fine.

If the baby comes out, and I still feel nothing, Posy will never know. She doesn't want to believe that I might not care for our child, and she's very skilled at denial. I swear that if I look at our daughter, and she's like everyone else in the world to me, I will never let on.

Her mother is the world to me. That will be enough.

I step across the threshold, and it's a blood bath. There's a pool of red on the tile floor, stains on the sheets, dripping from the women's gloves. How can she survive this? The midwife has her arm halfway up—holy Jesus. My stomach heaves. I can't look.

"Dario," Posy whimpers, holding out her hand. Her blonde hair is matted to her head with sweat, she's too pale, and her lips are cracked. Where's the damn doula? She said she'd take over giving Posy ice chips.

I take her small hand and hold her tight, try to transfer my strength.

"What's happening?" I choke out.

"We're having a baby, silly," Posy flashes me a wan smile, dropping it instantly as a contraction seizes her.

"Bear down!" the midwife barks. "And push, push, push—"

There's a terrible, wet sound. Then the women gathered between Posy's splayed legs all break into coos.

Posy's eyelids are drifting shut, but she's smiling again. Her body is so limp. Is she bleeding out?

The midwife is shuttling a tiny, shivering bundle toward us, and thank the lord Posy has the wherewithal to take it. She nestles it right to her chest, and it kind of huddles there, eyes squinched shut, little fists balled.

"Do you want to cut the cord, Daddy?" The midwife is offering me the handles of a pair of surgical scissors. I shake my head. I said I would when we did the birth plan, but that's only because Posy seemed to expect it. There's no way I'm doing it now. I'm not cutting my wife, and they need to focus. Staunch the bleeding. Now.

I look around the room helplessly for someone, *anyone* who appreciates the severity of the situation. A nurse is erasing a white board and adding a time of birth in loopy letters. The doula is in a chair, checking her phone. The midwife and a nurse are chatting as they work—with no sense of urgency—between Posy's legs. Jesus and Mary, what kind of operation are they running here?

"Dario, look," Posy says. "She has hair on her ears."

Posy's voice is hoarse but it shines with delight. She sounds—okay. Happy. Completely exhausted but not like she's fading into a coma or anything.

I check out the baby's ears. Posy's right. They're furry. The hair's very fine, but it covers the shells and the lobes.

"Are we gonna have to shave that or—"

The midwife, the nurse, and Posy all burst out laughing.

"You're not shaving our baby's ears," Posy giggles. It's a beautiful sound.

"It's called lanugo. It's perfectly normal. It'll go away in a few weeks, tops." The midwife is back to working on Posy. Did she lose a watch up there?

"Did you get the bleeding stopped?"

The midwife dumps something in a pink basin. "Posy can expect heavy bleeding for up to ten days and light bleeding or spotting for up to six weeks." She says this like it's no big deal.

She pats Posy on the knees. "You did great, Mama."

Posy flashes her a grateful smile. "Sorry about him." She glances up at me.

"Hey, he didn't pass out. I call that a good day." The midwife snaps off her gloves and washes her hands. "After we get you cleaned up, we'll leave you three to bond. Skin-to-skin and encourage her to nurse as soon as you're up to it, okay?"

Posy isn't listening. She's gazing at our baby, bemused. Blissed out. I've never made her look this happy.

Well, I guess I have. I helped make the baby who put the expression on her face. That's something.

The doula murmurs a few words to Posy, and then the room clears. Someone turns the lights down low. We're finally alone.

"Are you in pain?" I ask. She's stroking the baby's back. There's a fine layer of hair there as well. I'm sure the midwife would say that's normal, too.

"Oh, yeah," Posy answers. "It hurts like a son-of-a-bitch." She doesn't sound that bothered, though.

Posy brushes her nose over the baby's bald head—the only hairless part of her I've seen—and inhales. She makes a pleased hum. I've never seen her so captivated.

A loud voice echoes in the hall, and I tense. I don't want them disturbed. Soon enough, the voice fades, and it's quiet again except for Posy's babbling. She's talking to the baby. Asking her questions. The baby considers Posy with big brown eyes. She has a very serious expression for something so small and wrinkly.

"So what should we call her?"

It takes me a second to realize the question is directed at me. I'm watching the baby's hand. She's unfurling her tiny fingers and slowly waving them, as if she's trying them out for the first time. Seeing how they work.

I reach out, extend a finger close to her little palm, and she grabs it, squeezing. She's clearly holding on as tight as she can, but as small as she is, she has no strength.

She'll need very close watching until she's big enough to defend herself.

Adrenaline shoots through me. Is she safe enough here?

Lucca has crushed all challengers to his leadership. Ivano was operating alone. Turns out the Sicilian held a grudge. I can respect that even if he was a rat.

Since we dumped Ivano in the river, it's been quiet. That's why I left Sal home. His recovery still isn't one hundred percent. He bled out a long time in the snow. The cold is probably what saved him.

No one knows we're here. Everyone will assume Posy's giving birth at St. Ignatius. I know I haven't told anyone about this place. They'd think I was crazy to allow it, and they'd be right, but Posy cried, and I don't handle that shit well anymore.

The adrenaline is ebbing. It's safe. Ray's in the waiting room. I'm here. Nobody is going to hurt my girls.

I bend over and brush my lips across the baby's tiny knuckles and drop a kiss on Posy's cracked lips.

"You need water."

"Baby needs a name." Posy gazes at me expectantly. Names are one of her favorite conversations. She throws them at me when we're playing games, and I'm supposed to act like I have a preference.

I consider the little thing curled up like a shrimp and

dozing between Posy's breasts. Is she cold? I tug the sheet over her until she's covered to her tiny, pointed chin.

And that's when it hits me. It's so natural, I almost didn't notice.

"I love her," I marvel. It's the same feeling I have for Posy. The warm glow that makes Posy a beacon in the dark also comes from this tiny oblivious being. It's a miracle, not in a trite way, but in the sense that it's so unlikely it rearranges reality.

I love this baby as much as I love Posy.

I *love*.

It's a strange and marvelous thing.

"I like Mira," I finally answer her question. It's one of hundreds of names she's run past me, and I didn't think anything of it then, but now, it sounds perfect for this person we've made.

"Mira," Posy whispers in her ear. "Mommy and Daddy love you."

It's the truth. And it's as beautiful as this woman and this child of mine.

~

THE SERIES WILL CONTINUE in *Nicky the Driver*, coming in 2022. In the meantime, check out *Charge,* book 1 in the Steel Bones Motorcycle Club saga.

ABOUT THE AUTHOR

Cate C. Wells writes everything from mafia to motorcycle club to small town to paranormal romance. Whatever the subgenre, readers can expect character-driven stories that are raw, real, and emotionally satisfying. She's into messy love, flaws, long roads to redemption, grace, and happily ever after, in books and in life.

Along with stories, she's collected a husband and children along the way. She lives in Baltimore when she's not exploring the world with her family.

She loves to chat with readers! Check out the The Cate C. Wells Reader Group on Facebook.
For updates and bonus content, sign up for the newsletter at www.catecwells.com!

Facebook: @catecwells
Twitter: @CateCWells1
Bookbub: @catecwells

Printed in Great Britain
by Amazon